Also by Stephen Swartz

A Dry Patch of Skin

A Beautiful Chill

After Ilium

Aiko

The Dream Land Trilogy

I. Long Distance Voyager

II. Dreams of Future's Past

III. Diaspora

A Girl Called Wolf

A Novel Inspired by a True Life

Stephen Swartz

MYRDDIN PUBLISHING GROUP

UNITED STATES · UNITED KINGDOM · AUSTRALIA

ISBN-13: 978-1-68063-022-0

ISBN-10: 1-68063-022-9

unique electronic & print books

www.myrddinpublishing.com

Cover Design by Iris Schaeffer

Perhaps they are not stars, but rather openings in heaven where the love of our lost ones pours through and shines down upon us to let us know they are happy.

Inuit proverb

1

The Dark

In the dark the wind growls like ten hungry wolves. Mama says we are safe under the furs on the *illeq*, the sleeping platform in this hut. The wind-wolves only roar, never bite, she tells me. I smile at her, the only human I know. She is warm and soft. That is my first memory.

Mama tells me everything begins and ends with the dark. It covers the world and it fills every belly and every heart. We wait through many months of the dark. Then a silent spark flashes between the mountains on one special day and we know the sun will return. Little by little the sun rises and the dark slips away for a few months. I arrived on the day the sun returned, Mama always told me. I was like the sun coming back to the world, driving away the dark.

I remember watching Mama weave the beads together in the flickering light of the soapstone oil lamp. She puts the beads into rows and puts the rows together to make a picture. She stitches them together so they will stay in place. On the tapestry, the night is white and the moon is blue.

The fire in the pit crackles as the wind shakes the hut like an ice bear's paw slapping the walls.

In the tapestry is another mama bundled in furs, tugging at the cap of another baby. Mama smiles. She tells me the tapestry is her and me.

The fire crackles, spits —

Pounding on the door! Mama looks afraid. She tucks me under the furs on the *illeq*, hurries to the door.

The man with the red beard returns. He is angry, slaps at Mama. I don't know the words they shout. He takes Mama in his arms, pushes her on the furs beside me and drops over her like a big bear. She cries and shouts, then falls silent.

Mama looks at me as he covers her, all his weight on top of her. Her eyes are red. I know she is going to the dark place and I cover my face with my hands. I hide under the furs.

I hear Mama scream. I hear hard things hit soft things.

When I look out from under the furs, Mama is on the floor. Her naked body shakes, her head turning back and forth. The man with the red beard is gone. I climb off the *illeq* and hurry to close the door. Snow blows in before I can close it.

The tapestry is also on the floor. The man with the red beard stepped on it, broke many of the beads. I know Mama will fix it better than before.

Mama is still shaking on the floor. I grab the stick and put it in her mouth like she taught me to do. I throw a big fur from the *illeq* over her. I sit on her until she stops shaking. It is like riding the sled over the ice, the dogs pulling hard, the sled breaking over the rocks.

Later, I awaken in the bed, Mama beside me, whispering a

song. It was not a dream, she tells me. When the winds blow cold or the sun burns bright, he comes. The man with the red beard returns to this hut whenever he needs to release his evil spirits. It's a lesson, she says, and I must learn it if I am going to follow her into the spirit world, or else I must stay in the world of humans and live by their rules. Soon the time will come for me to choose.

A storm rattles the hut like the howling of ten wolves. Mama holds me close, skin to skin under the furs. She pushes her nipple to me and I suck. The world is new to me, still warm and soft. Yet I have seen cold and rough. That is the true lesson, says Mama.

Later we go outside. Holding me inside her sealskin *amautik*, the hut blocking the wind, we watch the night sky over the fjord. We wave at the dancing green lights above us that paint the glacier, the lights that tell our destiny. We also wave at the stars that are all our ancestors watching us.

"They are waiting to see you do great things," says Mama in the language she is teaching me. "So you must find the star that will guide you. There are many to choose from."

I tell her I want the brightest star and she points to the one in the north.

"That one is yours."

The first time I remember the man with the red beard coming to hurt Mama, I had almost three years. She let him in every time he visited, though always with the shouting and slapping. Better than letting him freeze to death outside, she said. We must be kind to everyone who comes here through the dark. Yet her eyes turned red each time he visited. He always left when she lay shaking on the floor. She was no use to him that way.

Mama was the crazy woman, I learned later from humans in the village. She was blessed or cursed with the sight of beyond. A few humans came to ask questions and she would answer. She chanted and sang strange words. She tossed bones into the air and watched them hit the floor. She saw pictures in the bones there, told them what she saw. Yet no humans came to ask her questions now. They were afraid.

That was the reason the others left, Mama told me. There used to be more huts around ours. There used to be more people living on this point of land across the fjord from the big ice. A small village of mostly fishermen, seal hunters. One by one they left, moved across the island to the larger village. Mama took what she could from the abandoned huts, built of whale bone beams and turf walls, wooden floors, skins and furs, ice blocks and snow roofs, adding them to this hut — the same hut where I was born, where I lived until Mama died.

The village all those humans moved to was far away. It took three days to walk there, going over the mountains and through the valleys, across the snow and ice. Even by dog sled it would be more than a day — if the snow was right for a sled. The rocky ground and the high mountain passes didn't make going by dog sled so easy. Better to walk.

The humans in the village on the other side of the island wouldn't let Mama live there. Yet they would give her food and the things she needed to live in this hut on the rocks. She would go to the village once or twice a year and exchange beadwork or other crafts she made for food and supplies. Sometimes one of the villagers came to this hut with gifts of food and supplies to trade for her prophecy.

Sometimes men came to the hut just to hurt her. One man hit the side of her head, she told me, and I saw the scar where it healed after she sewed the skin together. That was before the man with the red beard swept onto the shore. That was before I was born — before the other babies were born, the ones asleep in the ground behind the hut. Ever since those men attacked her, she fell a lot and shook against the floor.

The people in the village had many names for her, she said. I never knew Mama's name. She was always Mama to me. The man with the red beard called her Woman. When Mama died I still called her Mama. I had to cut into the hard ground to make a pit for her body to rest in, so deep the bears would not smell her and dig her up as food.

I said, "Goodbye, Mama" and watched her for a few days.

When humans from the village came later and dug her up to move her to the village, they asked her name.

I just said, "Mama."

"She's your mama?" they asked in my language.

I nodded.

"And what is your name?"

I told them.

"Wolf? Who is Wolf?" they asked me.

I pointed to my face. "I'm Wolf."

They laughed.

"Mama called me," I said.

The tall man with the badge said, "A girl called wolf? Hah! You're too small to be a wolf."

"I'm only thirteen. I will grow big as you."

"Let's hope so," said the man. "You don't want a real wolf to eat you! Not enough of you for one good meal."

And they led me away from the hut where I was born. Where Mama was born. Where the man with the red beard came one day, and many days after. I never looked back as we hiked over the ice and snow. I looked forward.

The first time I killed I was five years old. The man with the red beard sat me on a rock to watch him cut up a seal. He told me to watch closely so I would learn how to do it. Someday I would need to get my own food, he said.

The next seal he pushed between my feet. He handed me a club and told me to hit the seal's head with the club. I did not hesitate. *Whack!* More hits. Blood ran from the mouth of the seal and it lay still.

"Good girl," the man with the red beard said. "You've got deadly hands. The seals are afraid of you!"

I went out with him often to hunt. Sometimes the man with the red beard visited only a single night yet in good weather he might stay several days. When he took me out on a hunt, Mama stayed in the hut. She cooked whatever we brought back—fish, seals, birds, hares.

In summer we gathered berries and bird eggs. I went with Mama up the mountain slopes and along the shore. She said the man with the red beard was sailing on the sea during summer. On the big kayak he would catch many fish, she told me. He would visit later and bring some fish.

And he did, always when the wind blew hard and the wolf's howl was loud. He pounded against the door and Mama would look afraid, then get up and open the door. He burst in like a blizzard with gifts in one arm and a rifle in the other. Sometimes Mama was happy to see him, sometimes she wasn't.

I waited in the corner as the man with the red beard wrestled with Mama on the *illeq*. I never could see who won the fight. After a while they lay quiet together, the fighting done. As he lay there, Mama would get up, pull on her clothes. She would make a drink for him. Even though they always shouted at each other she always gave him something to eat. Unless she went to the dark place and her eyes turned red and he would leave.

He never asked her questions, never wanted to hear answers. He had no interest in seeing the pictures in the bones. He only wanted her to take away his evil spirits. During those moments he made animal noises, looked like he was dying. Then the evil spirits left him and went into Mama. She told me she would pee them out later and they would be gone.

One day after the man with the red beard threw Mama hard on the *illeq* and knocked me off, he got rid of his evil spirits and took his meal. He had a bottle and drank the rest of what was in it. Then he walked out, leaving the door open. Mama hurried to close it tight before too much snow blew in.

She came over to me, sitting on the floor, and pulled me up into her big arms.

"We must be good to him," she said. "He brings food for you and me. Also because he is your papa. When I am gone he will care for you."

I looked at her. Her eyes were not red, so I didn't believe.

It is truth, she said. She told me the story without using the bones to make pictures. She made pictures with words and I saw them in my head, behind my eyes. She found him one day on the rocks along the shore. He was asleep so she put him on the sled and brought him to the hut. He was sick from the sea. She cared for him until he was well again. Soon he could hunt and catch fish. He grew strong. One day he pushed her on the *illeq* and told her to take away his evil spirits. He said he was full of evil spirits for the things he had done. She did not want to do it yet he put his hands around her throat and held her tight until she opened her legs to him.

She told me the story often, changing some of it with each

telling. Yet in every telling at the end I am born.

The man with the red beard was afraid when Mama went to the dark place. He always ran out. Each time, Mama thought he would never return, yet he did.

Mama told me he went to the village. The other humans lived there. Mama and me were not the only humans in the world, I learned. He was from the village and needed to live there among his own kind of human. Mama and me were a different kind of human, the kind that needed to live on the ice. So he seemed like a ghost to me. From a secret place far away, he came like the wind and arrived like a bear, then left like a dog.

One day Mama knew the moment arrived and she let me out of her belly. She said the moon told her when to push. I was born on the sleeping platform in this hut, the same place where I was made. It was the same place where my Mama was made, and her mama, and back to the starting of time.

All of us were made in this hut. It was dug into the ground and built up with blocks of turf braced with wood, covered with skins and bones, and topped with more turf and wooden boards from abandoned huts nearby. Everything was done to keep out the wind and keep out the animals. It was one room for both of us, four corners and a fire pit, a raised platform at one end for sleeping, the door at the other end, a bench on the side, a cabinet, and some bins stacked up and shelves along a wall. A soapstone oil lamp sat on the stool. There was a bucket for the pee that we took out every few days.

The man with the red beard returned one summer day and saw this baby sitting among the furs on the *illeq*. He thought Mama had played with other men, so he cursed her. Mama told him all about me, the truth, yet he didn't seem happy. He beat Mama, then stood over me, looking down on me. He frowned and drops of water fell on my face. He wiped his face. Then he ran out of the hut. He did not return for many weeks.

The first time I shot a rifle I was seven years old. The man with the red beard visited again and stayed many days. He seemed happy, smiled at me. Mama was sick, laying under the furs, her body swollen, her head thumping, so he took me out on a hunt.

We greeted the dogs, ten of them at that time, and got them harnessed to the sled. I rode on the sled with him, out over the ice as far as we could go, right to the edge. Beyond was the deep blue water that nobody could cross. We turned and ran the sled in the opposite direction and reached the other end of the world.

We were on an island, he told me. He drew a circle in the snow. He put a pebble where the hut was. He put a small pile of pebbles where the village was, so far away on the other side of this world. Between the hut and the village were tall mountains and wide valleys, narrow draws, and ice, snow, and patches that were lakes in summer yet ice in winter. There were five paths to the village, he told me, two around the shore in each direction, three through the mountains.

Then he drew another circle apart from the first circle and told me he also came from an island, a different island, farther away than the village. I knew then I was small in the world. As big as Mama was to me when I first opened my eyes to her, the world was that much bigger than me. The village had ten huts and the world had ten villages. And the world had different kinds of humans, like different kinds of birds or fish. Some were good and some were not good.

He showed me the rifle, taught me how to put in bullets, how to prepare it for shooting, how to aim at the center of the target. He made a stack of stones for me to point the rifle at and told me to squeeze the trigger with no breath in my throat. I felt a big kick to my shoulder. He told me to hold it tight and squeeze the trigger again. The bullet went out of the rifle and knocked off the top stone. He patted my head.

Later we saw a fox and he put me on my belly in the snow and told me to point the rifle at the fox. I did as he said yet I missed. He told me to try again. Yet I missed and he cursed me for wasting the bullets. He grabbed the rifle from my hands and shot at the fox, hit it in a rear leg. I jumped up from the snow and chased after the fox until I caught it. I brought the bleeding fox back to him and he told me to club it, to end its life quickly.

Mama was happy to have fox but she preferred seal or fish.

In those days Mama went to the dark place many times. For a few weeks she went there almost every day. At first, the man with the red beard would be angry and shout at her. He did not want to lay under the furs with her if she was going to disappear into the world of spirits. In time, he recognized when she was about to leave and he put the stick in her mouth. Sometimes he held her tight on the floor. Sometimes he asked her questions and when she returned she brought answers.

Like where did you come from?

"I came from across the big sea," said the man with the red beard, "from a land of ice and snow not so different from this place. It is a land where people live in handsome cities and drive big cars on paved streets."

He seemed happy to tell a story, holding me on his lap while Mama rested on the bed, tired from her trip to the dark place.

"I did many bad things there," he said, "so I had to leave. I got on a boat and sailed away. Then I was caught in a storm and I lost the boat. I was in the sea until another boat found me. They brought me to this island."

"And Mama found you on the shore!" I liked filling in the

details that I knew.

"That was later," he said. "The boat that rescued me brought me to Tasiilaq. That is the village I told you about, on the other side of this island. No one knew me there so I could start a new life. I got hired as a deck hand. I'm good with nets and fish."

He looked at me, maybe checking if I believed him. At that young age I liked all stories. Mama did not speak much in those days though sometimes she chanted to herself.

"When you first meet Mama?" I asked him.

"It was another time I went out on the boat to catch fish and we hit a storm. I fell into the sea and they could not find me. The big waves threw me on the rocks near this hut." He swung his arm in the direction of the shore. "I was in a deep sleep when a woman pulled me onto a sled and a team of dogs brought me to this hut."

I understood. He came to this hut from the sea. He came here before I came out of Mama. First Mama, then the man with the red beard, then me. It all made sense.

"This is a good woman," he told me, pointing his long arm to the *illeq* where Mama slept. "She has special powers. She talks to the gods. She brought me back to life, so I can do no harm to her." He wiped his eyes. "Yet I have done bad things to her. I know this." He brushed my hair with his hand as he talked. "I promised the gods I would be a different man here."

I sat on his lap at that moment. He wrapped his arms around me until I could not breath. After a moment he released me.

"In that other land where I once lived, there was a child like you. I left her there. The gods torment me every day and make her fight with me in my dreams. It is my punishment."

I stared at him. His red beard was wet with tears.

Then he lifted me up, took me to the *illeq*. He set me beside Mama and grabbed his coat.

"I must walk," he said and left, pulling the door closed.

When the man with the red beard visited, he acted like the hut was his home. Mama never liked him acting that way, yet we shared what we had with him. Sometimes he brought things for us, food and supplies. Now when he visited, he didn't share the *illeq* with Mama. He let Mama and me sleep under the furs there. He slept on the floor like a dog. He only used the *illeq* for getting rid of the evil spirits inside him.

One time when Mama left on a trip to the village, I stayed in the hut with one dog, Maqiiva, to look after me. Maq protected me. He was my favorite, all white with light brown fur on his face and paws.

I looked at everything in the hut, wondered where they came from. I knew the bones came from animals and birds. I knew the stones came from the beach or the mountains. I had walked as far as the mountain and as far as the beach in the other direction. I saw only the white of ice and the snow. And the brown of bare rock. And the dark blue of the sea. Metal things, wooden things, cloth things. I put on Mama's old clothes, pretended I was her. I jumped on the floor, shook against the floorboards, laughing. I wondered what it was like to go to the dark place.

Mama came home and saw me, asked what I was doing. She shouted and slapped me. She put me outside in the cold.

As I stood beside the hut, the dogs came around me. I got on my knees and they pressed against me. I held them close. Night came. And went.

I hit the door with my hand many times, shouted to Mama to let me inside. I was hungry and cold.

In the morning, I saw a human coming toward the hut. At

that distance, I could see it was the man with the red beard. I waited.

"What you doing out here?" he asked, arriving and panting from his hike through the snow.

The day was bright with sun and I squinted at him.

"Your Mama must be punishing you. So we all have lessons to learn." He laughed and went inside.

I heard them talking. Then shouting. I put my ear to the wall, shivering against the hut. Suddenly the wall banged as someone inside crashed against it. I heard screams. Then silence.

After a while the door opened. Mama came out, pulled me inside, closed the door.

The man with the red beard lay on the floor, his face covered in blood.

Mama told me to get on the *illeq*, cover myself with the furs so I would not see them. I obeyed.

I heard the door open and I heard the sounds of his heavy body sliding across the floor. The door closed and I looked out from under the furs. After a while, Mama returned but the man with the red beard was gone.

One day in my tenth year, I was alone in the hut while Mama went out on a hunt. I was weaving beads the way she taught me. The man with the red beard came to visit. He was angry to see Mama gone. He asked me where she went. I could not answer. He said he was full of evil spirits and I should be careful. He said I should go out of the hut.

I was too slow so he grabbed me, threw me on the *illeq*. He put me down on my belly, tried to push something into my bottom. It wouldn't go in so he slapped my bottom. He shouted many words. He turned me on my back and pushed his fingers into me. He pulled out his fingers and they were stained with blood. I started crying and he slapped me.

He stood, pushed his trousers down, speaking like he was already in his own dark place. It was a different language than Mama and I spoke. He swayed on his feet and took hold of the thing men pee out of. With eyes closed, he chanted. When he opened his eyes, he stared at me, asked if I knew what to do. I shook my head so he told me I should learn it.

He grabbed my hand, told me to hold his *usuk*. He grabbed my head and pulled me close. He told me what to do. I started then stopped so he slapped me again.

When he was done, he pushed me back onto the *illeq*, telling me never to tell what we did. His smile at that moment made me wonder if he meant it or not.

I watched him wipe his hands on his sweater. Then he pulled up his trousers and sat on the floor like he always did when he visited. Mama would give him a bowl of food, I knew, and he would eat like a wolf that had not eaten for weeks.

I went to the locker and got a chunk of seal meat and made a soup like Mama taught me. I gave him a bowl full of soup.

"Thanks," he said in a sad voice. I was confused. Maybe he said it for what happened before the soup. Or because he was alive again without the evil spirits inside him.

I didn't know about right and wrong, good and evil. Mama told me about the spirits that live in people, spirits that make people do things which are good or evil. I saw what the man with the red beard did with Mama. I wondered if he thought I was old enough now to do those things. Mama said we were supposed to care for him. I thought about that as he ate the soup.

I learned that I had my own dark place. When I told my story later to the Catholic Sisters, they cried and held me in their arms.

They chanted over me like Mama used to do. They told me one of their spirits would protect me. They waved a gold cross at me, just like the bones Mama tossed in the air so she could answer questions. She let them drop on the floor and saw the picture the bones made. Instead of bones, the Catholic Sisters saw pictures in the air and in their heads.

So I made a picture in my head of the day when the man with the red beard visited no more.

It was his habit to visit us every few weeks. He hit the door like a storm, as though he was waking the spirits of the hut. Mama would let him inside. He got food. Sometimes he brought his own drink, a bottle of something that wasn't water. He would sing loudly after finishing the bottle.

Then he would push Mama to the *illeq*, laying over her. Sometimes he would turn his head and look at me. He would be on top of her yet look at me.

Other times I was there alone in the hut so he pushed me to the *illeq* like he did to Mama. He said I must obey him or Mama would be angry with me. He said it would only hurt if I was afraid. Yet I was afraid.

I stayed still as he did what he wanted. He got rid of the evil spirits. He patted my head when he finished.

When he would awaken from a sleep, or after finishing the bottle, he would be a different human. He smiled like the sun. He ran his hand over my head, tugged at my hair. He said I was *pretty* yet I did not know what that word meant. If Mama was there, he would be kind to her, dance with her in the middle of the floor. They looked happy. It must be good to lay together under the furs like they did. Then he would leave.

If he stayed for several days, he would go out on a hunt and most times he took me with him. Mama taught me how to care for the dogs and how to harness them to the sled, yet it was the man with the red beard who taught me how to make the dogs go fast. I liked the wind in my face as we ran up the valley.

He let me shoot at hares and foxes, and seals on the beach or at air holes on the ice. He said I was a good shooter. We would bring food for Mama to cook. One time we saw a reindeer and he shot it dead. Then we had meat for a few days. One time he let me shoot and I got a hare with only one shot.

Then one day Mama returned to the hut and saw him on top of me. She shouted at him, hit him with her fists. He got up from the *illeq*, reached for his clothes. Mama took the rifle and put it to her shoulder. She pointed it at him. She told him to get out. He begged to put his clothes on first. It was the darkest weeks of winter then. She repeated her demand. They turned around in the middle of the floor, growling like two bears deciding who was stronger.

He grabbed at the rifle yet Mama held it tight. They fell to the floor, wrestled. The rifle went off. I saw blood run from under the man with the red beard. Mama looked back at me, told me to put on my clothes and help her.

Even in the dark of winter, everything so black, we went out of the hut and took his body on the sled to a place she knew that was far off any trail. We worked through the night to dig a hole in the snow. In that season there was no morning or afternoon so I didn't know how long we worked. After a very long time the hole was big enough to roll him into it with his legs bent. We covered him with blocks of ice we cut. We piled snow over the ice. We put rocks over the snow.

It was colder than I ever felt before yet Mama took time to chant over the rocks.

Then we went home, the dogs complaining all the way.

Once inside the hut, Mama took my clothes off me and took me in front of the fire pit. She looked me over, checked every part of me. She asked if I knew what I was doing. She asked if he forced me. She asked how long he did that with me.

I was too slow to answer so she slapped my face.

"He said I'm old enough to help him get rid of evil spirits," I said in a rush. "He said you would be angry if I didn't help."

Mama slapped me many times. I thought she would put me out of the hut, into the cold and the dark again, yet she did not. She pushed me into the corner instead and threw my clothes at me, told me to put them on and never take them off.

As she finished speaking, her eyes turned red and her body shook and she fell on the floor. She went to the dark place for a long time, singing a song that made no sense. I covered my ears. On and on she sang through the night, shaking against the floor or resting for a while, then singing again.

I wondered if the man with the red beard was singing to her all the way from the hole in the ground. He was sure to be angry at Mama for what she did. I knew he stopped being human. He changed into a bear, and she treated him like a bear.

"There's no peace when you're facing down an angry bear. All you can do is kill it. That's the only way to survive," Mama told me. "It's the only way. You understand?"

And the man with the red beard never returned except in my darkest dreams.

Mama took the silence with her, like a heavy stone, all day and night, every place she would go. She shook her hands, pointed her fingers, kicked her feet, nodded her head, rolled her eyes to communicate after the man with the red beard slept in the pit for many months.

At first Mama went out on a hunt and I cooked. Then Mama sent me out to get food. Later she told me she was losing her sight, her eyes getting cloudy. So I took the dogs and the sled and the rifle out to hunt. All day we searched for food but only got a small seal to bring back to the hut.

Every day I went out with the dogs, taking the sled along the shore, looking out at the fjord and up at the mountains. In this small world was everything I knew.

The man with the red beard said it was an island, water on all sides. And there was a village on the other side. Yet Mama never took me to the village. She never wanted to talk about the village.

When the summer came and the snow melted, I went out hunting on foot, the dogs following me. We could not take the sled without the snow. I could get fish or birds and Mama would cook them and we would be happy.

More and more Mama went to the dark place. I could only hold her until she stopped shaking. I cried for her to come back. I told her I needed her, the only human in my life.

When she lay still on the floor, I lay beside her and covered us with furs. I saw the twitches in her face, under her skin, like birds were pecking at her.

"Mama? You alive?"

She opened her eyes, stared at me like she did not know me.

When she spoke, I listened close, my ear to her mouth. She told me to go to the village and tell them my mama died.

"Ask them to look after you," she said.

"Why you say that?"

"When I'm gone you must go to the village. They will protect you and give you food and shelter."

"I don't want that. I want you always be with me."

"You are child. I'm old woman. Impossible for me to take a long journey with you."

"Where you going? To another hole in the ground?"

"No, Wolf. You never talk about that. Agreed?"

"Yes, agree."

"He is never to be bothered," Mama said in a hard tone. "His spirit must not be disturbed."

"I won't say anything."

"Promise every morning."

I nodded, tears filling my eyes. She tried to wipe them away. Her hands didn't move as she wanted. Her fingers curled into frozen claws, and she could not straighten them. Her arms could not raise. She looked in pain.

"Mama!"

"Promise me you will do everything to survive."

"I will." I sniffled back tears and held her tighter.

"I call you Wolf so you will always be strong and clever," she whispered, "so you will make your own path."

She stared at the ceiling, at the beams of the hut, like she saw spirits waiting for her there. I looked up, too, yet I only saw the smoke curling up from the fire pit. When I looked back at Mama, her face was quiet.

I was twelve years old when Mama died.

2

The Ice

I pulled Mama onto the *illeq* and covered her with furs. I waited for her to return from the dark place. I held her for many days and nights. She lost her warmth. As I got hungry, I went out on a hunt. Sometimes I got food and sometimes I didn't. Whenever I returned to the hut, I called her name to see if she came back to this world. She never answered me.

When her body was firm as a whale bone and began to smell bad, I took her from the *illeq*, took her out of the hut. I pulled her on the sled and harnessed the dogs and we went up the valley to the far shore, trying to keep on the snow. It was the same trail Mama used when the man with the red beard went away.

I could not find the same place, yet I knew he was near. It was almost summer so much of the snow was gone. The rocks were bare. It was hard to push the sled. After I found a good place at the edge of a snowfield, I tried to dig in the ground but the tools I had didn't cut well. I could only make a shallow ditch. I knew I had to go back to the hut for different tools, so I pulled her off the sled and slid her down into the ditch. She did not fit. I covered her with fur.

The dogs were whining, getting worried.

I gathered some rocks and set them around her, over her. I tried to cover her but I didn't find enough good rocks. I searched all day for loose rocks to put over her.

The dogs barked, pulling at their traces. I stopped putting the rocks over Mama and looked at the dogs.

Above the ridge were three wolves. They smelled Mama and came for food. At that moment I realized it was already a few days since I last ate anything.

The dogs growled, pressed together in front of me. I wanted to let the lines go so they could run free. Yet I could not let the dogs fight with the wolves and be hurt. I needed the dogs for the sled.

I watched the wolves sniff the air, stepping down the slope as I reached for the rifle on the sled. The man with the red beard told me always take the rifle when I go out of the hut. Mama told me the same words.

Raising the rifle to my shoulder as I was taught, I put my eye to the sight peg and aimed at the center wolf.

They stepped further down the slope, not afraid of a small human. My dogs were making a great noise, jerking at their traces, moving the sled away.

My shot hit the front foot of that wolf. It barked and turned away, hobbling up the slope. The other wolves followed it.

I aimed again and hit the wounded wolf in the butt. It was crippled and could not run. The other wolves ran away.

Rushing up the slope, I jammed the rifle barrel against the wolf's head. It looked up at me, soft-eyed like a puppy.

"I'm Wolf," I said. "Only one of us can eat today."

That shot seemed to fill the whole sky, echoing against the distant mountain slopes. I wondered if the humans in the village could hear it, if they would come looking for me. The echo that hit me broke the ice on the shore and shook the rocks covering Mama. It stayed in my heart.

I looked down and the wolf was still. The dogs went silent. As the wind touched me, I smelled bad meat. It was not the wolf. Others would follow the scent to Mama.

I took off the rocks I already put over her and moved her out so I could dig more into the ground. I made the ditch deeper, enough so her body fit inside. I worked hard gathering more rocks, walking far and carrying them back, one after another. Then I put all the rocks over her so she was covered completely.

When we put the man with the red beard into the ground, Mama chanted over him. So I climbed on top of the rocks and chanted something I remembered her singing. I was not sure if I got the words right so I sang it again, louder.

The dogs whined, tired of waiting. They were hungry, too. It was getting late, the sun dropping behind the mountain crests, throwing the valley into shadow. The wolf carcass lay beside the sled. I was going to take it back to the hut yet we were already hungry.

So I took the knife and cut the fur and skin away from the shanks. I scraped the meat clean, wiped blood off the knife every few cuts. The dogs got excited, barking at me. I told them to be ready. I was almost finished.

I took pieces of meat and tossed them to each dog and they were happy to gobble it down. They barked for more. I cut off more pieces, moving down the hind legs of the wolf and tossing a piece to each dog. My belly called to me too, so I took my share of the meat and sat among the dogs to eat.

We watched the sun kiss the mountain peaks, little flashes of light as the sky melted into black. Then the sun would rise again without ever disappearing. I sat on the sled, the dogs around me, rifle against my leg.

Pictures filled my head, Mama and me in every moment we were together. My eyes let out streams of tears and my chest thumped harder until I didn't think I could keep going. I took big breaths and I howled at the mountain peaks, as loud as I could in every direction, and the angry echoes rushed back at me! I shouted until I lost my voice! My dogs joined me howling, then they took over for me.

Looking at those little lights high in the blackness, above the low-hanging night sun, I wondered how many lights there were. They seemed a lot. Maybe enough for every human in the village to have one—and everyone in all the other villages wherever they might be. I only needed one, Mama said. Find the one star that will guide me through my life. I knew then I really needed it. Because I was alone.

Mama never took me to the village, never told me anything about it. Only how the people there were cruel to her. Still, she went there for food and supplies. She sold the beadwork she made and later the beadwork I also made. She always hesitated going there.

When Mama went to sleep for a long time, I thought about what she said. Go to the village and ask for help. They will take care of you, she said. Yet what help did I need? I had a hut to live in. I had food when I went out on a hunt or catching fish or birds. I could get crowberries and bird eggs in summer. Every day I could do as I wanted. I had five dogs, too.

Most days I would harness the dogs and run the sled up the shore in search of food. One time, I found a small whale on the beach, already dead and half-eaten. I could cut away some good chunks of blubber and meat. We ate until we had full bellies, me and the dogs. I broke away some bones to take back, before I even thought how I would use them. Then, back in the hut, I cooked more of the meat, put the rest of it in the locker, and ate another meal with the dogs. That was a good week—a good month, until the meat was all eaten.

I knew how to hunt. I took the rifle and went into the gorges or up mountain slopes. I saw foxes, hares, and birds. I missed a lot. So I tried putting out some food to attract them and when they took it, I shot them and took them back to the hut. Or, I walked among the bird nests covering the ground and gathered some of their eggs. Not all the eggs, just enough for a few meals. I picked a lot of crowberries, too. I tried other plants but I got sick. I lay in the hut for a few days each time, unable to eat, unable to go out on a hunt.

In winter, when the fjord froze, I could get seals on the ice. They would lie on the ice under the sun, easy to get. Or I had to be quick and get them when they popped up at an air hole. I knew how to skin animals, too. I knew which parts were good to eat. Seal liver was the best. I would eat the meat uncooked or take it back to the hut and cook it. I shared everything I got with my dogs.

As winter got darker and colder, I stayed in the hut more and more. The cold and the wind and the storms kept me from going out on a hunt. We usually kept the dogs outside and they curled up in the snow. Yet being alone, I let them into the hut and the dogs kept me warm. We also talked. They were my friends.

Sometimes I could feel Mama in the hut, standing beside the *illeq* or over there by the fire. The dogs would whimper, feeling her near. I called to her, waited for an answer.

"I'm good, Mama," I would speak into the frosty air.

I missed Mama yet I always knew where she was.

The days were dark and the winds blew hard against the hut. The walls shook and the roof rattled. I was afraid the hut might blow down. The storms made it too dangerous to go out. Food got short. There were a few cans and jars on a shelf. I broke them open and ate until everything was gone. The dogs snarled with each other, hungry more than me.

After the worst of the winter passed, the light returned little by little. I took the dogs out for a run in a new direction. We headed to the village I always heard about. I didn't know the way so I followed Mama's spirit and looked for signs. I went one way then back again, looking for a village. The man with the red beard told me it was on the other side of this island. An island is round so if I traveled along the shore I would come to the village eventually.

"A village is many huts all together," I reminded myself one cold night under a big canvas tarp, hidden between the rocks. "It's not just one hut sitting alone beside a fjord."

My dogs stared at me, tilting their heads like they never heard anything so strange. I didn't speak much after Mama left.

"You understand?" I asked them.

Two of them yawned, then the others followed.

Back in the hut, I had a few books. The man with the red beard brought one, then another, and another, many of the times he visited. They were books for a child. They had strange writing I did not know yet I could look at the pictures and understand a lot. If one hut was a home, then more than one hut was a village.

Finally we got to the crest of a ridge, farther than I had ever gone before, and I saw the village in the distance. Many huts, sitting in snow like pretty beads. From the higher ground where

I was, I could see fingers of the sea stretching between me and the village. In this deep winter, the sea was ice now and I could run the sled over the frozen water to the land on the other side. I could reach the village quickly that way. Maybe it was an island, yet crossing this little bay would be shorter than going farther around the shore, out to the point and back along the other side.

Looking at the lights, I counted as high as I could. One to ten. One to ten. One to ten. There were about three tens of huts. Some were small like my hut and some were big. They all had bright colors—red, blue, green, yellow. Squinting, I could see humans moving between the huts. Several of them. Or maybe they were dogs. I counted one to eight. I watched for a long time.

A dark feeling swept through me like cold wind. The humans there didn't know me. I didn't know them. I remembered Mama telling me to go to the village, yet she never told me what to do when I got to the village. Do I say my name? Do I ask for food? Will they give me food? Or will they try to hurt me like the man with the red beard did.

I could not decide. Yet I was hungry. My dogs were hungry. It was impossible to go on a hunt or catch fish in the dark.

So I moved the sled down the slope and out to the shore, pushing it over the rocks there, onto the ice. I pushed the sled across the frozen bay as the dogs pulled.

The ice cracked under my footsteps and the rails of the sled cut the ice. Under us was a deep watery world where Neqivik, goddess of the waters, would keep hold of all the animals, not let them be hunted, if we humans were not good. Yet I knew I was good, even if I made a mistake sometimes.

The sled hit a rough patch of broken ice and turned over. I righted it, put the bundles of things back on it. The ice cracked under my feet, made loud noises. I thought a lead might open right there and swallow us! We hurried on—but steady so we did not hurt the ice. It was farther than I first thought. The dogs complained. I told them to be quiet so nobody would know we were coming.

Once we reached the other shore, the dogs struggled to get the sled up the slope, onto the shore, even with me pushing. We found a level spot and got the sled off the ice.

I left the sled there with the dogs and kept going on my own by foot. I took the rifle, slung it over my shoulder. I also took a sealskin sack with some old beadwork in it that Mama and I made, and another, larger leather bag that was empty.

I hiked over the first low hill, marking my path in the snow, and stumbled over hidden rocks. Every few steps I got another look at the colorful huts and I knew I was getting closer.

Then I came around a hill and I saw a trail. It was wide and there were two tracks side by side running on to some huts. I walked between the tracks, my sealskin *kamik*s making a new line of tracks in the snow.

I came to the first huts and stopped to look around. A big red hut on my right side, a medium blue hut on the left side. These big huts made me wonder how many humans lived in them. And all the other huts here, too! This must be the biggest village in the whole world!

Suddenly, I saw another human up close. Just walked out in front of me. I jumped back. The human looked at me like that wolf looked at me when I was at Mama's resting place. Even in the winter dark, with light only spreading across the far horizon in the middle of the day, I could see the human smile. Then the human spoke to me. I was certain the words were for me yet I did not know them.

The human came toward me slowly, maybe afraid of me. I stepped back, then turned and ran a short distance away and stopped. I looked back at the human.

"I won't hurt you!" called the human.

I knew those words. I waved my hand. The human stepped toward me, both hands raised. I wanted to pull the rifle into my hands and be ready, yet if I did then the human might run away. The human might not know I was not hunting humans.

"Who are you?" asked the human, pulling a long cloth away from the face. It looked like a woman.

"I'm Wolf." I raised my voice to send my words to her.

"You're not a wolf."

I could not think how to answer as the woman came closer.

"You're not from here?" she asked.

I shook my head.

"Are you hurt?"

I shook my head again.

"Where you come from?"

I pointed behind me. I shook my hand like I was sending my fingers over the mountains. My voice was too tired to come out of my mouth.

She was only a few steps from me by then.

"Do you need help?"

Those words I knew, too. Mama taught me. They were the language of the humans. Yet I could not speak. I only spoke to Mama and the man with the red beard. And the dogs.

My heart pounded like a fist on the door of the hut.

"Food," I said. It took all my strength to speak.

She rushed up to me then, like a bear charging, grabbed my shoulders. I fell down on my knees in the snow. I tried to get up but she was holding me, trying to help me up, yet I only pulled her down with me.

She got up straight, laughing.

"You want food? That's it?"

I stood and showed her the empty bag, shook it so she knew

it was empty. I patted my belly.

"Come with me," said the woman.

I thought she knew where to find food. I looked back in the direction of the dogs and was ready to run to them through the snow and push the sled onto the ice and rush away.

The woman was talking but her words came too fast so I did not understand.

She led me further into the village. Other humans watched us from the openings in their huts or they walked past us on this trail between the huts. She went to one hut, big and blue, and opened the door, waved for me to enter. Inside were more humans and they looked at us like we were meat for them. One man greeted the woman.

She talked with them, pointed her hand at me. I thought she meant for me to sit. Instead of sitting on the floor, she held a tall stool for me and I set my body on it, still bundled in all my furs and skins, too bulky to keep from knocking things. I felt warm in that hut so I wondered if I should pull off my sealskin overcoat.

Another woman arrived from behind a wall and put a bowl of soup in front of me. Despite the steam rising from it, I grabbed the bowl and lifted it to my mouth, slurping the soup in a noisy way. The men laughed. I stopped and glared at them.

"Forget them," said the woman who was my guide. "They do not see many people off the ice."

I wanted to ask what she meant but I could not speak.

"Go on, finish the soup," she said. "It's free today."

This woman called the village Tasiilaq and said there were 1,529 humans, more than I could ever count. It was the largest village on the east coast of Greenland, what they called *Kalaallit Nunaat*, the big island I saw from my hut. Across the fjord from the big ice was this little island, and these humans called it Ammassalik. Yet some called it Angmagssalik. Some said the island had one name, the village the other name. I could not understand. All I knew was that this village was on the opposite side of the island from the hut where Mama and I lived.

On that day I first walked into Tasiilaq, I did not know what a heliport was, or helicopters, or cars or trucks, or motor boats, or telephone or television, or any modern machines like those. I learned that what Mama and I called *humans*—Inuk—was what others called us. We were all humans.

I listened as they talked, the woman who was my guide and the woman who gave me the soup, as well as some men there in that hut. Maybe they did not think I understood. I did not speak. I was too afraid to speak. Mama taught me words but they spoke many more words than I knew. Maybe they would laugh at my words if I spoke.

I didn't know how a village worked. Maybe like a team of dogs, each with a different purpose? What did each human do? Mama told me the village was evil and the humans would hurt me, yet she told me to go there after she went to her sleeping place. I didn't obey her. Not until I got hungry and could not go on a hunt. Maybe the humans in the village would be good to me even if they were not good to Mama.

And then I heard the words I feared.

"If she came from over the mountains she likely passed that crazy woman's place. I wonder if they met. Ya, or if this girl knows her."

They were talking to each other, taking turns looking at me. I ate another bowl of soup. The woman gave me pieces of fish. And something she called *bread*.

"It's likely," said one man, "this girl knows about the crazy woman."

"Or they are related." Some of them laughed.

"Ya, could be the crazy woman's child."

"A crazy child to become another crazy woman!"

They asked me questions yet I did not answer. They looked at me as though I was stupid, then talked about me as though I was not there, calling me stupid and crazy, saying they better be careful around me or I might burst into violence. I was carrying a rifle, after all.

I kept my head down, eating slowly yet ready to fight or run if they said the wrong words.

"Let her be," said the woman who was my guide. "She's cold and hungry. Not important where she's from."

"Where *is* she from? That's the mystery."

"And she's going back to where she's from? Is it safe there?"

"She's got that rifle!"

"But she's just a girl. How about her parents?"

They kept talking about me like I didn't understand. Mama taught me many words. She told me I came out of her and she came out of her mama, back to the first humans of this island. So where did these humans come from? They all had to have their own mama. So we were alike.

The woman who was my guide pointed to my sack.

"What have you got in it?"

I reached in the sack, pulled out the beadwork.

She smiled. "You made it?"

"Mama," I said. I could not make strings of words.

"So she does have a mother!" said one man.

"That's it," said another. "She's got to be the crazy woman's child. That crazy woman always trying to sell her beadwork to get food." He looked closer at the beadwork. "Looks like her style, too. Tourists like it."

"How could she get pregnant living out there?" a different woman asked.

"Haven't seen her for a while now."

"Remember that fellow come from Iceland, the one with the red beard? He went out that way often."

"He could have met up with the shaman."

"Shaman, eh?"

"Ya, a real *angakok*. She had visions, read the bones. She had the sight of beyond."

"True? Or was she mentally ill? I wonder."

I wanted to tell them not to talk about Mama that way, but the words froze in my mouth.

More important than soup, I needed to get food in trade for the beadwork, enough food to last until spring when I could go out hunting.

The woman held the beadwork in her hands as she talked with the men. She ran her fingers over the design.

"Like?" I asked her.

"What?" she said, turning her attention back to me. "Do I like it? It's very good. Yes, I do."

"Food," I said and pointed to the beadwork.

"You want food for this beadwork?"

One man pointed to me, said I was a stupid child, probably stole the beadwork.

I shook my head at that.

"See? She understands you!"

They all laughed.

"All right," said the woman who was my guide, "we can get you some food for this beadwork."

She thanked the woman who gave me three bowls of soup and the fish and the bread, then she led me outside. Some of the men followed, others stood at the window to look one last time.

The woman took me to another hut and inside was so much food already in bags and boxes, all in a row. I pointed to the fish and the meat.

The man in that hut with the food talked with the woman who was my guide. They made a trade. She asked me to give her the beadwork and I did. They looked it over as I walked through the hut, checking all the food on shelves.

The woman came to me, told me the man would give me two hundred *krone* for the beadwork. He said it was better than usual so he could sell it for more than most. I didn't know what *krone* meant and I could not count to a high number.

I nodded to accept.

The woman helped me gather whatever I wanted. I got a lot of food in closed bags, some supplies for the hut, and two boxes of bullets. Everything went to the shelf where the man stood.

"That's a lot more than what I give her for the beadwork," he said with a frown.

"You need to choose only the most important things," said the woman.

I separated what I put on the shelf. To the left side went what I would keep and to the right what I would put back. In the end I filled the empty bag I brought and waved at the woman as we stood a moment outside the hut.

"Thanks," I spoke in our language.

"You mustn't be afraid to come here if you need more," she said and patted my shoulder. "Remember, my name is Agneta."

I turned to go back to where I left the sled and the dogs.

A man called out, running toward us.

"Take care!" the woman sang after me.

The man stopped beside the woman. They talked as I hurried away, out of sight.

The evening was coming on in the winter night so I was soon

in the dark and stumbling through the rocks back to the shore of the frozen bay. I found the sled. My dogs were happy to see me. They jumped on me, barking. I hugged each of them. I took out some dried fish and they ate it up.

It was almost complete darkness by then yet I had to get far away from the village, even though we could not get all the way back to the hut. I thought I saw somebody hiding among the rocks, watching me.

So I turned the sled, pushed it down on the ice again and the dogs pulled. We got across the bay after some time.

On the opposite shore we stopped and made a camp. I dug into the snow and threw down a tarp and furs from the sled. I tacked up another tarp overhead. Between them I crawled inside and the dogs curled around me. They slept with me, keeping me warm. The tarp over us blocked the wind yet the noise kept me from sleeping.

After we awoke, we pushed and pulled the sled on through the rocks and up to the ice field. The way was easy when we ran over the ice. The day remained dark, only a sliver of light on the horizon at mid-day. By the next night we arrived back at the hut.

Inside, I unpacked all the things I brought from the village, organized the cabinets and bins.

In the hut, I felt Mama watching me.

"I went to the village," I said to her spirit. "A female human helped me. Men humans laughed at me. They said bad words about you." I wiped my eyes. "And I could not tell them to stop. Yet they did not hurt me."

It was true. It was not a comfortable place. Mama was right. I felt like I walked among wolves. I was afraid even though I was also Wolf.

When the snow stopped falling, I went out almost every day, my dogs pulling the sled under the bright blue sky and golden sun. We went on long runs. My dogs and I were happy. I could shoot a seal every few days or a bird or a hare. Living in the hut, I felt like the tall woman in the book who lived in the big hut on the mountain filled with many shiny things. I started to understand what happy meant.

Then the men came to the hut.

I saw them from a distance. They watched the hut, saw me come and go with the dogs and the sled. At first, I thought they were just wolves looking for a meal. Then I recognized them as humans and knew they must be from the village. It was many days after I went to the village so I thought they had followed me. Each time I saw them they were closer and closer.

I checked the rifle and counted the bullets. The man with the red beard taught me how to take care of the rifle and how to use it. I got ready for the attack.

Yet the attack did not come at the hut. They waited until I was out on the snowfield. Going around a curve the sled turned over. There was a stone under the snow. The dogs halted. Three men ran out from behind a snowbank, pulled me off the sled, held me down on my back. One man stared into my face and showed me his crooked, yellow teeth.

"You're the wolf girl, eh?" he asked in my language.

I did not understand why they attacked me.

"I'm Wolf," I answered in a strong voice.

The other two men stood over me, talking with the first one. I thought they had evil spirits in them. I struggled to get up but they pushed me down.

The first man climbed over me, sat on my feet, then put one hand to my throat. He put his other hand inside my parka. He grabbed at my chest. Then his hand went between my legs. He asked if it hurt. I shook my head. With both hands he pulled down my sealskin trousers, pushed it down to my boots. My bare skin burned against the snow.

He took out his little *usuk* and tried to push it into me. It was too cold and too soft for that and he got angry. I laughed and he slapped my face.

The two men standing beside me laughed at him, too, so he got up and fought with them.

I jumped to my feet, pulled my trousers up and got the sled upright. I whistled to my dogs and we rushed away, across the snowfield, before they could stop fighting and chase after me.

I checked the rifle on the sled as the dogs raced us home.

Mama told me about men. The man with the red beard was a good example of the bad ones, she said. He was weak in his heart and he could become a monster. When he let evil spirits take over his body, he was violent and angry. When the evil spirits left him and went into Mama, then he returned to being a good human.

The men from the village chased after me. I knew they would not stop until they could get me down and put their evil spirits into me.

I bolted the door of the hut tightly and stacked heavy bins against it. I slept with the rifle beside me. I awoke every time the wind howled or the door rattled. I had short dreams full of bears and falcons. The dogs slept with me, keeping me warm, and warning if anybody came close to the hut.

Finally the night came. I awoke from a light sleep when the noise started. Somebody pushing against the door. Not like the man with the red beard who hit the door with his fist. This was like a shoulder pushing hard against the door. One after another. The bolt held and they gave up.

It was more than a full day run south to reach the shore near the village. Too much rocky ground for a smooth run, stopping a lot to work the sled around or over the rocks. It was night, too, so the men would not go back to the village. Probably they would wait for me to come out.

I heard them walking around, boots crunching the snow, sometimes talking to each other.

"Hey, wolf girl," they would call. "Come outside and play with us."

A few more nights they shoved against the door yet it held strong. After a few days I didn't hear any more noise from them. Set in the ground, the hut had no windows so I could not look outside yet all was quiet, not even the wind to make noise.

I moved the heavy bins away, unbolted the door. I opened the door and the morning sunshine hit my face. I stepped away from the hut, the rifle in my hands, and two dogs beside me. No sign of the men. They got tired of waiting.

I knew they would return. The hut was known to them now. So I had the idea of moving away. I could make an *igloo*. Mama had shown me how when we went out on long runs away from the hut and could not return the same day. When the snow was deep we could cut it into blocks and build a hut of snow. I made some temporary shelters when I was out alone, too. I could bring supplies from the hut with a few runs and build a new home.

First I took the dogs on a long run past where Mama rested and we found a good place with rocks to block the wind and not far from the fjord. I dug into the snow and cut into the ground. I shaped the base. What I took on the sled I unloaded and built a frame of wooden boards. Then we returned to the hut.

I slept that night in the hut and the next day loaded the sled again. The sled was small so it could not carry too many things. It would be too heavy for the dogs to pull. I only had five dogs, and with me pushing, there was not a lot we could carry.

We ran the sled out to the new place by midday. I worked all through the afternoon to build the new home. Then we returned to the hut. I ran the sled around the hut a few times, then sent the dogs out in different directions so the men would not know which way we went from the tracks.

Working all night, I packed more supplies, then slept.

In the morning we made another run to our new home. It did not have a door with a bolt like the old hut. I put up wooden boards for the walls, set in the ground. The roof had to be built. I hung a tarp over the top of the new hut and stayed overnight there. The wind blew against the tarp. The flapping was noisy in the night.

The next day I kept building the hut. Most of what I planned would need to wait until summer, after the snow melted. Then I could cut peat and stack it to make better walls. I needed to bring a few metal sheets from some of the abandoned huts near my old hut to use as a roof, then cover it with the tarp and more turf. It would stand strong by then and keep out the wind and animals.

The third night there, sleeping under the tarp and some seal skins, I heard a bear sniffing outside. I felt the unfinished frame shake, like the bear was testing it with a paw.

I got the rifle ready.

The dogs were quiet as we waited. This new home was not secure, not fully braced yet, so I knew one hard slap by the bear and it would collapse on top of us.

The frame and the tarp shook overhead and I knew we were about to be discovered. I lay on my back, the rifle butt in my shoulder. I aimed upward. The rumble of the bear's throat gave away its position.

Then the tarp tore open and there was the black nose and

white face of the ice bear poking through. The bear looked down at me, growled like it was disappointed I wasn't a seal. It turned its head away, then came back with a roar, showing its teeth.

I didn't have time to scramble up and get out of the way. I pulled the trigger and the bullet hit the bear in the throat. A line of blood dripped down on me from the white fur. The big body of the bear jerked back a moment, then the whole body fell down through the tarps and skins, breaking the frame, and into what was going to be my new home.

The bear's head landed on my legs, black snout toward me, a surprised face frowning at me, but most of its body landed on top of Paqaulik, my lead dog.

I tried to pull him out from under the bear's heavy body as Paq howled with pain. I was not strong enough to get him out. He squealed like I never heard before. I knew then he would not survive. His hips were crushed and he was in pain. So I loaded another bullet and made him sleep.

After that night, I was not sure of making a new home. I took what I could from the new home and loaded it on the sled. With one dog less, it was harder to pull. I pushed from behind and it took two days to return to the hut.

The smell of a bear carcass would attract wolves and prey birds from everywhere so I returned to the new hut and took more of whatever I could get before it was gone. Already a pair of foxes were snipping at the meat. I scattered them and went to work.

I tied a rope around one foreleg and had the dogs pull the bear over onto its back. I took a knife and cut at the footpads. I cut along the forelegs and across the shoulders, stripping away the skin from the fat and muscle. I worked the same way on the hindlegs. When the meat was exposed I noticed a pair of wolves appeared, watching me.

I tried to cut across the belly but got the knife into the guts. It had a strong smell. Out poured some partly digested seal. More creatures came for a meal.

After cutting chunks of meat from the legs and fat from the belly, I wrapped them in skins and cloth. I cut as much skin from the bear as I could manage. I could make clothing from the fur. I packed all that on the sled and we got going as the wolves and birds and foxes attacked the carcass.

We stopped some distance from the bear carcass, settling in a narrow draw, safe from the wind, and calmly ate our meal, the dogs and me. We rested under a bright sun and blue sky. Our bellies were full for once.

I thought of Mama. She was with me. I knew she was smiling at how strong I was.

"See, Mama? I make my own path."

After our rest we headed on to the old home, the hut where I was born.

As we got close, I saw two sleds and teams of dogs beside the hut. There were four humans walking around, calling out. One of them saw me, pointed. The others looked at me.

I halted my sled where I was and watched them. I got the rifle ready, checked the bullets. Then I walked beside the sled as the dogs pulled it slowly toward the hut.

"We won't hurt you," called one of the men.

I didn't trust his words. I slowed more, then stopped. They stood between me and the hut. I did not recognize them. Yet I saw they were not the same men who attacked me on the ice before, who tried to break into the hut.

"You live in this hut?" the man called.

I squinted against the bright sunlight. I held the rifle to my shoulder so they would know I was ready for them.

"No need for that," called the man. "Don't shoot. We're not here to hurt you."

I kept the rifle up. "Why?" I shouted back.

"Why?" He seemed to laugh. "Why are we here?"

"Why here?" I repeated.

The man stepped forward, hands up.

"We're checking on you. On your well-being."

He knelt in the snow, making himself look innocent. Down in the snow he could not spring up suddenly. We both knew that. I lowered the rifle to my hip, still pointing it at him, and took a few steps forward.

"We heard about you from the people in Tasiilaq. You know Tasiilaq? The village you came to a couple months ago? You met Agneta, remember?"

"Why here?"

"We came to see if you are all right."

I didn't know what he meant. Why would I not be all right? I got everything I needed. What did those people in the village of Tasiilaq think of me? I'm Wolf. I make my own path.

"It's not good for a young girl to live alone out here," he said. "How long you been on your own?"

I took two more steps closer. He shifted his position, dropped his butt into the snow, crossed his legs. I knelt where I was yet kept the rifle ready, low against my lap. By then, we were about the same distance as the lead dog's nose to the rear of the sled.

"Mama died."

"Your mama died? I'm sorry to hear that. When? How?"

"Mama danced with spirits then she slept."

The man turned to the others, far behind him, said something and waved his hand. They sat on the sleds.

"These men came with me to check on you. One is the head

teacher. You know what 'teacher' is? The other is our priest. You know what 'priest' is? Do you know about God?"

I could not answer. I never heard those words before.

"It's all right if you don't know. I'm Olek Jensen. You know Agneta? She helped you in the village. I'm her husband. I work for a Danish company in Kulusuk. You know Kulusuk?"

I shook my head.

"It's another village, across the sound from Tasiilaq."

I could not make sense of his words. Maybe he thought he was tricking me. It didn't matter. They came to get me, I knew. They even brought a man from a different village to talk to me, now that Mama was no longer with me.

"It's time for you to come live in the village and go to school. You will like the school. Lots of games and toys. A girl like you should live in a village, not out here on the ice."

"No village," I said.

"You can't live out here by yourself. How old are you?"

"Thirteen years."

"Only thirteen? You've been living out here since when?"

"I was born here. In my hut." I pointed to it.

"Ah! Then you're quite comfortable here. I understand."

"My home."

"Yes, I understand it's your home."

He glanced back at the others as if waiting for a sign.

"Come with us back to the village. You can go to school and there is lots of food for you there."

"Here my home."

He kept saying I should go with them to the village. I kept saying here was my home. Again and again. Even so, they could not convince me to go with them.

They set down a box of supplies from one of the sleds, saying it was a gift. They probably saw the bear skin wrapped up on the sled and maybe they wondered how I got it. My rifle made them stay back.

"See? We didn't hurt you. We're checking you are all right."

He pushed the box forward in the snow with his boots.

"This is for you."

I nodded. Gifts from men usually mean I better take a rest with them, let them get rid of the evil spirits. These men didn't do that. They left the package in the snow, then stepped away. I watched them get on the sleds and leave.

I walked to the box and put it on the sled. We went on to the hut and unloaded everything.

Inside the box was many different food things. I tore open the wrappings and bit into some of them. Some things I knew, some I didn't. Very sweet. Hard to chew.

One gift was a book. Inside I saw many pictures. Some were like pictures inside my head when I sleep. The book had writing on the pages. I could read the characters of the syllables because Mama taught me how to speak them. The pictures were children like me — Inuit — playing in snow. Other pages showed a village like the one I visited. I saw the children in a big hut, all of them sitting on wooden things. At the front of the room was a woman holding a book.

Another gift was a small folder. Inside were pictures drawn on cards. Humans from the village. Places in the village. I saw the face of the woman who was my guide when I went there. Agneta, wife of Olek. I saw a picture of the hut where I got soup. I saw the picture of the bay when it was not frozen. Seeing that view, I knew I could not cross it in summer.

I returned to the book and looked at each page carefully. I got to the last page and returned to the first page. The dogs sat with me, looked at the pictures with me. Maq lay his head on my lap, his nose wetting the page.

"You see this?" I spoke to Maq. "This is a village. You didn't get to see it like I did."

Maq just stared at me, like he thought I was telling lies.

I tried to speak the words written on each page. Mama taught me this mark was said this way, that mark was said that way. The dogs listened to my voice without complaint.

"It's a story," I told the dogs.

When we got hungry I cut more pieces of bear meat for the dogs, and a piece for myself, cooked over the fire. After a rest, I ate one of the food gifts, something brown and square that melted in my hand. It was sticky. I licked off my fingers. Maq took a lick, too. The wrapper said KIT-KAT.

More than ten days later, I returned to the place where I planned to build my new hut. The ice bear was now just a pile of bones. Many tracks in the snow showed all the animals that fed off the carcass, thanks to me. I stood looking at the bones, thinking how dangerous it was that night, yet I did not feel fear.

I gathered more of the supplies that I took there before. They filled the sled, yet not too much for four dogs to pull with one girl pushing. Nothing of the bear carcass that was worth taking now. I let the dogs chew on the bones, getting whatever meat remained. I had enough fur to make clothes.

Knowing I would not return to this place, we ran fast over the snow, back to the hut where I was born.

When we arrived, the men who gave me the gift food in a box had returned. Three of them stood by the door of the hut. I think they were pounding on the door. Yet if they did not see my sled they should have known I was away.

I slid up close to the hut, jumped off the sled with the rifle in my hands.

"Go away!" I cried out, pulling the rifle up to my shoulder.

"Hold on!" shouted the man who spoke to me before. "We won't hurt you. Remember last time we met? I told you about the village. We did not hurt you."

"Why come back?"

"Did you like the gifts?"

I nodded.

"Did you see the photographs of the village? It's a good place to live, don't you think?"

Again I nodded.

"You like the pictures? What do you think of the village?"

The wind bit my face and I could not speak. I lowered the rifle, put the butt down on my sealskin boot. I knew a bullet was ready to fire if they attacked me.

"How about visiting Tasiilaq again? Would you like to?" He smiled. "Plenty of soup for you. Food for your dogs, too."

I knew what he was saying. His words sounded strange yet they were the words of my language. His voice was like summer breezes. He was setting a trap. I could feel it. They wanted me to go with them to the village. That was the reason they sent this half-Inuit half-Danish man out here to talk to me.

"Only a visit. You can come back here then, if you want to," he said.

My dogs crowded around me. They bared their teeth at the three men. Utaak growled, always the first dog to sound the alarm. I pulled the rifle up into my hands again.

"Nothing to be afraid of, miss."

His words seemed true yet I never trusted men humans since the man with the red beard hurt Mama and me. And the other men who followed me out on the ice, wanting to play games. If I went to the village, what would happen there?

"It's sad when a girl loses her mother," said Jensen. "I lost my mother at a young age, too. I know it's difficult for you living out here. You can be proud for surviving such a long time. You don't need to work hard from now on. Come to the village with us. Live in the village."

I didn't say anything. His smile did not go away.

"You can go to the school each day, be warm, have plenty of food. If you liked the book, there are other books at the school. And you can still visit this place any time you want to. There are other children there, too, so you won't be alone. You can have friends. You won't be lonely."

He stepped forward, his hands held out, reaching for me.

Utaak didn't like the man's voice, barked at him. I called Utaak back yet suddenly he leaped at the man. I ordered Utaak back but he bit the man's leg. The man fell down in the snow, crying out and slapping his hands at Utaak.

Another man pulled out a small gun from a pocket and shot at Utaak, laying him down.

I screamed and that same man shot at the other dogs, hitting Qai in the hip. Susik and Maqiiva ran off and I ran after them as fast as I could through the snow.

Another shot whizzed past me and hit Susik, dropping him in the snow. I got to Maq and wrestled him down. I held him tight in my arms.

The two other men chased after me, got to me before I could get up. One man put the pistol to Maq's head.

"Call off your dogs!"

I held Maq against my chest. "No hurt!"

The two men took hold of my feet and dragged me across the snow. I held on to Maq. I told him to be calm.

"I'm sorry about your dogs," said Jensen when we reached him. He sat in the snow, blood leaving a red spot. He pressed a cloth against his ankle. "Not a serious bite. Those dogs love you, it's clear to see. They are too wild for the village. Probably they will fight with other dogs there."

Suddenly, one of the men shot at Qai, a bullet to the head, to end his pain.

I held Maq tight against me. "No hurt!"

"All right, no more hurt." He held up his hands like he was pushing me away.

The two men who pulled me across the snow lifted me to my feet. One of them handed my rifle to Jensen. I dropped it when I ran after my dogs.

I set down Maq, kept my hand on his head. He whimpered. I told him to be calm, stay with me.

"You can take this dog with you."

"No hurt!" I cried out.

He waved his hand. The two men came at me with a rope.

"This is the best way," said Jensen. "Come along, young lady. We'll take you to the village. That's where you belong."

They wrestled me down, finally got my hands together and tied rope around my wrists, then around my waist. I kicked at them and they tied my feet. They tied Maq against me. They put me and my dog flat on the sled.

Jensen took the rifle and unloaded it, put the bullets in his pocket and hung the rifle over his shoulder.

"Be a good girl and we won't hurt you. Or your dog."

3

The Village

Covered in a red dress with white beads and lace, I sat on a hard wooden chair and listened to the adult speak at the front of the room. The words were mostly my language. The people in the village said Mama spoke differently yet some words were the same. I should learn the real words, they said.

To each side of me were other humans, young ones like me, girls and boys, all wearing clothes which did not come from seals or reindeer or bear. Without my furs I felt naked. I wanted to hide yet no place could fit me. The adult was the teacher, a female human who smiled a lot. The room was warm, the air dry and made me sleepy.

They called it *school* and I must visit every day, they said. Sit quietly and listen, learn to write and read. Answer questions. Keep clean. It was the place where I belonged, they said.

When they took me to the village they gave me to a woman

and a man. They had a child already. They had dogs, too. The woman spoke to me yet it was not always my language. She saw I didn't understand and chose different words. She made me feel calm. She was called Maria. They were Danes.

First she took off my sealskins. Parka and trousers and boots. Maria washed me with a wet cloth. I did not like it and wanted to run out but I could not go out in the cold without clothes. She was washing me, she said, because it seemed I didn't have a bath for a long time. I smelled like dogs. On the ice there is no time for a bath, all the water only melted snow, and the air so cold.

She untangled my hair and put bubbles over my head. Then she poured water over my head. She combed out my hair like Mama used to do.

"You have brown hair," she said as I stood in the basin. "Not black like other Inuit. Not blond like Danes."

I didn't know what she meant. Mama had black hair. The man with the red beard had red hair. Black and red mixed into brown. I knew that.

Later I heard Maria telling Per, the man in the house, about my hair. He said there was a man with a red beard in the village yet he went away a couple years past. I thought they knew the man with the red beard was my papa. They wondered where he went. I didn't say anything.

They put me into soft clothes made of something I did not know, not furs or skins. The cloth had pictures all over it, from my chin to my feet. I was told to wear these clothes when I slept. They took me to a different room and showed me where I must sleep. It was a long bench called *bed*. I sat on it, the covering soft as hare's fur, and waited for the moon to shine in the window.

In the hut, as I waited to sleep, I always put beads together like Mama showed me. When I got tired I went to sleep in the same place. Now there was a separate room that was only for sleeping. And I didn't have any beads to string into a picture. I stared out the window at the moon painting the snow-covered mountains blue across the bay from this new hut.

When we arrived in the village, Jensen handed over my rifle to the man in the store. He paid Jensen for it with money. Jensen gave me some of the money. He said the rest of it he would put in a *bank* and I could get it later when I was older.

I did not know about money, never used it. It was just paper and shiny metal things. Yet I knew the value of the rifle. If I ever had to get food, I needed the rifle. If I ever had to defend against attackers, I needed the rifle. It was not his rifle to sell. It belonged to Mama.

"It's better this way," said Jensen when I tried to argue. "A girl doesn't need a rifle. You can sit at home and make clothing. Be comfortable. Let the men do the hunting."

He did not know I hunted a lot out on the ice. Even through the winter dark. I only came to the village one time when I was hungry. I could be hunting again if they didn't capture me and take me to this village.

I got to bring my last dog with me. Yet Maqiiva did not fit in with Maria's dogs. Maq was from a different team so they fought with him or shunned him. So Maq was given to another family. I could visit Maq after school. When I did, I always gave him some meat or fish. He whined so loud when I had to go to my house. Maq continued to bark after I was out of sight.

Maria always checked on me like she thought I would not be in that room when she looked in. Where else could I be? There was no place to go or hide. There was nothing to do. I did not like the sounds or the smells. She had me lie on the bed like I was dead and pulled a blanket over me like I was in a ditch dug in the snow, covered with rocks.

Water came from my eyes and I knew I could not stay in the village any longer.

On the first morning, Maria awoke me and got me dressed in the red clothes, then took me to another room for food.

"Today I will take you to the school and you can meet the other children," she said. She was trying to speak my language yet her voice was strange. "Doesn't that sound like fun?"

I smiled because I knew it was a polite thing to do. They told me to be polite and thankful to any human who helps me. I never wanted anybody to help. I make my own path. They captured me. It's not the same as helping.

I ate the food she gave me yet it didn't taste good. Pieces of wood in a bowl full of milk.

At the school the male teacher knew me already from when they came out to the hut to capture me.

"Good morning," he said in my language. "How are you? Ready for your first day of school? Where should we begin?"

Another teacher, the woman, led me to a room and showed me where to sit. On the *chair*, at the *desk*. I watched everything and listened to everybody, yet I did not learn at all. The other humans stared at me. The teacher told them not to look, that it was rude and Inuit were not rude humans. She smiled at me.

I felt strange among the little humans. I let my head turn to pictures of Mama and my dogs and the man with the red beard and the ice bear. If I had not gone back to the new home I was building just to take back whatever I could, then maybe I would not have been captured and taken to the village like a reindeer meant to last all winter.

I didn't speak, even when Teacher asked me questions.

Except when she asked about my name.

"Mama called me Wolf," I said.

Some children laughed and the teacher scolded them.

"*Anuka* is as good a name as any name," said Teacher.

I could not live in the house with that family. Maria tried to be kind to me but she was not Mama. Per always looked at me like I was a dog. The little boy, standing only as tall as my hip, feared me. Yet they gave me food and a place to sleep. And they took me to the big hut they called school, where Teacher pushed me to learn things I didn't need to know.

They didn't understand my life. You cannot capture a wolf!

One night I gathered all my things, as much as I could carry, and rolled it all up in a blanket to tie it to my back. I put on my sealskin clothes and left the house. I went to the other house and untied Maq. He followed quietly. We both knew we must slip away in the night.

Yet the night did not remember me. We could not find the path over the rocks. We got lost and hid among the rocks until morning. Then we continued up the draw, across the valley, through the mountains, over the snowfield, back along the ridge that led to the other side of the island where the hut was. It took two full days of hiking.

I was so happy to be home again! Inside were all the things Mama and I had. I jumped onto the *illeq*, the sleeping platform, and rolled under the furs. It smelled so good, like Mama and like my dogs! Maq jumped on the *illeq*, too.

There was no food. I took a few things from the house in the village. Only enough for a couple days. I didn't have the rifle now. In the corner of the hut were a few spears and a harpoon for seals. The next day we went out to one of the good spots for seals to come up. It was not a good day and we were hungry going home.

Another day we went out for food and I almost got a hare with a spear. Later I almost got another hare with a good spear throw. Yet we went home hungry.

In the hut were some cans which I got open by beating rocks on the metal to break it open. I shared the meat inside with Maq.

Every day we went out to get food.

A storm came and went so we stayed in the hut.

"Here you are!" a voice said a few mornings later, after the snow stopped falling.

The door to the hut flew open and a big man stood there. He grinned like a hungry bear. Behind him two other men waited. I remembered them from before, the men who attacked me on the snowfield.

"You're a wild girl," the man said, stepping inside. "Ya, the village is not for you. If you're going to live out here you need supplies. We brought some for you." He pointed his hand out the door. "I thought you'd return to this poor little cabin. And I was right, eh?"

"Home," I said.

I moved off the *illeq*. Maq sat up.

"Go away."

He waved the other men inside. They carried boxes and sat them on the floor. He picked up one item after another, showing them to me. Food packages. Tools. Bottles of drinks.

"See? We brought supplies."

He told me what each thing was.

"You like them? They are for you."

I didn't know what to say or do. They wanted me to come with them to the village, I thought. They decided I would go if they gave me gifts.

Give me a rifle! And bullets. That is all I need. I was not very good with a spear yet I could throw rocks accurately. I tried to say it but the words would not leave my mouth.

He laughed and I didn't understand why.

"We brought you these gifts," he said as he stepped toward me, "because we want you to live here. You do not belong in the village. So we visit you."

I was surprised. These men were going to be kind, after all. Finally some humans understood. This is my home. They would let me stay here. Yet I got the feeling of fear spreading through my belly.

"True?" I asked.

"Yes, true."

His grin was like the trio of wolves standing on the ridge above Mama's resting place. He told the other men to put the dog outside and shut the door. Maq barked for a long time.

The man pushed me backward onto the sleeping platform. His arms held me down. Not what I wanted. I shouted curses. Maq barked louder outside.

"For the gifts we brought, you should give us something."

He pulled at my parka and got it off over my head. He tore at my shirt. He pushed my trousers down to my boots as the other men laughed behind him. They stood at the edge of the *illeq* and helped him tug at my clothes.

"Shut that dog up!" the man shouted.

The other man opened the door enough to hold out the rifle. There was a shot. Maq didn't bark any more.

I screamed after the gunshot. I could fight no more.

The man was on top of me, hurting me. Then he got off and the other men got on me. When they finished, there was blood on the furs.

"Now you're a woman," said the first man.

That's what he thought. Already some blood came out of me for no reason every full moon. It did not matter if a man got on me or not. Maria helped me clean it. She explained that bleeding was both blessing and curse. So I was already a woman before this man got on me. He thought he was the first man, smiling at the sight of the blood, acting so happy.

The others didn't like that I was bleeding. They wanted to leave but the leader insisted they stay. They argued for a while as I lay on the *illeq*. Then they decided they hiked too far to not do it again.

When they were finished, they tossed a big fur over me.

I learned later what this game is called. It's a game called *rape* and nobody wins. Those men understood it. Outside the village, nobody would know what they did. That's what they wanted. It's not allowed in the village. Not unless two people agree to it and they live together. Then it's called *sex*.

"We'll visit again," said the man. He sounded proud, like he did something good for me. "We'll bring you more food. That's the deal, eh? You can stay out here. And today, the game we played...? Not too bad? Didn't hurt much? You didn't make much noise." He laughed and the other men joined him. "Your mother was good at this. My uncle said so. But it's our secret now. If you tell anyone, we will have to hurt you."

I thought of Mama, how men came to ask her questions and get rid of their evil spirits. If they passed their evil spirits to me, then I would become evil. It made me realize how she got hurt every time somebody visited her. Now I was in the hut and men from the village visited me. Yet I could not see beyond the night like she could. I had nothing to give, no answers to questions.

"You're a good girl," said the leader, patting my leg. "You didn't fight us, so you can have these gifts. Like we promised. We'll return another day and play with you. We'll bring you more food."

When they left, I pulled on my clothes and went out. I carried Maqiiva in my arms as far as I could, until I could not carry him any more. I dug a place for him at the spot where I fell to my knees, unable to go on. I buried him and chanted over him.

After returning to the hut, I braced the door as best I could.

Then I cleaned myself.

And I sharpened the spears.

I knew they would return, so I broke off a sliver of wood from the edge of the *illeq*. I rubbed its point against a rock to make it sharper. Then I lay on the *illeq* and put a bundle of furs on top of me, imagining it was a man. I hid the sharp stick under the furs beside my hip, then pulled it out as fast as I could. I tried stabbing at different angles, aiming for the ribs, the throat, the belly. I saw that the man's arm would block a thrust to the ribs, so I aimed lower, below the ribs. I practiced swinging the stick up, stabbing the bundled furs, until I was ready for them.

Mama tossed the bones on the floor and saw the pictures they made. So I gathered the bones and tossed them up, let them fall on the floor and I saw the picture of a village. Many huts and many paths. If Mama saw the picture, she would say I was going to the village someday. Yet that was not where I wanted to go. That was where the men lived. I could never go there now.

I was really alone.

No dogs. No rifle to hunt with. No food except what the men left for me. And that was soon finished.

I called to Mama yet I didn't hear any answer.

So I watched the sun come and go, listened to the wind, and I counted the days until I could go to the resting place and join

Mama and my dogs. I didn't want to do anything else.

Many days later, Jensen and the other men who took me to the village the first time returned to take me to the village again. They did not use ropes this time. I went quietly. I understood I could not stay in the hut, not without a rifle and dogs.

"Can you show us where your mother rests?" he asked after I agreed to go with them.

I thought it would be better to have Mama close to me, so I showed them the place. They pulled her from the ground and took her to the village along with me.

On the edge of the village, they cut a hole in a yard of crossed sticks, and she joined the others resting there.

"Now you know your mother is close," said Agneta, putting her hand on my shoulder.

"Mama is always close," I whispered.

When I arrived in the village again, I saw the three men who attacked me. They were surprised to see me there. The leader waved at me. Maybe they worried I would tell their secrets. I worried they would hurt me if I told anybody. As I walked by them, they grinned at me. I guessed they would not attack me while I was with a group of people.

I was taken to a new house. Brigita, the woman there, had long yellow hair. She took away my sealskins and dressed me in clothes like she wore. Danish clothes. Before the clothes, she put me in a big basin of water and washed me. She cut my hair. She told me I was pretty.

If pretty was a good thing then I liked it. If it meant I looked the same as them, then it was not true. If it meant I was different yet I could still live among them with nobody hurting me, then I accepted it. *Pretty* is a polite thing to say.

I started going to the school again. I was supposed to learn how to write the words of my language. What Mama taught me was different from their language. I got the idea how to change one to the other. Mama taught me only short words, yet I could see they were really part of the long words these young humans were speaking and writing.

I was older than them so I felt lost in the room. I could not think like them. I wanted to be on the sled again with my dogs running across the snowfield, skirting the frozen lakes, finding a good air hole and then get a seal to eat.

So I ran away again one night.

I could not go far in the Danish clothes they gave me. I only had a long dress and stockings, buckle shoes, a scarf and coat. Those clothes didn't keep me warm or protect my feet. The hike through the mountains was hard. The shoes broke apart, so I went on without them. I fought against the rocks and against myself. Half of me wanted to go ahead, half wanted to turn back.

The sky darkened around me, the winds slapping against me. I found shelter between some rocks. I wanted a dog to hold tight during the night, to keep warm.

The next day I found an old trail made by my sled. I followed it to the hut.

Inside, the hut was a mess. Like somebody visited and threw everything around looking for something. I put everything right again. I mended my cut feet, then took some fox pelts left there and sewed a pair of boots. They were not good for hiking yet they would keep my feet warm.

As I admired my new boots, I called to Mama yet she did not answer. The hut was all mine. Not even her spirit lived in it any longer. She slept in the village now.

With no dogs and no sled, no rifle and no spears, I could not live there for long. I knew that. Hunger would come soon. Then the winter dark. And everything begins and ends with the dark, Mama always said. *Everything ends with the dark.*

I sat on the *illeq*, saw the blood-stained furs still there, and thought of all the days I lived with Mama in this hut and all the days I lived alone after she went to rest. I wondered what to do.

I knew they would come again, the men who attacked me or the other men who wanted me to go to the village. I did not belong out here on the ice, that Jensen told me. The men who attacked me wanted me to stay here. I was born here yet I did not belong here. Maybe I did not belong any place. It was like fire and ice fighting with each other. The fire melts the ice and the water puts out the fire. The world was crazy.

Feeling the emptiness of my belly and the cold wind blowing through cracks in the walls, unprotected by these Danish clothes, my eyes settled on the old metal harpoon leaning in the corner. I thought about how it must feel to be a seal popping up at an air hole and suddenly the harpoon cuts through its body and stops its life. It was always quick.

I got up, grabbed the harpoon and cut my finger on the sharp point. I returned to the *illeq*, sat on the edge with the harpoon between my knees. I pulled off my coat and opened my dirty dress, put the point between my breasts. I breathed hard.

Water dripped from my eyes. If I just slipped off the edge of the *illeq*, the tip would cut straight through me. Then I would be with Mama—

Suddenly, I heard the long howl weaving through the wind. Another wolf joined the first wolf. And another. The howling grew louder than the wind. All the howls coming together as one. It matched my breathing.

I let the harpoon drop to the floor. I stood and howled with them. I ran outside and howled as loud as I could. The distant wolves howled back at me. I howled so loud the whole sky full of stars rattled and shook!

They arrived after several days, knowing where to find me. It was the good men, not the bad men. I had to wonder how much difference there was.

"We're getting tired of chasing you," said Jensen. "It's a hard trip over the mountains. Longer with the sleds going around the shore, like we did this time. You must come back and stay in the village. That is where you belong."

I understood what he said, yet I needed to be in this hut for a while. I shook my head.

"Will you return with us to the village?" he asked.

I breathed deeply and nodded. The clouds were around me and I heard wolves still howling in my head.

"Good. In time you'll forget this place. Life will be better for you in the village."

Maybe that is what Mama meant when she told me to go to the village after she went to rest.

"Be a good girl and come with us. Stop this foolishness."

I'm not a good girl! I didn't want to be that. Good girls always let men do whatever they want to do. That was not me.

"I'm Wolf. I make my own path," I muttered.

"What did you say?" asked Jensen.

I looked away.

To be sure I didn't return to this hut where I was born, they took anything of value out and set fire to the rest. The wooden beams burned. So did the floor boards. The turf walls collapsed inward, leaving a big smoldering pit where my home once sat.

"You won't need all those old sealskin clothes," said Jensen. "In the village you will have wonderful new clothing. And new boots. You can keep a few things for your memories. But it's likely you won't want any memories of this terrible place." He turned to the other men. "Can you imagine a girl growing up in this place? Not even a wooden house. Really, just a hole in the ground with some floor boards and a tin roof overhead. Like a wolf den."

"To think she was a baby here, born here! How unsanitary! An awful place for a baby."

"I'm amazed she was not sick from disease or starving."

"Her mother probably fed her fish. Or hares. And not much of any of that. No vegetables."

"Can she read and write?"

"They put her in the primary class. She might catch up. Even so, maybe she will never be a good member of the village."

"She seems good at beadwork. Have you seen it?"

"At least her mother taught her a useful skill."

"Hard to imagine a child growing up here. Hard enough in the village. So many of our youth leave for the capital. Or even to Denmark."

"This one won't leave. She could never survive in a city."

They laughed together. Jensen caught me watching them.

"You understand us?" he asked in my language.

I nodded. I was not a stupid child like they believed. Mama taught me many words and the man with the red beard showed me books and read them to me.

They took my home from me. But I would find another. Or make another. I would always survive. *I'm Wolf. I make my own path.* They did not know that. They thought I was just a soft little bird to sing for them.

Brigita shook her head, frowned at me. She did not want me, I could see. I did not want her. Yet she accepted me again.

Same as before, she told me to take off my clothing. I had a bad smell, she said. I must wash then put on clean clothes. She was a Dane and they had special ideas about keeping clean. The Inuit didn't care, she told me. They lived with all the smells of nature. In the cold and the dark nobody washed or bathed. No laundry either. Same bodies, same clothes for months. Keeping safe in the cold was more important than being clean.

I got down to my skin. This woman told me to stand in the basin on the floor again. I was cold but the water she poured over me was warm. I held my arms around myself.

"So this is where you are!" said Mikkel, her husband, as he entered the room.

He spoke my language. They continued in their language. He kept looking at me and I held my arms in front of me. The way his eyes touched me was cold.

"This is the wild girl?" he asked, using my language again. He wanted me to understand him.

"I agreed to give her room and board for one year — or until she gets in trouble again. She can go to school and help around the house." She cleared her throat loudly. "After all, we are a good Christian family."

They spoke more with each other. Mikkel continued looking at me. He pointed his hand at me, said something, laughed.

He left the room a moment. Then he peeked around the door as my bathing continued.

Brigita raised each of my arms, washed under them. She cut the hair there. She gave me soap and a cloth and told me to wash between my legs. She poured warm water over me again. I liked the warm water against my skin.

She asked me to lift up a foot so she could wash it. I tried to keep my balance on one leg as she ran a cloth between my toes, yet I could not and I tumbled down, knocking the basin over.

Water rushed across the wooden floor! She shouted at me, even though I fell on my hip and got hurt.

She left and returned with a big cloth, told me to get the water up. Already on my hands and knees on the floor, I took the big cloth and let the water soak in, moved the cloth across the floor. Then I could get the new clothing she promised.

Mikkel watched as I cleaned the spill on the floor. He liked looking at me. Maybe because I was wild, like everybody said. I was not like them, I understood, so I was not treated like they treated each other.

He stopped sneaking looks and entered the room holding a new cloth.

"Here, dry yourself," he said, tossing it to me.

I caught the cloth and held it against my body. He waited while I dried my skin with the cloth.

"Go to the next room. She's got clothing for you. Something lovely from Copenhagen."

Living with Mama on the ice, I wore only seal skins or bear skin clothes.

Brigita held up pink and white clothing, another dress.

"First, you must learn what proper garments to wear," she said. "I know you have never worn undergarments before now but a proper Danish girl always does. So first the panty, then the pantaloons, then the brassiere. Then the camisole and petticoat. You already need them. Don't want the boys to get too excited, eh? You're only thirteen. No need for boys."

Every day I had to dress like a proper Danish girl. I pulled long white stockings up my legs. They covered my toes, my feet, and all my legs from above my knees. They were very slick and they sometimes rolled down. I had to wear panty and pantaloons, camisole and petticoat, Brigita said, or else the men would not be able to control themselves. I didn't want to get attacked again, so I obeyed her. Maybe there was magic in these clothes. I had to put my breasts into a brassiere, too, and it hurt so much I hated it. After that, she would drop a dress down over my head that stopped below my knees. Last, I slid my feet into shoes made of the skin of cows. I never saw a cow but they live in Denmark and have horns and give milk. Brigita would comb out my hair and usually said she couldn't do anything to make it look how a Danish girl's hair should look. Her hair was yellow so I guessed she thought my hair was ugly.

Brigita always complained about me yet she let me stay. She couldn't have children come out from her belly so she thought I could be her child, yet I was so difficult to teach to be a proper Danish girl. I wondered what *proper* meant and how Danish girls could be so wonderful. I thought they must have a difficult life, always putting on so many clothes then making their hair pretty. Then what do they do? Go hunt seals? Or maybe they hunt those cows and take the skin for shoes. It might be a good life, after all. I dreamed of being a Danish girl.

Yet Brigita always told me I could never be a Danish girl, not a proper girl, either. So I never tried. My life, she said, was to go to the school every day and learn the language. She meant my language that I already spoke, not her language from Denmark. That would be impossible, she said. I was not smart enough to learn Danish. I was not even smart enough to learn *Kalaallisut*—official Greenlandic. On the east side of Greenland, where we lived, they spoke another language called *Tunumiit*.

Mama taught me the same words she spoke and her mama spoke. That was her own language. Some of her words were like *Tunumiit* but not always. We didn't need to speak much anyway.

Yet this woman from Denmark always spoke too much, never stopped talking. And I could never understand her.

So I did what I was supposed to do. I sat on the chair at the back of the classroom and listened to Teacher telling us about everything. She showed us numbers, told us how to put them together and take them apart. If we wanted to count how many seals we got or how many fish we caught we could use numbers. Before I came to the village I only knew ten numbers. Now I knew a hundred numbers. I wrote them in order every day.

Teacher showed pictures of other places and other humans. Some lived in villages like Tasiilaq, some lived in big villages called *cities*. Some humans had white skin and yellow hair and some had brown skin and black hair. All shapes and sizes of humans. They wore different clothing and ate different food. Some humans lived where there was never any snow. In that place there were walrus with long noses that walked on the land and instead of wolves they had big cats. It seemed like a terrible place to live so I was happy to be in this village.

We went through the winter dark keeping to the same school schedule, always counting on a *clock*. Then we went to a *church* every seventh day. I never counted days before, yet in the village they thought it was important.

On the ice Mama called to Sila for answers. Sila was the spirit that made the weather. Sila also gave wisdom, Mama told me. Weather and wisdom were the same, and if you did not obey you would die in hundreds of terrible ways. Yet in the church everybody sang to a different spirit and they sounded happy, especially during the winter dark. The tall man with the white beard put on a robe and stood before everybody to tell stories of the spirit that watched over Denmark. Although it was a small land far away, they had a king that was the leader of this place called Greenland. Denmark didn't have any ice but sometimes had snow. There were no bears there and no dark. And because of the spirit that lived there, the cows gave milk and humans could make *chocolate* from it.

One day I went into the house after the school finished and I saw a small golden thing on the table. It was square, about the size of my fist. I picked it up and it smelled good. I tore open the paper around it and inside was something brown and sweet. I took a bite of the corner and it tasted good. So I ate all of it.

But I left the paper on the table.

Brigita found the paper. She shouted at me for eating the chocolate she was saving for everyone. It came all the way from Denmark, she said. It was worth a lot of money. I did not have money, she told me, so I could not pay for it. She was planning to give me one bite so I would know how wonderful Denmark was. But I ate all of it so nobody else could have a bite.

So she beat me, called me selfish. I remembered when Mama hit me, when she was in the dark place, so I took it until the woman got tired. I never wanted to eat chocolate again, no matter if it came from Denmark or not. Better to chew seal fat or whale blubber!

I lived with the Danes for a few months. Each time I went to the first meal of the day, Brigita would scold me for not being dressed properly or for being late. Then, later in the day, she would tell me she was only trying to teach me how a proper Danish girl should behave. Each day she checked how I dressed. Sometimes she watched me put on the clothes to be sure I did it right. Sometimes Mikkel watched, too.

The woman taught me to put plates on the table and to take them off the table. She taught me a lot of Danish words. I learned to obey her when she said the words. I got my hair cut short. She wanted me to look Danish yet I had the skin of Inuit.

The sun went away and it was the dark time. Day and night

the same. We got up when we felt rested and went to bed when we felt sleepy, no matter what the clock showed.

When I was sleeping, Mikkel would enter my room and get under the blanket with me.

"If you're living in my house," he said, "you should be kind and help me sleep."

He took my hand. I knew he had evil spirits in him. He told me what to do, yet it was no different than I did with the man with the red beard. He left his evil spirits on the sheet.

I started to expect him any night. He put his hands on me, all around my body, squeezing my skin. He asked if I wanted to be his second wife. He said it was allowed because I'm Inuit. I said yes. It was good to sleep with any warm body in the dark. The world grew darker and there were more evil spirits.

Brigita found stains on the sheet. She shouted at her husband, almost killed him. She shouted at me and slapped me. I was not a Danish girl after all. Not proper in any way, she told me. Just a wild girl from the ice. I didn't deserve the fine things she had shared with me. No chance to have a civilized life for me here in the village.

I was sent to live with an Inuit family.

"What are you thinking, Anuka?" asked the woman who tried so hard to teach me everything I did not know.

She knelt beside my desk.

I stared far ahead into another world, feeling how close the walls were and how warm the room was with the other children sitting around me. I liked that Teacher called me Wolf, the name Mama gave me. Mostly Mama said *Ka* if she wanted to get my attention.

Now Teacher and I spoke Greenlandic.

"I remember running the sled with my dogs," I said after a moment to enjoy the picture in my head.

"You miss your dogs?"

"Yeah, miss a lot."

"Sorry for that. Plenty of other dogs here."

She studied me like I had clues painted on my face.

"Thinking of that makes you happy, doesn't it?"

"Yeah, happy pictures."

She got up, stood beside me and my desk. She put her hand on my shoulder.

"I know something else that will make you happy."

"What is it?" I thought I might get a snack treat.

"You've made a lot of progress. Perhaps I can go ahead and tell you. We're going to promote you to the next class soon."

I stared at the book in front of me, the lines of words set like wolf teeth on the paper.

"I see you like books. Lots of stories in books. You can learn a lot reading books."

"I like books."

"Then we should let you run the library." She laughed. "Not so many books we have in Greenlandic. More books in Danish. If you learn more Danish, you can read more books."

I nodded, partly because I learned to do that when asked a question, and partly because I really wanted more stories and if I had to learn another language to read more books then I would learn it. I could see the patterns and knew how to change words around, so my list of words grew longer and longer. Teacher was very happy with me.

Outside of school, I helped in the house where I lived. The house was always cold and Opik, the woman there, was kind to me. She asked many questions yet I did not answer loudly. I had a small voice. She could not hear my words. That made her angry sometimes. A few times she called me stupid even though Teacher said I wasn't.

I helped wash the clothes of the Danish families. That was the work Opik did. She said it was fair exchange for giving me a bed and the clothes that belonged to her eldest daughter who died, drowned years before when the ice broke under her. I did the washing following her instructions. If I didn't wash the clothes correctly, she called me stupid. She said her two young children could do it better than me yet she never made the children show me they could do it better. I promised to try harder.

And her man, Arnauyq, always going out for work or for drinking and never at home. When he was at home, he would get angry at Opik for anything he didn't like, then he would beat her. Sometimes her crying would keep me awake at night. Yet I didn't tell anyone what happened in that house. I was a guest so I could not tell their secrets. Someday I would leave the house, I knew. Then their secrets could melt away like summer snow.

After the sun began to shine again, little by little across the sea and over the mountain peaks, Opik sent me to the store to get a few things on a list. I stopped before I went in, to kick the snow off my boots.

There were a lot of people inside. They didn't see me, so I stood by the door and listened.

"Has to be one of the men in this village," said a man.

I thought they were talking about the men who attacked me at my hut. I was ready to tell them about it if they knew their names.

"Who else could go there?"

"But look at her: brown hair, like she is mixed."

"I remember a Danish man in the village for some time."

"Ya, I remember him."

"Not Danish."

"He spoke Dane, I recall."

"Red beard, red hair."

"Ya, I know who you mean. The man from the sea. Brought on a ship. From Iceland, I heard. Strange man, kept to himself."

"Except when he hired on a fishing boat."

So it was not the men who attacked me they were talking about! My belly felt empty. They meant the man with the red beard. Yet he was gone.

"You think he went all the way over the mountains for her, the crazy woman?"

"Perhaps. Who can be sure?"

"Maybe he went away for his own reasons and happened to find her. Or, I heard —"

"He went overboard. Then he returned some months later. Like nothing happened."

"Could be he made it to shore there."

"He was fighting on the boat. That's what Finn told me, so they put him on the shore, left him there."

"You think he raped that crazy woman?"

"How else to make a child like that?"

"He disappeared for a few days every once in a while. I know that much. He hired on fishing boats, but when we looked for him again he was gone."

"Gone to the north side for some whoring, eh?"

"There's an ungodly pair!" said a woman with a laugh.

"So the girl is their progeny. Who else could be her father? Look at her hair, brown not black. Only half-Inuk."

"What to do about her?"

"She loves to look at the books." I recognized Teacher's voice.

"Can she read? Did the crazy woman teach her anything?"

"I think she reads. She is clever though quiet."

"Her Greenlandic is terrible. No doubt her mother was an illiterate so she doesn't know our language well."

"She learns quick," said Teacher. "She wants to learn. She has a big heart."

"She's too wild. I'd never let her near my children."

A man laughed. "Your children are just as wild. And they never lived out on the ice."

"As long as she's no trouble she can stay."

"Why you think she'd be trouble? She keeps to herself, or she plays with the dogs."

"See? An animal herself."

"That's so cruel!"

"Well, she does have that name. Wolf! What kind of name is that for a girl?"

"I asked her if she wanted a new name," said Teacher.

"And her response?"

"Her mother gave her that name because the wolves howled when she was born. That's what she said."

"You can never trust those who live on the ice."

"I showed her a list of names in a book, asked her to choose one. And she did."

"So she took a new name?"

"Not exactly. She did point to one. Aynur."

"Aynur? What's that? Not an Inuit name, sure. Not Danish, either."

"I think it's Turkish. It was a book of children's names from around the world."

"That's no name for a girl in Greenland."

"Unless we all came here across the top of the world like her ancestors did. All the way from Asia, from central Asia. You know, where Turkish people lived."

"Oh, so like Siberia, like Kazakh, like Mongolia…."

"I suppose."

"See? She is clever."

"So that's how we should call her?"

"I think she still prefers Anuka."

"Ya, Wolf! Now it's Aynur-something."

"I call her 'Hey you' — and she gives me a look!"

"So cruel, Jorgen!"

"Whatever her name, she's going to be trouble soon, as she gets older. You know — the boys, I mean."

"You shouldn't even be thinking that way!"

"She's a virgin?" asked a woman.

"What kind of question is that?" said Teacher.

"It's a legitimate question. A girl of her age should be."

"Ya, if not now or already, then soon enough. When she gets to sixteen…."

"Not like your daughters, eh? So pure and saintly. Naw, they are such whores!"

"Quiet now! They're the prettiest girls in the village."

"And most popular!"

"We are a small village. Not many choices, eh?"

They all laughed.

"Even that wild girl will be pretty to someone. Not me, sure, but someone here will want her for a wife — a temporary wife, at least."

"Shush now! She'd better not hear you talking like that," said Teacher.

"Marry her to someone and be done with her."

"The elders must decide something like that. Can't force her into a marriage."

I turned away, holding my breath. They were planning to sell me to somebody or hurt me, I knew then. They always had this plan! Change me into a Danish girl, then give me to the men.

So I returned to my room and gathered my belongings. I had to get away. Yet I had no place to go.

I could go back to where the hut was, maybe build it again. Or I could cross the fjord to the opposite shore and get away. But I did not have supplies. I needed dogs and a sled and a kayak and a rifle and bullets. Yet all I had was pretty pink dresses and stupid brassieres.

There was a boy called Happy who lived in this village. Actually his name was the Greenlandic words for Happy Eider Duck but I called him Happy. He was older than me, two levels higher in the school, but he was no taller than me. I met him at a party the school had for me when I started my fourteenth year. They celebrated my birth day on the same day as the first day of the sunrise after the dark.

We ate cake with chocolate sauce. Teacher gave me a book about the world and the people, animals, and plants in it. It was very heavy. Brigita gave me chocolate and a blue dress with white buttons down the front. For the party, she asked me to wear a pink dress she made instead of a traditional Greenlandic costume. There was music, too. An old man sang folk songs and Happy crossed the room to ask me to dance. I did not know how to dance but he pulled me around with him in the middle of the room. People laughed at us, so I ran out.

Happy liked throwing snow at me whenever I walked by. One day I chased after him and knocked him down. I pushed his face into the snow. I cursed at him. He rolled us over so he was on top of me in the snow, holding me down. I thought he was going to attack me!

Instead, he stared into my eyes. Then he put his mouth on my mouth. He didn't spit, didn't pass food like Mama did when I was a baby. He held his mouth against my mouth. Then he climbed off, said he was sorry for doing it.

On days when he walked with me, I saw the men again, the ones who attacked me at the hut. They sat outside drinking, or I saw them leaving the drinking house. They seemed to ignore me now, like they knew they couldn't attack me in the village. I still wished I had the rifle with me.

One day Happy and I walked to the store and I saw the men who attacked me crossing the road. I took Happy by the arm and turned him around.

"Let's go this direction," I said to him.

He was surprised. "If you wish."

"Hey, wolf girl," the man called after us. "Is that your new boyfriend?"

I hurried us on, turned a corner behind the buildings.

After we got to my house, Happy said he liked the way I held his arm, like we were a couple. Then he put his arms around me, squeezed me in his arms.

"Who were those men calling to you?" he asked in a serious tone when he released me.

"Just some men I don't like." I frowned, not sure what to say. "They hurt me before."

"Who would want to hurt you?" said Happy with a big grin.

"Some people do."

Happy was not like those bad men. He always looked at me in the school and in the village with a big smile on his face. He waited for me—even after extra lessons with Teacher, learning to read books—just so he could walk with me to the house where I lived. He always asked questions as we walked. If I didn't seem to listen, he kept talking anyway. Then he would answer the questions he asked. He wanted to show he knew everything.

We walked along the shore. I pulled him that way a lot, away from the eyes of people. I liked to pick up some of the smooth round stones as he talked.

He said he would go to Denmark someday, like his father did a few years before. He would be a prince and wear a crown, ride a big horse, and even kill a few dragons if I commanded him. He explained about horses—"They're like dogs but bigger."—and about dragons—"They fly in the sky and spit fire at children."

Another day we looked at some books in the school together and he showed me pictures of horses and dragons. You can find all kinds of things in books. We saw pictures of princes, too.

I told him he was dreaming, that all there was in the world was ice and snow, and a month of wildflowers and sunshine.

So one sunny day he gathered a bunch of blue and red and pink wildflowers in his arms and gave them to me.

"Here, Aynur! This is the best of the world here," he said, grinning brightly, "and now you have it."

I held out my arms but they were not big enough to hold all the wildflowers.

"All these from this island?"

"Not all. But most of them! I left some for next year."

I liked him walking beside me. Sometimes he took my hand and pulled me along with him. Upon the bare rocks, down to the shore, behind the houses, into the shadows, and he kissed me a lot whenever we were alone. He was a good man, not bad. In my heart a flock of birds flew into the sky whenever I saw him!

Then one day he asked me if I loved him.

"What's that?" There is no Greenlandic word for what he meant. He spoke Danish for that word.

"It's like a feeling inside your heart that's like the sun shining on the first day after mid-winter," he said.

"It feels warm? It feels bright?"

"Better than that," he said. "It's what I feel every time I see you, Aynur."

"Like you get hungry?"

"Bigger than hungry. But it's a good feeling. It's like after you eat a good meal."

"A big, good feeling of sunshine in your heart...."

"That's it!"

"I know I love Mama. I get that feeling inside me whenever I think of her. And she is always with me."

He frowned. "I know you love your mama." He stared at me. "Do you love me? That's what I want to know."

I couldn't answer.

He took my arm, pulled the glove off my hand and slid his fingers between my fingers. He leaned close, gazing deep into my eyes. I thought he was going to press his mouth against my mouth again.

"You like books, don't you?"

I nodded, clenching my fingers tighter around his.

"Then you know most books are about love."

"Are they?" I never thought of it but I had not read all the books in the school.

"Searching for love. Or...losing it."

"Then I should write a book," I said.

"About love?"

"About losing it."

"You're losing love?"

"Maybe. Or I never got any of it."

"But I—"

He stopped us right there in the street. Some people passing by looked at us.

"I can say it in Danish. Want to hear?"

"Teacher says I'll never learn Danish."

"It's *Jeg elsker dig.*"

"What's that mean?"

"I told you. It's 'I love you' in Danish. Papa said it to Mother before he left for Denmark."

"He's still there?"

"Ya, but probably he never comes back."

"Then you won't be happy."

He smiled. "Happy is my name. So I'm always Happy."

I leaned against him, bumped his shoulder so he knew I was beside him, that he wasn't alone. Our eyes met. Suddenly, he stepped up against me. I thought he was going to kiss me. His hands slipped in my coat pockets and found some of the stones I had gathered.

"You're always carrying stones, Aynur."

"I like them."

He took his hands out, held up one stone, gray with a white crystal seam. "It is pretty, I guess. They make you happy?"

"Someday they will."

"I hope so." He grinned. "You know why I'm Happy?"

"No," I said, gazing back.

"Because I see you every day!"

He kissed me hard on my mouth, then ran away. I watched him go behind a house and he was gone.

That night I thought about how his lips felt against my lips.

Maybe he would join me when I ran away. We could find a place to start our own village and we would help each other. It would be good to have another human to stay at the camp while I went out on a hunt. Maybe we could keep each other warm on the *illeq*, too. This man I liked.

I liked how I felt when he put his mouth to my mouth, when he held my hand, when he got close and I thought he wanted to put his hand under my dress yet he didn't.

I laughed to myself. I thought he was happy because he liked eating eider ducks!

During the next couple of weeks I didn't have time to collect many supplies. I took some things from the house that I thought would be useful. I looked around the store for what I needed. I slipped some small things into my parka or a sack. The priest said the spirit that watched over Denmark would forgive me for anything.

I talked with Happy about my plan. He was ready to go.

"Then you and me can be the prince and princess!"

"But you gotta protect me from dragons," I told him.

"I will!"

"And I will protect you from ice bears."

I waited outside the drinking place. I snuck out of the house after I was supposed to be sleeping. In the dark I could hide. When the three men came out of the drinking house, laughing among themselves, I stepped out of the shadow of the building, weighing the stone in my hand.

The leader noticed me.

"Hey, wolf girl! Why you out so late?"

I didn't hear what the other men said because I hurled the stone at the leader. His hands went to his face and he cried out. The other two saw what I did and cursed at me. I threw a stone at the next man and struck his head. He fell to the ground. The third man I hit in the mouth with the stone, maybe knocked out some teeth. I threw more stones, hitting them with almost every one—as hard as I could throw!

Then another man rushed up to me from the side and he grabbed my arms, held them against my chest.

"You stop that!" he shouted at me.

The three men were on their knees. Under the lamplight I could see blood running through the fingers of the leader, hands covering his face. Another man held his hand over his mouth. The other man rubbed the back of his head. They were cursing!

The man who grabbed me called to the people who came out to see what the noise was about. He asked them to help the men get over to the clinic. Then he took me to the house where I was supposed to be sleeping.

Opik was surprised and shouted at me for sneaking out. The man told her what happened.

"You could have put out his eye!" said Opik.

Maria, who I lived with first in Tasiilaq, followed us to the house. She was a witness.

"You can't throw rocks at people," said the man who acted as constable. "We know you come from the ice but it's not allowed here. You should know it's wrong."

"Oh, Aynur," said Maria, "why'd you throw rocks at them?"

I had a scowl hammered onto my face.

"I didn't throw rocks."

"Come now! We saw you."

"I was putting the stones in my pocket and they slipped out of my hand."

The adults scoffed at me. The constable shook his head.

"Why did you throw at those men?" he asked. "Do you know them?"

I looked sideways at Maria. "They killed my dog."

"Killed your dog?" asked the constable.

"You mean Maq?" asked Maria. "I thought he just ran away.

Haven't seen him for a long time."

"And they attack me."

Maria stared at me. "Attacked? What do you mean?"

I could not hold back my anger. My eyes let go all the tears I was saving. Maria came over and hugged me, held me tight. Opik asked the constable to step outside so they could talk with me. After he went out, I told them what happened at the hut.

A few days later, I was awakened early by Opik. Teacher was there, too.

"Aynur," Opik called me, "a lot of people here think it's best if you go to a special house for orphan children all the way over in Nuuk."

"It's the capital," said Teacher. "It's practically a city. Almost ten times the size of Tasiilaq. It will be like heaven."

"There are many people, lots of children, too."

"You can go to a big school and someday, if you wish, you can return here."

"On the west coast everything's better, warmer."

"We want you to be happy. Maybe there is only trouble for you here in this village. Already people talk."

"The elders decided."

"After you move to Nuuk, you can learn more. Someday you can do something great."

"Nuuk is better for you, Anuka — sorry, I keep forgetting to call you Aynur now. Aynur, the wandering jewel."

"Either way it's best for everyone that you leave this village."

"I'll write to you. And you can take your favorite books."

"Nuuk is the place for you now."

"And you will never be bothered by those men again."

In less than an hour a bag was packed for me. I was taken to the far end of the village. A big red bird they called a *helicopter* was sitting there and some people got into it.

"The heli will take you across the sound to Kulusuk," said Teacher. She hugged me. "That's where the airport is. You get to ride on an airplane!" She hugged me again. "I'm going to miss you, Aynur! My best student! You are going to do great things, I know!"

I couldn't say anything. Words sailed above me, out of reach.

Brigita came to say farewell to me. She gave me a package of chocolate. She told me to be good and bathe at least every seven days. Then she hugged me.

The women started walking away from the helipad.

I didn't get to say goodbye to Happy so I shouted after them.

"Tell Happy Eider Duck I love him!"

The women were bent down, keeping their heads low.

"Tell him *'Jeg elsker dig'*!"

Teacher looked back, waved, saying something.

The helicopter whirred over my head and I could not hear her words. Maybe she could not hear my words. Yet words are not thoughts, not feelings, not anything important. Words are only dreams that disappear as soon as you open your eyes. That is why people put them into books.

4

The Town

From the window of the big red helicopter I looked down as we rose into the sky and I saw the whole world where I lived. Never before did I think there was so much land, so much sea around me. I was only a small human. I lived on a small island beside a big island. And we were only a corner of the whole world.

I searched through the mountains and glacier valleys for the ruins of a hut I called home for almost all my life, but I could not find it against the white snowfields and the brown rocks. Below was the dark blue sea spotted with chunks of ice, like a bag of white beads had been spilled over a table.

The helicopter never went above the clouds so I could see the island of Kulusuk all the way until we landed there.

Teacher put a red and white tag on me, hung it around my neck with a cord. She wrote the address on it where I was going. If I got lost they could find me, she said. Someone would meet me in Nuuk.

At Kulusuk, I was on my own again. The airport was small, one room and six chairs. I sat like a proper Danish girl, holding my bag on my lap, knees together. An Inuit woman in airplane clothes introduced herself. She took me to get a few snacks. She bought a Kit-Kat for me.

As I waited, I thought of writing a letter to Happy. I thought of the words. Then I got a fog around my head and I could not remember how to write the marks. I also did not have any paper, just the pages of a few books Teacher gave me. She told me to treat books like special treasures so I dared not tear out a page to write on. Someday I would write a letter to him, I knew.

After a while the woman in the airplane clothes returned to lead me to the airplane. I sat in the seat they told me to sit in and pulled the belt around my body. Then the world suddenly fell away and there was nothing outside the windows but the sky and the clouds and whiteness everywhere below. I saw only the ice cap that went forever across the world below.

The woman in the airplane clothes visited me at my seat and asked me questions. Yet I could not say many words. She patted my head. She gave me a can of *cola* to drink. It bubbled so hard in my throat I could not finish it. When we landed, it spilled. I got down to clean it up but the woman said she would do it. I had to get off the airplane, she told me. I had to meet the people I was sent to because I had no mama and no papa.

The two women said they were *Catholic* sisters yet they did not look alike at all. Except they dressed alike. They wore long black dresses and big white hats. They looked like Danes, one with yellow hair, one with light brown hair. They spoke Danish to me until they realized I didn't understand. The brown haired sister went out and returned with a woman who looked Inuit. She wore the same black dress and white hat.

The sister with yellow hair was Margret. Sister Margret, she said. The other was Sister Katerina. They were the leaders of this school. It was more than a school, it was a home for children who had no mother or father. Orphans. This was the Children's House. Sometimes parents in a far away settlement might die from accidents or while hunting or they got sick, so there were orphan children. This school had thirty-six children. And me.

Here, said Sister Margret, I could learn everything I needed to know to be a good Christian woman, get some job skills, and prepare to be a good wife and mother. If I wanted, I might even become a Sister like them. For that, I would have to go away to Denmark for training. That was where their spirits lived.

When I lived in the hut with Mama, I never thought about my life or what I would do the next day or the next season. Time moved only with the seasons. Sila, who made all the weather, decided everything. I went along like an ice floe on the sea.

Now these sisters were happy to decide everything. But they said the Denmark spirit was the highest spirit in the world. He was the one that really decided everything. So I should say good words to him every night, ask for wisdom and advice, like how to be a proper Danish girl. They didn't say 'proper Danish girl' but I heard those words in my head from Brigita. It seemed so long ago now.

Suddenly, I was in Nuuk, a town that was the capital of a country called *Kalaallit Nunaat*—called *Greenland* by people who didn't live here. This town of Nuuk, what proper Danish girls called Godthåb, was the biggest town on this biggest island.

So I was an even smaller human!

"We have your teacher's report," said Sister Margret, sitting behind the big desk.

I sat on a chair in front of the desk, my knees together, my bag on the floor and my hands on my lap.

"However," she continued, "there is some information that has been left out. Perhaps you can help us make it complete. First of all, what is your official legal name?"

I did not understand, even when the Inuit Sister spoke to me in my language. Her name was Sister Louisa, which was not an Inuit name. She did not seem happy to see me, like I reminded her of when she was living in a village somewhere, maybe got captured like me.

"What do you call yourself?" asked Sister Margret.

"Anuka," I said. Louisa spoke in Danish to Margret.

"Your name is 'wolf'?"

"Mama called me Wolf."

"That is certainly not a good Christian name. Let's see...."

The sisters talked among themselves.

"How would you like us to call you 'Anna'? There is a saint named Anne. Your Inuit name sounds like Anna so we shall call you Anna. How about that?"

Sister Louisa spoke their words to me and I nodded to agree. I didn't know what Anna meant but maybe they were speaking *Anuka* the wrong way, so I let them. Mama didn't speak correct Greenlandic, I learned at the school, so the Sisters did not speak correct Greenlandic either.

"It's not likely you have a family name, is it?"

I shook my head after hearing the translation.

"Do you know your mother's name? Your father's name?"

I did not answer even after Sister Louisa spoke their words.

"Did you know your father at all?"

Sister Katerina leaned over, whispered to Sister Margret.

"Oh, I'm sorry to hear that," said Sister Margret. "Even so, the Lord protects and blesses even children born from rape. All are equal in the eyes of the Lord."

They talked among themselves. Then Margret wrote words on the paper. Mother's name: unknown. Father: unknown.

"Given that you have no family name, shall we give you a name? You came from the village of Tasiilaq, so everyone can call you Miss Tasiilaq. How about that? All official records must have a given name, preferably a Christian name, as well as a family name."

Sister Louisa had a lot of words to say to me. Sister Margret got impatient before Sister Louisa finished. I got the message. This was their house. They would share their food with me. I would work to pay them for everything. Like a family. I had to agree to everything. To start, they gave me a name they liked.

"Now then, we understand you were born outside the village of Tasiilaq. Do you know the date of your birth?"

I told them I was born on the first day of sunrise. Mama said so. That was sometime in the spring, they calculated. Sometime between the end of February and the end of March, Sister Louisa explained. Sister Margret turned the pages of the calendar on her desk. Calendars are like books, marking the time of each season, I knew. Yet the pages did not say the day of the first sunrise of the year.

"All right, we will have to assign you a birth day. Then you will be official and legal. Perhaps it doesn't matter exactly when you were born, as long as we have the year correct and thus your true age. Similar to our Lord and Savior's birth date. Some say December twenty-fifth, some say in the spring."

Sister Louisa told me what they said.

"Today is April twentieth, the day you arrived in Nuuk. How about we say today is your birthday? It's a spring day, after all. Beautiful weather, for once. Much better than some ungodly cold day in the dark of winter."

I nodded after Sister Louisa told me what she said.

From then on my birth day would be April twentieth, the day I was born again and started a new life in Nuuk, a new life with a new name: *Anna Tasiilaq*.

"Anna, you forgot the toilets again!" cried Sister Katerina. "It's your turn this week. Come back and finish the lavatory. Put the book away."

I slipped the book under my pillow and jumped up. I was not used to these long dresses they made me wear. I could not run wearing a dress. Nor with the slippers we wore to walk on the wooden floors of the house. But I hurried as best I could to the lavatory at the end of the room where all the girls slept. There were beds on each side, all in a row, and the twelve girls there were about the same age as me. There were other rooms for the younger girls and rooms for the boys.

Sister Katerina showed me where I missed cleaning and told me to work on it during the evening rest time. She would check it the next morning. Instead of reading, I had to clean the toilets. Again. And finish it before the time for turning out lights.

Each day we awoke early and said a greeting to the spirit that lived in Denmark called Jesus. We also called him Lord. It meant the same thing. We could ask for something, too. I always asked for a new book. Sometimes I asked for a dog. Then we cleaned our area in the sleeping room and went to the breakfast. We ate the food without talking. Eggs and bread mostly, Danish food. Then we had classes just like I had in Tasiilaq. Except the teachers at the Children's House were not as kind as Teacher was. Some of them came from the town. They taught at a regular school and only came here for special lessons. Other classes were taught by the Sisters. I had classes to learn numbers and classes to learn words. I had classes to learn about the world and this country. There was also a class to learn more about the Lord of Denmark and the book he wrote.

One day I was called to Sister Margret's room. I knew I did something wrong.

"She's not progressing in Danish," said the teacher with the bald head and the yellow beard.

He spoke to Sister Margret as I stood before her desk.

"She hardly speaks at all and when she does it hardly makes any sense. Better to let her focus on Greenlandic. That's poor enough. Sounds like an illiterate who never learn it correctly."

"Our Anna is a child of unusual circumstances," spoke Sister Margret in a voice as smooth as a sheet of ice. I was picking up the Danish words they thought I couldn't learn. "She needs our compassion and understanding. As long as she keeps her area clean and follows her work tasks faithfully, we might have to let her studies slide."

"As you wish," said the teacher. "Then perhaps she can learn English. She already has a fine grasp of babbling."

"Indeed." Sister Margret thought for a moment. "How many English books do we have in the library?"

"At least a dozen, possibly more. They are simple books, for children."

"If she is a beginner then they would be perfect for her, even at age fourteen. She has to start someplace."

"You're serious? English for her?"

"If she can learn English she could be a tour guide one day. That's a fair job, isn't it?"

The teacher nodded. They both looked at me like I did not understand. The teacher spoke to me in Greenlandic, explaining that they were giving up on me learning Danish and would start teaching me English, the language of the Americans who had the airplane base up north.

It did not matter to me. No language outside my head could stop the words of Mama inside my head. I knew the purpose of the Children's House was to make us fit for society. Teach us the language and get us some job skills. When we turn eighteen we go out on our own.

Nuuk is built on rocks that were carved by glaciers, beside the ice cap many years before, long before humans came across the north and down the coast. The town sits on a point of land that is like the forgotten foot on the withered leg of an old crushed goose whose giant beak is covered by the vast ice cap. Scratched and cut by ice over a thousand centuries, all that is left of this point of land are stubby ragged fingers extending from a rough, opened hand. All around is dark water, or ice for half the year: the Davis Strait, the fjords going back up to the ice cap, and the harbor.

On top of those remnants of rock where Nuuk sits, somehow rows of apartment blocks were built. The long buildings line the rocky shoreline. Inland are the older buildings in Danish style. In the middle is a shopping center. Newer buildings have modern style that looks like something from a big city.

Away from the town are the same Greenland scenes as on the east coast: bare rock, tufts of grass and sprigs of lichen, pockets of snow, patches of ice. You can work your way up the rugged mountains to the edge of the ice cap if you got the energy. The ice cap is like the thick layer of frosting on a birthday cake. Sometimes the frosting slips down onto the plate, breaks into chunks that float away down the fjord and out to the sea.

You can see all of that from the top of the mountain.

And then when you get back to the Children's House after running away to climb the mountain, just to see where you are in the world, there are the Sisters waiting to scold you just for wanting to go have a look. So they give you extra work to do. And you think about your hike, what took you all day and part of the next, sleeping outdoors among the rocks, not caring if an ice bear comes by or a wolf takes bites out of you, not worried if people are looking for you, just happy to be away from that big house and free to think as you like — then you know getting a little more work to do was worth it.

Then it was time for lessons. I liked lessons because I wanted to know everything. The man who taught English was kind but he was a hard teacher. Mr. Johnson was from America but he had an Inuit wife so he lived in Nuuk. He used to be a soldier at the Thule airplane base. He liked Greenland so much he stayed.

There was a lot to speak every lesson. Repeat after him!

"The Catholic Sisters were kind to me," I recited.

"No, no. That sounds like they *used* to be kind but they aren't any more. Use 'are' not 'were'! You see, 'are' is present tense, 'were' is past tense. Remember?"

"The Catholic Sisters *are* kind to me." I put an extra push on 'are' so he would believe I got it.

"Good. Much better. Keep improving like this and someday, Anna, we'll send you up the coast to the American air base. If you can speak English, you can get a job there."

"What a job I get?"

"No, what *kind of* job *can* I get."

I repeated and memorized it.

Sister Katerina took me to a room one day and showed me a machine. It was a square box yet it had small petals on the front and each petal had a letter or a number on it. In the back was a piece of paper with no words marked on it.

"This is called a typewriter," she said.

She had me sit down on the chair at the table. She showed me how to put my fingers over the petals, one finger for each petal. She called them *keys*, but there were more keys than my fingers. She said I had to change my fingers as I spelled the words. She showed me how to push down the keys to make a word appear on the paper. It was fun to put words together that way, like writing a letter.

"Can I write letter?" I asked in English.

"*May* I write a letter?"

"If you wish, Sister Katerina."

She frowned. "Don't be impertinent, now, child!"

"I want to write a letter. Please."

"To whom?"

"To my friend."

"All your friends are here. You can speak to them."

I wanted to tell her about Happy, the boy I liked in Tasiilaq, yet I didn't think she would want me writing to him. He was not a Catholic boy.

"Let's continue."

She had me type all the letters on the alphabet list. Again and again. Until the paper was filled. She took the paper out, turned it to the back side and put it into the machine again. Type, type, type, all the letters.

"If you learn to type, and you can also speak Greenlandic, some Danish and some English, then you can get a good job as a secretary. You can work in an office. You are very good with words and numbers, so it will be a good job for you."

So I practiced every day, sometimes twice a day. I typed the letters, then the words. Again and again.

One night I got out of my bed, went to the typewriter room. I put a piece of paper in the machine and I typed a letter.

```
Deer Happ y
I mis yu . I am good heer. yu miss me ???
This is eNglish . Plees understanit .
sinser ly
          Anna
          - they cal me Anna  now
```

I heard a noise so I ran back to my bed.

The next day I was told to go see Sister Margret. She held up the paper I typed.

"Is this something you wrote, Anna?"

I nodded.

"It's a good letter." She laid it on the desk. "However, Sister Katerina took the liberty of correcting the misspelled words."

I carefully picked up the paper from the edge of the desk. All my words were marked in red ink.

"I want you to practice," she said. "Type the letter again with the correct spellings. Then we can send it to your friend."

My mouth burst open. Was it true? I could send a letter to Happy? I wanted to jump up and hug Sister Margret.

I typed the letter three times, until I got every word correct. I added a few more words, too. Then Sister Margret gave me an envelope and I wrote his name on it. I wrote his Greenlandic name but the only address I knew was the village name.

"I'm sure once it arrives, they can find his house. There's not many people there, as you know."

So finally I got to send a letter to Happy. Even written in English he might understand it. Or he could find someone who could read it to him. Teacher could help him understand. Then he would really be happy!

For some reason that only their spirits knew, two little girls came to me one day and called me Sister Anna. I corrected them. I was not a Sister like Margret or Katerina. I told them to call me Anna. The girls looked exactly the same and probably they were at the Children's House before I arrived.

I was cleaning the hall after lunch time and they watched me sweeping with a broom, then came up to me, one of them taking each hand. They spoke my language.

After that, Aqatsaq and Arnarulunguaq always followed me around the house or in the play yard. I called them Aq and Arna. The Sisters called them Mary and Martha, names from the Lord of Denmark's big book. The girls waited for me after meals and they visited me before sleeping. They asked me to help them with things like dressing and cleaning. Sister Louisa said they adopted me so I had better be good to them.

It was close to the time for the dark to arrive and everybody was getting ready for three months with no sun. Already the sun only shone a couple hours in the middle of the day. It was like the winds blew stronger and they could finally blow away the sun completely.

Then came the special days for celebrating the birthday of the Lord of Denmark. He was born in winter. We gave gifts to the baby statue laid in the crib beside the winter tree. My gift was a pretty rock with a picture of a seal I scratched into it. We sang Catholic songs and read parts of the book the Lord of Denmark wrote. Every child got a gift. Mine was a new copy of his book yet I couldn't read it because it was in Danish. I traded it for a story book. Then we fell silent and whispered our words to the Lord of Denmark, asking for next year's gift. I wanted a dog.

And books. And a friend.

Of course, in a big town like Nuuk there were always lights on. In the winter you could not see the difference between day and night. Always dark, so the lights were always on. You had to set a clock to stay on a schedule. The Children's House had one of the loudest clocks ever made! I awakened every time it went *bong*.

On the ice you sleep when you are tired. You hunt when you are hungry. You run when you feel too full of energy. There is no clock or calendar, just the sun and the moon and the dark to let you know if you survived a season or not. If not, then clocks or calendars didn't matter. If you did, then you thank Sila for letting you go on. The seals will come to be your meals again.

I missed having a dinner of seal. In the Children's House we ate the kind of food they ate in Denmark. Lots of chickens and pigs, vegetables, and brown bread. Never any seal or reindeer or bear. Sometimes we had fish. A lot of potatoes and too many green things. Aq and Arna liked or didn't like the food based on if I liked it or not. If I frowned, they frowned. If I smiled, they smiled. If I ate it, they ate it. Sister Louisa told me I had a big responsibility to show them how to live right.

Yet I did not know for myself how to live right. I thought I knew it back in Mama's hut. The spirits there took care of me and I never starved for long. I shared what I got with my dogs. At night I would lie awake in my bed in the Children's House and think about my life on the ice, in that hut, before and after Mama died. My eyes got wet. I wanted to return to it, just to see it again, even if all there was to see was a pile of turf and broken burnt timbers and narwhal bones.

I learned later that Aq and Arna lost their father when the ice broke under his feet. He was pulling a narwhal onto the ice floe. It was up north where the ice is more dangerous. Under that ice, thin or thick, broken or smooth, was a lot of deep, dark sea and you could never touch the bottom and come up again. So their father went into the cold sea and couldn't pull himself onto the ice again. It was the way things happen in the north.

Their mother died from illness later, too far away for a doctor and no shaman close by to perform any magic. Without a man to hunt they did not get enough food, eating whatever food people might give to them. The twins were sent to live with a family in Uummannaq, up the coast from Nuuk, but after a while they could no longer care for them. Young girls are so hard to live with, they said. So they came to the Children's House and they adopted me.

Sister Katerina liked how I treated the twins, so she thought I could be a good teacher. I never thought I could do that because I didn't know much. Even reading some books I didn't know a lot. Sister Katerina said I was not required to know a lot, just enough to teach the children. It would be a good job for me after I got my eighteen years.

Gradually, I got more responsibilities, watching the younger children during play time. I also checked them after meals and at sleep time. I cleaned them and dressed them like I was a mama. At fifteen, I was like a small Sister in the Children's House.

More young children came to me. They liked my stories. I told them about life on the ice. They understood what I meant. Going on a sled with my dogs, hunting seals by their air holes, running after hares and foxes, shooting at ducks, catching fish in the fjord, or picking berries on the hillsides. I sat them down in a circle around me and I told the stories. I told all the true stories first so then I had to think of new stories.

So I imagined everything and said it like it was true. I asked the spirits to forgive me, most of all the Lord of Denmark. He could be mean to people who told stories that were not true,

Sister Katerina told me once. I knew there was truth that was real enough to be written in big words but was not written at all, and there was truth which was written in books yet not meant to be believed as real. The children didn't mind which kind of story I told them. It became a regular event each afternoon. Sometimes one of the Sisters watched me telling stories to the children and she would smile.

As the dark came over the world, Aq and Arna often came to my bed in the older girls' room and wanted to sleep with me. It was custom in the north to share our body heat, so we got under the furs, all of us together.

There were no pajamas or nightgowns in the north. Clothes hold in body heat, so for sleeping you have to take off the clothes if you want to share warmth. Sleeping naked that way doesn't mean anything else. Unless you are a couple. Then you have to make a different kind of body heat. Sometimes it can get so hot that a baby comes out of the woman's belly. That is the way it is in the north.

I let them join me and we slept. Then we were told we were not allowed to sleep without wearing nightgowns, even if we were covered with quilts and blankets and sheets.

I had to go talk to Sister Margret about Inuit ways. She knew about them yet she wanted us to learn Danish ways. We were not going back to the ice, she said. We were learning how to be Danish. That was the goal of our training.

It was not a problem for me. I followed the rules. Yet the twin girls wanted to sleep with me and they only fell asleep if they felt comfortable. She allowed them to sleep with me yet we had to wear nightgowns.

The world is full of rules, said Sister Margret, and our first job at the Children's House was to learn them.

We followed the rules exactly and we still got punished. I

never got pushed down onto an *illeq* but I stood in a corner for a while. I had to clean more places in the house. Yet Sister Margret always smiled at me when I finished my punishment. Then she would remind me it was never as bad as being bitten by a bear.

I told her about shooting the ice bear at the new home I tried to make, but she only laughed and said I had a big imagination. I should tell that story to the young children, she said, so they would be entertained.

At night, all of us together in my bed, Aq and Arna asked me why I was crying. I said I wasn't but they said I was. So I had to believe them. I told them about shooting the ice bear yet nobody believed me. I told them what happened and they were afraid, then they cheered quietly for me. They believed me. Not every story is a story.

I told them how I cut up the bear and took as much meat as I could back to the hut on my sled, my five dogs pulling hard. It was a heavy sled with the bear meat. No—I caught myself—one dog was killed when the bear fell on him, crushed him. So only four dogs pulling the sled. And me pushing it.

The girls could not sleep after that, afraid of the bear. In the morning, they didn't think hard enough in their lessons so I was scolded again for telling stories that scared the children.

When the dark broke one afternoon for a few minutes, we all went out to celebrate. It was very cold but it felt so good to breathe in that air. It cut through my body like a sharp knife, filled my body, and out I sent it again into the world. It was like I was on Ammassalik island again, outside my hut, or on the sled running hard up the valley with the snow flying into my face, and the stars over my head. That was my dream every night.

We turned off the lights and saw what night looked like in the middle of the day. The young children, from three years to twelve, gathered around me like I was their big sister. We all hugged each other under the dark sky full of stars. Only a small spark cut the horizon, and for only a short time, though each day it grew bigger and stayed longer. At last there was no dark at all, only sunshine for three months.

One day my wish to the Lord of Denmark was granted. A new girl arrived at the Children's House. She was about my age but did not speak. She had been sent by her father. He could not care for her any longer. Every day he was out hunting. None of the family members wanted to care for her, either. There was a new wife, after this girl's mama died, so his old family didn't like him and the new family didn't like the girl.

I was telling stories to the children when she arrived and was shown around the house by Sister Margret and Sister Louisa. I saw them watching us yet I continued the story of a woman who hunted bears by moonlight and then she built an igloo for herself and the bear. It was like a story Mama told me when I was very young. The woman and the bear became a couple and their child was very strong and covered in white fur.

This new girl was called Tuglik, but the Catholic name they called her was Ruth. I called her Tuglik when we were alone but I said Ruth if other people were with us. She came down from Ilulissat, a small town north of Nuuk along the coast, yet she was born farther north in a settlement with no name. Being from the far north and knowing nothing of a town, she was very wild and cried out loudly all day. She refused any food given to her, just slapping the plate to the floor or ignoring it. She sat in the corner by her choice and stared at the wall. She was trying to not see this new home.

I remembered feeling that way when I arrived, yet I did not

act the same as she did. Maybe it was easier for me because I got a year and a half living in Tasiilaq before I arrived in this town of Nuuk. It was as scary as being surrounded by ice bears and all you have to defend yourself is a handful of snow. You throw it at the bears and then you have nothing.

Ruth liked story time. She always stood in the corner yet now with her face to the rest of us. She never smiled yet she stopped screaming and crying. She listened. I spoke in our language so she understood. I think she relaxed listening to my stories. The Sisters liked that I helped her, so I became her teacher in the Children's House.

As Inuit do in our homes, we shared the sleeping platform called *illeq*, everybody getting under the furs and sharing their warmth with everybody else. We need to share body heat or we die. I always slept with Mama that way. So Ruth began coming over to my bed after lights out time. She could not sleep alone in the Danish style bed, so she got under the blanket and quilt with me. She fell asleep next to me, her hands always holding me.

Ruth started to listen better in the lessons. She tried to follow the instructions. She always looked to me for what to do. She still did not speak, only grunts or moans or sighs or sounds that were like words yet were not any words I knew. I took her outside to the play yard and we had our own lesson. I told her about this place, the Children's House, and the town of Nuuk. I held her hand, told her I came from the ice, too, but on the east coast. I was in a village. She hugged me and wouldn't let go.

The younger children were afraid of Ruth. They wouldn't come close if she was with me. I had to divide my time between the younger children, story time, watching them clean and get ready for sleep, and the time I was with Ruth, helping her get used to this new life. She never spoke and the children never spoke to her, everybody looking at each other like we were rocks or ice or a whale carcass on a stony beach.

Then one day during story time I got everybody in a circle and I asked what story they wanted me to tell. I pointed to each boy and girl to give me an answer. Some of the children asked for a story I already told them. They just wanted to hear it again. Other children wanted a new story, so I would have to imagine something for them.

When I pointed to Ruth, her face broke into a smile for the first time I ever saw!

"Sleep," she said in a low voice, like she wasn't sure if she was saying the word correctly or if it was even the right word.

I guessed she meant a story about sleeping.

"Tell the story of the sleeping bears," one boy called out.

So I remembered the story I told them before, and I acted it out as I told it. Two bears met in a mountain valley and instead of fighting they decided to live together. They had to fight the hunters and hide from an airplane! Yet they liked each other so much they built an igloo to live in. One day a human saw the igloo. He thought there must other humans inside. Only humans build igloos, of course. So he entered it and saw the bears. The bears were asleep on the *illeq*, the sleeping platform at the end of the igloo, off the ice floor. With their own fur covering their bodies, the bears did not need furs over them like humans did. Humans were always naked unless they wore another animal's skin. The human saw the bears were sleeping and he thought they looked so happy and comfortable together. So he thought he might as well sleep there, too.

The children shouted out the end of the story. They heard it before and wanted me to tell it again. The bears awake and see the human sleeping there with them. They decide to eat the human. End of story. So if you go into an igloo and you see two bears asleep on the *illeq*, don't sleep there with them or maybe you won't wake up again!

Ruth got the story. She smiled through the telling, then she stood beside me and would not go away. All day she followed me, holding my hand. I talked with her yet she only gave short answers. The Sisters noticed her talking to me and nobody else. Sister Margret called me into her room, thanked me for helping Ruth.

So I got privileges. I got an afternoon free each week to do whatever I wanted. Mostly I read books. Later I went out from the Children's House and just walked on the streets. The Sisters liked me.

And Tuglik liked me. At night, she slept with me, even if we had to be close against each other or else fell off the narrow bed. We got out of the gowns, kept warm together under the blanket. We got good dreams that way. In the morning we put on the gowns like we had worn them all night, then got ready for the day as usual.

It was like the girl in the book called *Jane Eyre* that I read to learn English. The Children's House was like the place Jane Eyre lived, and she also had a friend who slept with her. Eventually Jane Eyre left that place and got a job teaching the daughter of a rich man. Later they got married, Jane Eyre and the rich man. I thought of my life in Nuuk, wondering if there were any rich men living here.

Father: unknown.

My father is not unknown. I knew him. Good or bad, I knew him. The man with the red beard. Mama said he was my papa and I believed Mama. So he is my father. Mama called him Man so I only called him Man, too. Did he have a name on that other island where he lived before coming to the hut?

"Anna, I have good news," said Sister Louisa one day after dinner.

I finished washing the dishes. It was not my turn but I was helping Tuglik. It was her turn. So we ate quickly and hurried to the kitchen to start the soapy water. My hands were in rubber gloves and I was scrubbing off the old food from the plates. We were told to eat everything, never waste food, so the plates were not too dirty. Yet they had to be made wet with the soapy water, then let them dry during the night to be ready for breakfast.

Sister Louisa showed me a letter as I was washing the dishes. I thought it had to be from Happy. He wrote a letter back to me!

But the letter was from Teacher, not Happy. It was written half in Greenlandic and half in Danish. Teacher was half Inuit, half Danish, so I thought she wrote it twice because she wanted the Sisters to know what she told me.

Sister Louisa read it to me.

My friend Happy got the letter and was *happy* to get it even though he could not read it. He showed the letter to Teacher so she translated it to him. He likes to call you Anna, by the way, wrote Teacher.

"But I have other news," Sister Louisa read to me. "I got new information for you. I did some checking and talked with many people. I got your mother's name. She was called Qavigarssuaq."

I smiled at Sister Louisa. She knew the name, an Inuit name. It was usually a man's name, though. Teacher explained how she got the story from the oldest woman on Ammassalik. When Mama was born, her father was out hunting and heard his wife delivered a boy so he sent the name for the baby back with his friends. When he returned later he saw the boy was actually a girl but he already got used to that name so it stayed.

Long ago when Mama was an ordinary woman she had a

name. People called her that name. When she began going to the dark place and seeing beyond the world, they left her alone and only called her the crazy woman. But she had a name!

"And I found the name of your father, too," Sister Louisa read. "He registered in the village office to be a fishing boat deckhand. His name was Magnus. And he came from Iceland. That's right: all the way from Iceland, across the sea, and came to live in Tasiilaq. So I wrote letters to some offices in Reykjavik, the capital city, to see what anyone knew of him."

Teacher explained people didn't use family names in Iceland. They used their father's name. His father was called Mathias, so he was Magnus Mathiasson. He was born in Akureyri, a town in the north of Iceland. Then he lived in Reykjavik.

"One other thing you will want to know," Sister Louisa read, "is he has a daughter, another daughter. She is older than you, but now you are related. You have a sister, Anna!"

Instead of jumping up so happy and hugging Sister Louisa, I sat still on the stool beside the wash basin. I didn't know what to say. I never thought there could ever be another person in the world like me.

"Aren't you happy?" asked Sister Louisa.

I nodded. I always nodded no matter what they said because I have to agree with everything. I agreed to come to this town and live in this school, learn how to write on the typing machine and speak a language called English. Everything was decided for me. Now it was decided I have an older sister.

"Yes, I'm happy," I said, just to be polite. I didn't know how I felt. I had so many feelings at that moment, all mixed up like a soup. My voice was not happy and she heard that.

She told me she would leave the letter on my bed.

I finished washing and cleaned up the kitchen. Then I went to the sleeping room and the letter was there. I read it for myself and used a word book to find the meaning of all the words. It was close to what Sister Louisa told me.

Now that I got a sister, I'm not an orphan. Am I? Is she also an orphan? Happy Eider Duck was not an orphan because he still had his mama. Maybe this sister had her mama, too. So we only shared a father. If the man with the red beard had another daughter, did she have red hair too? Did she think I had red hair?

That night I dreamed of taking a kayak across the sea to a land of red-haired people. They tried to keep me from coming onto the shore because I had brown hair. Later, Happy rode a white horse along the shore and pulled me up from the kayak. The sea swallowed the kayak right then yet I was safe. We rode the horse together all the way to a giant typing machine. It was like a mountain! The machine typed by itself. And the word it typed was MAGNUS. Then from somewhere flew a dragon and the dragon spit fire over the typing machine and it burned until I awoke screaming.

At sixteen years I was one of the oldest guests in the Children's House, so Sister Margret gave me the job watching the younger children. Tuglik got responsibilities, too. She helped the children bathe in the evenings. So we worked together. Then we slept together, feeling so tired from our tasks during the day.

The Sisters thought I was good with children. They always told me. The children were happy being with me. I talked with them and we played games in the yard. I was good at herding them. The Sisters thought I could get a job as a teacher or be a child care helper at a school or in a rich Danish family's house. I heard a clock ringing in my head. It was like that Jane Eyre's life!

She lived in an orphanage, too. Then she was hired to care for a child at a rich man's house. Later she loved the old man because he was blind. Yet I could never love an old man.

The Sisters tried to take care of me but I always had to go out and climb a mountain. I had to play with dogs. I had to sit by the shore and stare far away. They understood me. I was like Maria in the film *Music Sounds*. Maria was a Sister, too, and she cared for the children at a rich man's house. Then she married him! Just like Jane Eyre did with her rich old man. I wondered if that was my path, too. Like her, I wanted to belong someplace and find love with somebody. Having one special person to think about and be with every day seemed like the best thing.

I typed more letters to Happy but he never sent letters back to me. Maybe he didn't know how to write, or he didn't have paper. Then I got the idea that maybe he met another girl in the village. I knew he made friends easily, so he probably forgot me. I stopped sending letters, but I thought of him every day for another year.

There were some boys in the Children's House who spoke to me. They did not seem happy. A boy called Dirk said he felt like a girl the way he had to stay indoors and do housework. The boys wanted to be with their dogs and go hunting like their fathers. They were not being trained for a job using a typing machine or caring for children. They would not get a job in a rich Danish family's house. All they could do was help on a fishing boat or go hunting on the ice.

One day, I got permission to go out for the whole day. I had to be back to the house by dusk. Yet it was still summer so dusk was after midnight.

As usual, I went to the store for snacks. I got a little money from my work at the Children's House. I had my tasks to do but if I did more they gave me some money. It was partly a lesson. I had to learn to use money, the Sisters said. I learned to count the money, both paper and coin, and count up the difference if what I was buying cost less than the money I had. So I would not be cheated. Buying something at a store was a lesson as much as a reward.

I bought a Kit-Kat. Actually, I got two this time. I got a bottle of juice also.

Then I saw Dirk there. He got a day pass, too!

Dirk did not get any money, so I bought a bag of dried fish for him and a bottle of cola. I suggested he try the cola but I warned him it could be too bubbly, maybe hurt his belly. He said he was strong enough for that.

We decided to ride the bus to the end of the town. Then we hiked on the trail that started there and went up the mountain which rose across the harbor from the town. I went there a few times before. It was my favorite place. I could see the whole world from there. I wanted to show it to him.

Dirk followed me because I knew the way. I felt responsible for him because I was used to watching the children. Dirk was a year older than me yet he seemed younger. If he did anything bad I must report him to the Sisters. He laughed when I told him and said he had no plan to act bad.

We sat high on the mountainside, just bare rocks and some grass here and there. We watched a ship come into the harbor below. We could see very far across the sea. It was called Davis Strait. It connected with Baffin Bay to the north. To the south it connected to the ocean of Atlantic which flowed all the way around the world.

On the other side of Davis Strait, Dirk said, was a country called Canada. He had been there, but farther north. He crossed the ice to get there with his father and uncle when he was young. Some people related to his family lived in Qaanaaq, which was in the far north near the American airplane base. In the winter, in the dark, the sea froze all the way across and they could take a sled over the ice to Canada.

"Is that place where you want to return?" I asked. We spoke in Greenlandic even though he was also learning English.

"If I want a job, I have to," he said in a rough voice. "I can go hunting there, too."

"Yeah, I used to hunt where I lived."

He did not believe me. He said only boys could hunt. Women had to clean the skins and cook the meat. I told him I did that, too. I did everything because I was alone.

"What's it feel like being alone?" he asked.

I stared out at the sky, as big a sky as I ever saw. I pointed to a small cloud floating out there, way out there, over the sea, almost so small we could not see it.

"It's like that cloud," I said, pointing. "You're just there. And nobody ever touches you."

He sighed like he understood, then leaned back on the rock.

"But you got all the children around you."

"I care for them," I said. "It's a job. Not the same as friends."

He spit down the side of the mountain. "Not the same…. Ya, nothing is the same." He looked at me. "I don't have anyone."

"The children are the only people I know."

"You had a friend. That girl you always slept with."

"You mean Tuglik? I guess she was my friend. More like I was her big sister, always taking care of her."

We couldn't say more. Tuglik, who the Sisters called Ruth, killed herself one night. She got out of the house and went to the harbor and jumped in. The water was cold and she could not swim. Nobody talked about it after a month passed.

"I was her friend. Maybe she thought I was her friend."

"Weren't you?"

"I don't know." I wiped my face. "What is a friend? Someone who takes care of you? To look after you?"

He gave a quick frown. "I had other family members looking after me, just not my parents. I never had friends."

"I had my mama. Sometimes my papa would visit."

The wind gusted, pushing us against the rocks and against each other.

"What happened to them?" he asked after a moment.

"They died, of course. That's why I'm orphan."

He laughed. "What happened to make them die?"

I blinked, unsure what to say. "Nobody ever asked me that."

"You don't have to say it."

The wind blew strong again. The sun was warm but clouds formed on the northern horizon, half over the mountains, half over the strait.

He leaned against me, then put his arm around me.

"I want to say it. I have to say it to somebody. Might as well be you."

He held me tighter and then his face was close to my face and then his lips were close to my lips and then I kissed him. It was very quick, like my mouth did it before my mind could decide if I wanted to do it or not. He was surprised. Then he grinned.

"That's our first kiss," he said softly.

"I'm sorry. It was accident."

"Then let's do it purposely."

So we kissed more, and nobody down in Nuuk could see us. We were too far up on the mountain. Only the clouds and the sun could watch us.

Later, I told Dirk how one day the man with the red beard hurt me, so Mama shot him. We buried him under rocks and snow. A year after that, Mama went to the dark place once more and went to sleep. I buried her under rocks and snow, too. Then

I was orphan.

Dirk felt sad for me. He held me close.

The sky was changing. We were changing. I had tears in my eyes so he asked if there was anything he could do to make me feel better. I kissed him again and asked if we could do what the married people do.

"You know it, don't you? That sex game they play."

"Are you sure?" asked Dirk. "You're too young."

"Don't worry," I said. "I did it before. Yeah—when I didn't want to. This time it's my choice."

I thought of those men in Tasiilaq. Mama said the sex game was supposed to feel good. I saw how Mama and Papa could be happy sometimes after they played it. So I wanted to change my memory. I wanted to have a good memory of being with a man. I had to start again. I had to make a new life.

"You won't tell anybody?" he asked.

"Nobody." I hugged him, kissed his cheek. "But you gotta be nice. Don't hurt me."

"I can be nice, but...."

"But what?"

"I'm not sure what to do."

I just smiled. "I'll show you."

He was nice, didn't hurt me, but he got finished before I got started. I felt better, anyway, just putting our bodies together. A good memory for both of us. I told Dirk he would always be my first. Only the Lord of Denmark saw us.

We fixed our clothes and went home.

Sister Louisa met us at the door. It seemed like she knew everything we did. Dirk and I held each other's hand yet we let go at that moment. It was late even though the sky was still light at midnight. She sent us straight to bed. In the sleeping rooms the dark curtains were closed against the light.

I couldn't sleep, though. I kept thinking of Dirk and what we did on the mountain, and how I wished it was Happy who was with me. It was the last time I thought of him.

One day, the Children's House was too quiet and I worried that everybody left me and went away. I had lived alone on the ice for a year yet now that I was surrounded by people all the time, I got used to hearing them doing something.

I walked carefully through the house, listening for sounds.

Where did everybody go?

I went to the younger children's classroom—

"Surprise!" they shouted.

I fell back like I was attached by wolves. Everybody called to me and children ran up to me, grabbed my hands and my dress like I was Lord of Denmark. The Sisters said "Happy Birthday" in English and Danish, then everybody sang an English song to me. It was about having a happy birthday.

Of course, I did not remember the day I was born so I didn't know if it was a happy day or not. Mama said it was a happy day for her. She got three seals on the ice that day, she told me, and then I came out of her after dinner.

The Sisters told me to make this day a happy day. So I sat where they told me and everybody gave me gifts they made, like drawings on paper or something twisted from metal or a tooth that came out, or a long falcon feather that was found, or a shiny stone, or a piece of leather cut into a picture.

Sister Katerina gave me a square gift wrapped in pink paper. She thought I liked pink, a girl's color. Danish girls liked pink, she always told me. I tore open the wrapping and there was a book: *Jane Eyre*.

"I read this already," I said in my language. Before Sister Louisa could translate, I said it again in Danish.

"Perhaps so, Anna," said Sister Katerina, smiling. "This is the real book. It has all the words. What you read before was only a simple version for young readers."

"Does it have different end?"

"No, I think it's the same ending. There's more words in the middle. Since you're studying English, I thought you might like to have the entire book."

I seemed unhappy to her. Sister Louisa stepped forward, put her hand on my shoulder.

"You don't want to have only a flipper," she said, "when the whole seal is right there on the ice for you to eat, do you?"

I laughed, understanding.

Sister Margret handed me a gift, too. I guessed by its shape it was another book. They knew I liked books. They encouraged me to read them and take care of them. Sometimes, they gave me time off if I said I wanted to read a book, so I liked to read just to get off from work.

I opened the blue wrapping paper with stars on it. Yes, it was another book: *Wuthering Heights*. Sister Margret said this book was written by the sister of the woman who wrote *Jane Eyre*, so she thought I would like to read it, too. They were the "classics" of English books. She said "classics" meant a book nobody reads any longer but they keep on a shelf so everybody thinks they read it.

"Thank you," I said in English.

We ate cake with sauce on it and drank sweet red water. I ate a lot and my belly hurt later. I saw Dirk standing to the side and I knew he wanted to kiss me. Yet the children made me dance with them. We sang songs, both Greenlandic songs and Danish songs. It was great fun.

After the party, Sister Margret called me into her office and had me sit down. Sister Louisa joined us to translate. It must be important, I thought. Maybe I did something wrong and I had to be punished. Yet not on my birthday! Please not today!

"We have received a letter," Sister Margret said softly. She held up a plain white envelope. "It arrived yesterday. However, we waited to decide what to do with it. You see, it is addressed to you, Anna."

Sister Louisa patted my shoulder, like it was good to get a letter. I knew by looking at the letter it was not from Happy. He didn't know how to write that style. Not from Teacher, either. She always writes with big, looping letters.

"We have not opened it," Sister Margret continued, "but we want to be sure you wish to read it. Sometimes we get letters from the relatives of our children. Rarely does it mean the child can go live with that relative. We want you to be aware of how these situations can go."

Sister Louisa translated to me.

"Perhaps you cannot even understand the words inside or what the words mean. What they really mean regarding your status here," Sister Margret continued, raising her eyebrows like hawks looking for hares. "We do not know even what language it may be written in."

My heart was beating as loud as ice calving from a glacier.

"I understand."

"We only wish to warn you the letter may not be good news. Some letters only confirm that the relatives cannot take on the responsibility of caring for the child. We see so many children hurt by such letters."

Sister Louisa translated as Sister Margret slid the envelope across the desk to me.

I stared at the envelope, then held it in my hands. It was not heavy. My name was written on the front: *Ms. Anna Tasiilaq.* Not written on a typing machine but with a pen—a blue pen—by a hand. Under my name was written The Children's House and the street name. And the town and country: *Nuuk, Greenland.*

"Where did it come from?" I asked. "Who knows I'm here?"

Sister Margret smiled, one of her rare moments.

"The letter appears to be from…your sister. See the return address in the corner? That's where she lives."

"My sister?"

"Indeed. Remember? Your teacher in Tasiilaq was searching for some of your relatives? Perhaps she found one. This is likely the daughter—the other daughter, that is—of the man who… mmm…was with your mother. Your father, that is."

"This is his other daughter." Sister Louisa could not wait. "The one in Iceland."

I didn't know what to say, what to think. I had a sister. The man with the red beard had a daughter already, before I was born. He told me about her one time. I recalled his stories of how he fell overboard and landed on the shore and Mama took him to the hut and cared for him until he was well. He said he left a child back in Iceland.

Now she wrote a letter to me!

"It seems by the address and these stamps that she lives in Canada now," said Sister Margret, pointing. "You see? That's the flag of Canada on the stamps. That's Canada across Davis Strait from us. Think of your geography lessons."

I stared at the stamps a while, wondering if my new sister lived in a hut on one of those islands across Davis Strait from Greenland. Was she half-Inuit like me? Did she have dogs and a sled like I used to have? Did she want me to come live with her?

Sister Margret told me I had the rest of the day free to read the letter and think about whatever it said. I could get help from

Sister Katerina if it was written in Icelandic. Perhaps it was in Danish. They teach Danish in Iceland schools, too, she said. If it came from Canada, it likely would be in English.

I thanked her and walked out slowly, my eyes stuck on my name on the envelope, knowing that my life had changed again.

"Miss Anna! Miss Anna!" the twins Aq and Arna called to me.

They ran up to me, grabbed my hips and hugged me like they had not seen me for a month. Actually, they were at the party only a little while before. We danced already but they were always chasing me. I was their big sister!

Now I had a big sister for myself.

I showed them the letter and they were amazed. They looked at the stamps and asked if they could touch them. I said it was a letter from my sister. They were surprised I had a sister because nobody at the Children's House had any family.

"I just got this letter," I said to them. "I just now learned I got a sister."

They became worried. They thought now I would go home. Where is home? I still didn't know. I only remember one home and that was the hut on Ammassalik island, the one that was destroyed so I could never return to it. Now I'm all the way across the ice cap in Nuuk, living with so many people that I cannot breathe.

"I'm not going anywhere," I told them. "I'm still going to be your big sister."

They hugged me tight again and wiped a few tears.

"Now I got to read the letter alone. It's a rule. I got to do this alone so I can think about all the words. Maybe it's written in a magic language."

They were excited about the magic language so they were willing to wait to learn what the letter said.

I continued down the hall and out the back door into the play yard. I sat on the bench there. The evening was coming on, the peak of daylight long past.

I opened the letter, taking care not to tear the envelope. I slid out the paper. Three pages written by hand in blue ink. It was so beautiful I stared at it for a while. Then I looked at the top of the first page and began to read.

> *dear anna,*
>
> *my name is iris. you don't know me but it seems we*
> *have something in common.*

The letter was written in English, all the words written in small letters like she didn't want anyone to see them. Yet I could see her words and understand them. I knew that's the language of Canada. Maybe my teachers had a dream about Canada. Maybe it's the reason they switched me from Danish to English. There always were spirits around me, guiding me.

Iris. My sister's name. I knew it was the name of a flower. It didn't grow in Greenland but I saw it in a book. My Mama called me Wolf. Her Mama called her a flower. Where she was born must be a whole garden of flowers, I thought. A beautiful place with sunshine all day and lots of fish and seals to eat. She had to be beautiful, too. As beautiful as a flower!

We had something in common, she wrote. Her father ran away from the house in Iceland and went fishing, got caught in a storm, and was saved by another boat. Yet my sister never knew what happened to him. She thought he drowned and that was the end. Then Teacher in Tasiilaq explained the story to her by letter, so now she knew. Her father did not drown in the sea but was rescued and taken to Greenland, to Tasiilaq. Now my sister was happy to know the end of the story.

Yet she was not happy to know that he lived on a few years more. There were problems in her family, she wrote, and he was not kind to her, so finally he left. I remembered in the hut he said he was bad there in his homeland and that was the reason he came to Tasiilaq, to get away and start a new life where nobody knew him. Before he arrived in Tasiilaq, he acted bad and my sister told me what he did to her.

Tears filled my eyes because it was the same as what he did to Mama and then to me. All those memories came back into my head like crashing ice. Right then I knew my sister would never want me. I would remind her of this father. Just me being alive would remind her of that man.

Sister Margret told me most letters do not result in an orphan going to live with a relative. It made sense.

I still liked getting the letter and knowing I had a sister in the world. That was good.

I read slowly through all those English words. Two times. I could understand most of them. There were no words too big for my head. My sister probably had to learn English like me when she went to Canada. She was not any better writing big words than me. So we also had that in common.

Then the words changed and the blue ink got darker, became black ink. The writing got messy.

I went inside the house to get the big dictionary out of the classroom. I turned the pages back and forth to find the words I was looking for. I read the letter again. This is how you learn, my English teacher told me. If you don't know a word, look it up and memorize it.

Leaning over the table in the classroom, I got the meaning.

i would like to meet you. while i have no love for my father – our father – i want to do the right thing for you. we are sisters no matter how we came to be. if you want, you can see if you would like living here in canada. toronto is a very large city and very different from where you are but you can visit and see what you think. if you like it here you can live with my family.

She wanted to meet me! She even invited me to live with her family! I never knew this person yet she liked me already. She never met me yet she liked me!

I ran to Sister Margret's room but she was gone. I passed by some children I usually watch and told them I had a sister. They were surprised yet happy for me. I went to Sister Louisa's room and showed her the letter.

"I got a sister," I sang out to her. "She wants to meet me, maybe let me live with her, too!"

"That's wonderful, Anna!"

"She lives in Toronto. Her name is a flower. She likes me."

I was dancing by that time and Sister Louisa was clapping.

That night I could not sleep. I tried to see my sister in my dreams. If the man with the red beard had a daughter then she probably had red hair, too. In my dream the woman I saw had red hair and rode on a white horse across a field of snow. She got to where I was standing and stopped. She reached down for me to take her hand. Then a falcon flew by and shit on my hand. My dream sister was angry at my dirty hand and rode away.

I awoke covered in sweat, shaking like it was winter and I had no clothes on.

Something would come to destroy my dream again. The men burning the hut. The helicopter taking me from Tasiilaq. Now this sister promising a place to live. Probably the airplane would crash and it would never happen. I could not return to sleep the rest of the night and in the morning I was too sick for my lessons.

We hiked up the mountain again, Dirk and me, just so we could look down on Nuuk and stare far out to the horizon. I tried to see Canada from there but it was too far away. The ice was long ago broken up and melted, the harbor clear and the strait was open sea. The sky was blue and the sea was blue. The land was as green as it ever got, not all brown rocks or rocks covered in snow and ice like the rest of the year.

Getting another day pass, I left after breakfast and walked along the streets, happy to be out of the house. I listened to dogs barking, the bus chugging, people talking on the streets and outside shops, and the cars swishing by me like sleds racing over ice. I went by the wharfs to see the fishing boats unloading their catches. Then I went to the store I always visit and bought candy and snacks. I liked the dried meat best, fish and cow. I always got Kit-Kat for my treat. I put it in my bag to save for later.

As we planned, I met Dirk at the corner of Rinksveyj Street and the street leading to the Snow Arena. He was a member of a team that played hockey. I did not know about that kind of game but I knew that if you hit the rock into a net with a stick you get to hug the members of your team.

Dirk was *emancipated* already, got to eighteen years and was sent out of the Children's House. He lived with some men who showed him how to work on a boat. Because of his job, he shared a room with three other men so there was no place we could go to be together.

So we hiked up the mountain.

We set out our lunch and gazed across the harbor and the fjord, counting the streets of Nuuk, seeing the people down there looking like specks of dirt. We ate our snacks and drank our cola bottles. He brought a bottle of beer, too, but I knew if the Sisters smelled it on my breath I would loose my day pass probably for a year.

"Yet maybe I'll leave before then, anyway," I told him. "Then it won't matter if I get a day pass again."

He was surprised I talked about that. Dirk had no relatives yet now he could go anywhere he wanted. He worked every day on the boat then played hockey in the arena in the evenings.

I told him about the letter and my sister and Canada. He was quiet, looking at me like he never saw a girl before.

"So maybe I'm leaving soon to live with my sister."

"Don't be so happy," Dirk said, frowning. "You know what Sister Margret says. Not every letter is good. Maybe you visit your sister but then she doesn't like you. Then back you go to the Children's House."

I thought a moment. "I'll be good. I'll keep my area clean. She won't have any reason to send me back."

"When you're eighteen you can go anywhere."

"If you can go anywhere, why not go north, like you always wanted to go before?"

"It's not that easy. You got to have money to go anywhere. Or you got to have a sled."

He was right. There are no roads in Greenland outside of the towns. People go from village to village by ferry or by helicopter or by sled over the ice. For any of them you had to have money. You could make a sled, but you had to have money to buy the materials. If you were in the north, you could find the materials, sure, but then you need tools to make the sled. And then you need dogs. Fifteen dogs for a full-size sled. If you are pulling a heavy sledge of supplies, you need more.

"I got some money saved."

"You spend it all on your chocolates!" He laughed. "Maybe the Sisters will let you get a job outside the Children's House so you can get more money. Then you can buy a ticket and fly on the airplane."

He had a great idea. But also he made me think. How am I going to visit my sister? I didn't know who paid for my tickets to ride the helicopter from Tasiilaq to Kulusuk and on the airplane from Kulusuk to Nuuk. Nobody in Tasiilaq had much money.

"If you want money, Anna, the men I live with would pay you." He pinched his lips, squinted. "If you did with them, you know, what you do with me. They would give you money for doing that."

My belly turned inside out. "Why you say that? Don't you want me? Don't you want me to be your girl?"

"Doesn't matter. You're leaving." He stared out across the strait. "I have to get another girl anyway."

I shook my head. "A girl who has money?"

"Doesn't matter if she has money or not."

"But you want to go north. You said it."

"I'll get enough money. Someday. Then I'll go north."

Everybody needed money. I thought about getting money from the men Dirk worked with. I knew what to do. If I closed my eyes, it would not be too bad. But maybe it still would not be enough money to fly to Canada.

"Tell them I can't do it, not even for money."

It was all paper, anyway, so maybe we could make some of it, whatever we needed. There were plenty of art supplies in the Children's House. I could draw some paper money good enough to use.

"You can't do that," said Dirk. "They'll see it's fake and put you in jail. That's worse than being in the Children's House."

I told him how I hated the Children's House at the beginning but now I liked it. I felt like a member of a family. The children always looked up to me and they liked me. The Sisters liked me, too. Sometimes they talked about me becoming a real Sister and working with them. I had to go to Denmark for training.

Now that my sister sent the letter, it seemed I was not going to Denmark but to Canada.

"Sister Margret says I show a lot of responsibility."

He let out a long sigh. "Responsibility...."

"What's wrong?" I asked him.

On the fishing boat he had a lot of things to do. All that work hurt his hands, made his back tired, and his shoulders sore. He hated it. He got sick on the boat and always lost his food. He was only doing it to get a place to live. Working on the boat allowed him to have a bunk in a room shared with other fishermen. And daily meals. It was worse than living at the Children's House.

"I'm going north as soon as I get money for a ferry ticket."

"Then you can find your relatives."

"They won't want me. But now I'm a man they may help me live on the ice, doing what I want, hunting walrus or narwhal, living on my own schedule."

I sat back against the rock, remembering the year I lived on my own. "Yeah, that's the life for me. On the ice. Hunting seals. Just do what I want."

"As long as you watch the weather. And watch the ice."

"I know. Mama taught me."

"The ice is different up north. You get the weather off the ice cap and off the pole, too. It's more dangerous than the ice on the east coast. And if you're hunting walrus, you gotta go to the ice edge, far from the land."

"Maybe so, but I could learn it."

"You could learn it, I know." He grinned. "You would be a great help. You could be my wife. You could go with me."

"If you let me hunt, too."

"Yeah, it would take both of us working together to survive up there. But I'm willing to give it a try. I mean, I'll give you a try. If you want to be my wife."

I looked at him and his eyes were different.

We always joked about being husband and wife whenever we went out on a day pass. Just because we play the sex game sometimes. Right here on the mountain. We liked how people in Nuuk thought we were married when we walked around. They treated us better.

"Do you really want me to be your wife? Or you just want to play sex games with me?"

"Isn't that what a wife is for?"

"A wife is for helping you. And sharing everything."

"And making babies and cooking the food and keeping the house clean."

"If you only want a wife for those things then you better look at somebody else. I'm not like those girls up north."

"You're not like anybody up north. Maybe that's why you should go live with your sister in Canada."

"I will!"

He was always trying to be the man, always wanted me to be the woman. Like the way he remembered his mama and papa were. Yet that was not me.

"I hear they use snowmobiles in Canada," he said. "No dog sleds."

"Then I won't go. I got to have dogs."

"You're a dog," he said, laughing.

I slapped his arm. "No, I'm not. I'm not a dog." I punched his shoulder. He cried out like it hurt. "I'm Wolf. Remember that!"

"You howl like a wolf when we fuck. I know that!"

I hit him again but he didn't flinch. Instead he put his arm around me so tight I couldn't swing my arm at him.

We knew one of us was leaving soon. Either Dirk was going up north to start his life as a hunter. Or I was going to Canada to live with my sister. It was a sad moment.

I did not love him, not like the knight and the princess kind of love, but he was a boy—a man now. And I never got many chances to hold somebody that close, so we played the sex game, just because we could—and maybe we never could again after we left the mountain.

It was autumn and the wind started blowing cold under the warm sun there on the mountainside. He covered me so I was warm, yet even with my legs wrapped around him and my bare feet up in the cold air, it felt so good.

Back in the Children's House I was nervous writing a letter to my sister. I wrote as best I could, showed it to Sister Katerina. She made a few corrections. I copied it on a different paper and wrote more words that I didn't show to her.

> Dear My Sister Iris Magnusdottir,
>
>   How are you ?? I am fine. Thank you for a
> letter from you. I wished for long time.
> Before I know you are alive. Just when I know
> about a country called Canada I get letter
> from you . Its very a happy day!!!!

I told her about my life in Nuuk, living and working at the Children's House, watching the children, learning English and how to use a typing machine. I told her about my life in Tasiilaq, too, and how I got this name. I told her only a little about Mama and the hut and living on the ice. Maybe she would not want to know that part of my life. Everybody's got a hard life, one way or another way.

I asked my sister many questions about Canada. I could read about Canada in a book, yet I could not think of what to write in a letter so I asked questions.

My teacher helped me read a big book about Canada. I saw pictures of my sister's town. It was actually a *city*. There were more than a *million* people living there! So many houses and tall buildings! In Greenland there were only about 50,000 people— and a million dogs!

It was getting dark again here, less sun each day. I went out once a week on a pass and I got snacks and watched the stars watching me or the snow falling. I went to the Snow Arena to see Dirk play the hockey game. He didn't know I was there. He got to hug the members of his team twice. I waited for him after the game yet I never saw him come out that door like the other players did. Maybe he went out a different door. I wanted to let him know I was going to Canada soon and he would not see me again. Yet it seemed like he already decided I was gone.

Through the dark months I wrote more letters and my sister always wrote back to me. A lot of short letters, sometimes only one page, just to ask or answer one question. We got to know each other as she planned how we should meet. She described her life in Canada, and I felt she was very different from me. She already was married and she had her own child!

It was a long story but over many letters I learned about her life. It was like my life but without ice. She was sixteen when her father went away and she thought he drowned in the sea. So her mother married a Canadian man who visited Iceland. Then she and her mother went to Canada to live with him. Now I was sixteen and about to go to a far away place, too. I was going to Canada like she did!

There in Toronto, my sister studied art at a college. She was a painter. She was so good that she got to go to America to study more. She met a man there and she got to be pregnant. Yet they argued a lot so she went all the way to Iceland and had the baby there. She wanted to stay in Iceland because it was her home. It was the only place she fit in.

She got a job in Iceland teaching art in some towns. When she went to the schools, her little boy stayed in the nursery. One day he fell off a wall and hurt his head. She tried to take care of him but after a few months he died. She said he went to sleep for many days and the doctors decided he died.

After her son died, she returned to America to find that man and make another baby. She loved her son so much she wanted another child just like him. Instead, they had a girl. So they lived together like they were married, and moved to places wherever he worked. Finally they went to Canada.

She said after their daughter was born they lived a wild kind of life, but that was done now. She and her man liked to be with other people sometimes or all the people together on the bed to play sex games. She warned me not to tell the Sisters about her life or they may not let me go to Canada.

It wasn't a wild life to me. If you are Inuit, you got a wife at home and if you go on a hunt you take a wife with you. If his wife at home is pregnant or ill then you take another wife, like the wife of your brother or a friend. She helps on the hunt like a wife at home. She keeps you warm at night. Whatever happens then is ordered by Sila and nobody can say anything against it. They accept any child that is born.

That was what Dirk talked about. He wanted to hunt and he

wanted me to be his traveling wife. I thought he still wanted a wife at home, yet maybe he never would have a home, never find a place to stay for long, always on the move across the ice, following the narwhal and the walrus, and he expected me to clean and cook for him. And sleep with him, keep him warm.

In Toronto, my sister Iris was a model for art classes and a model for artists and photographers. She took off her clothes and let them make pictures of her. Sometimes it was for magazines so people would buy something, or just for anybody who wanted to practice photography.

After she finished a *photo shoot*, my sister wrote in a letter, she planned to visit Iceland with her daughter. She thought she could fly over to Nuuk from Reykjavik during that trip and meet me. Yet it was just as far to fly that way as it was to fly to Nuuk from Canada. And the cost was higher. If I was still living on the east coast then maybe it would be a good idea, she wrote, but not with me living in Nuuk. So she decided the best way was to send me a ticket and I would fly to Toronto.

She would meet me there.

Sister Margret was cautious, yet Sister Louisa was excited. They worried that my sister would not treat me good, like I was only a child care girl. I'm good with young children, they said. I should be a teacher. Or I could care for a rich family's children. I told them my sister's family was not rich, so they could not pay for a child care girl.

"So what will you do there?" asked Sister Margret. "You're sixteen, almost seventeen, and you know three languages and you have secretary skills. Will you look for a job?"

"It's what I can do," I replied.

Actually, I didn't have any idea what to do, in Toronto or even in Nuuk. I only worked at the Children's House. That was my first job and my only job. After I got eighteen years and left the Children's House, what would I do? I could not imagine a whole day working, every day the same, and on Sunday going where I wanted and just looking at the sky and the sea and visiting my dreams again while I'm awake.

"Is that the only way people live?" I asked Sister Margret.

"Yes, everyone chooses a job. Whatever they like doing and they are good at. You work and the boss gives you money for your work. You use the money to get the things you need, like food and clothing. If you have extra money, you save it for when you don't have a job. Or when you want to buy something extra or for a special occasion. If you are lucky you meet someone you want to live with, and one day you may have a baby to care for. That is the life God has granted to us."

I frowned. It did not seem as good as running the sled up the valley with the dogs pulling hard or sneaking up to a seal at its air hole to get dinner. Or standing out in the cold to watch the green lights wave across the sky or feel the snow tickling my face. There, I did not need to work for money, just work when I wanted to or needed to.

"I'm almost adult," I said in a sad voice, "so I guess I have to change to the Lord of Denmark's way of living."

"It's not like that, Anna. He gives us the whole world to use. We have decided, as the people of this world, how we should live and how we should make use of the world."

"I want to be by myself in the snow, just do what I want."

"Those are the thoughts of a child, Anna. We know you have grown away from that thinking. You're quite mature now, so I'm surprised to hear you talk of childish play."

I didn't want her to say 'no' to leaving and going to Canada, so I changed my words.

"I know it's child's play. I was only remembering how happy I was then. I'm ready to be adult now and go to a job and get money and buy things and meet somebody and have a baby."

"I'm glad to hear you say that. However, Anna, you needn't do them all at once—"

"Just please, Sister Margret, please let me do all those things in Canada!"

She smiled, and I thought there was a laugh, too.

"Oh, dear child, of course you are going to Canada."

"Thank you, Sister Margret!"

"The papers are all signed. It's official. We only need to wait for your airplane ticket to arrive."

So I waited for the ticket. I got some letters from my sister as usual and she kept saying she was working on getting the ticket. She said it was complicated. Something about *adoption* process, even though we were related.

Then more than a whole month passed without any letters from her. I thought maybe she changed her mind about me. Or it was too complicated. I wrote again, told her I didn't mind caring for her child. I was trained for that and I got good marks from the Sisters.

"These things take time," said Sister Margret. "Didn't I warn you how sometimes these situations do not resolve happily? I'm sorry, Anna. Perhaps you should pray about it."

My sister changed her mind, thought Sister Margret. It was a big disappointment. I wanted to find Dirk and take him to the mountain and forget about Canada. I was ready to go north with him and be his wife. Yet he was always gone now.

I got passes every weekend and also for the evening one time to see an Inuit dance show. I walked along the snowy streets through the darkest, coldest days of the winter, watching green curtains waving overhead. I didn't dream of Canada. I tried to forget Canada. It was time to go north.

Then a letter came from my sister. She apologized for not

writing. She had to go on a trip. They went to California. She also had a lot of preparation for me to come live with her family. Also, she was going to have another baby. I knew then I would be caring for her children.

Along with the letter was a ticket with my name on it, a ticket to fly from Nuuk to Toronto in two weeks!

Sister Katerina thought we should have a party to celebrate graduation from the Children's House. I was not yet eighteen, not even seventeen, but when a relative claims you and you go live with the relative, it is like graduation.

She also thought I needed a proper costume to wear for them to remember me, so Sister Louisa got a traditional Greenlandic costume for me to wear at the party. Tall white *kamik* boots, red jacket and trousers, beadwork collar—like Mama and I made in the hut long ago. It was so beautiful. I did not think I belonged in that costume. They gave me flowers to hold. They got a camera and took a few snaps of me. I forgot to smile.

It was one of the first days of good sunlight after the dark months, enough to light several hours of the day. The pictures of me were dark when they arrived from the printer. It was almost time for my birthday party, anyway, when I would be seventeen. Yet it was a farewell party instead.

We ate a round chocolate Danish cake, drank lemon water. Everybody hugged me and some kissed my cheeks like I was their mama. I had to cry yet I didn't want to.

The Sisters gave me farewell gifts. One was a small book of photographs of Nuuk, the Children's House, the children I took care of, and my friends. I stared at the picture of Dirk when he was younger, a pudgy boy with long dark hair. I laughed at the picture of me holding Aq and Arna, all of us making scary faces. When I turned the next page there was Tuglik looking so plain and sad. Everybody got quiet. Sister Katerina took the book and started to slip the photograph out of the sleeve.

"No, I want it," I said. "I want to remember her."

I wanted to remember one who didn't make it out like me. I was a lucky girl. Not everybody gets to live with a relative. I felt sad for them, the children I left behind there.

So I had to work hard, Sister Margret told me. I had to do something good that people would remember for a long time.

5

The City

As many mountain peaks as there were in my homeland there were tall buildings in this new place! I stared out the airplane's window and could not believe so many people would live there. This really was a *city!* There was no snow, no ice, no bare rock, only buildings as far as I could see. Between the buildings were so many roads. And there were giant plants like wildflowers called *trees*, sprouting up all through the city. I never saw many trees in Greenland.

I started to get scared, not knowing what to do or what to say. I was dressed in the simple clothes the Sisters chose for me. They called it casual style. A white knit pullover shirt and gray canvas pants. I also had a red jacket but it got too warm so I took it off and carried it over my arm. I carried a small bag over my shoulder, some snacks and a few memory things.

After I showed the airport man all my papers, I went out and chose my big blue bag from the turning wheel and carried it out through the doors into my new world.

So many people, like a flock of auks blackening the sky! I stood in the middle of the airport, the world buzzing around me. People walking fast, never looking around, never stopping, not knowing where they were or thinking what they could catch for dinner or if they would die in their sleep tonight if it got too cold or an ice bear broke in. It was so amazing that I froze there, not knowing where to go.

"Anna?"

Somebody called my name, my Catholic name that the Lord of Denmark chose for me.

I turned and there was a woman with red hair. She ran up to me and hugged me before I could move.

"You're Anna, *já?*" she said when she released me. If I was not Anna then she hugged the wrong orphan.

We looked at each other. She was beautiful, didn't look like me at all. She had the red hair. Her skin was so white and her eyes were very blue. I was not sure this really could be my sister. I had brown hair and my skin was brown from looking at the sun. My eyes were dark. She was tall and I was short. She was thin and I was thick. Opposites.

I nodded my head.

She asked me again, to be sure. Probably I was not what she was expecting to come out of that airplane.

"Yes, I'm Anna."

"You look exactly like the pictures."

I was surprised. "Pictures?"

"Your teachers sent me pictures of you."

A smile spread over my face. She saw me in pictures and still wanted me. We did not look alike yet she welcomed me.

"I like the one of you sitting in your classroom, *já*, and all the children are sitting around you."

"Story time."

"Oh, you were telling them a story?"

"Read book to children."

"That's lovely!"

She put her arm around my shoulders and led me through the big building where the airplane people came and went. We walked a long way, over a hard flat floor, and the new shoes the Sisters gave me squeaked. I stopped and took them off, walked on bare feet until we got outside. I put them on again because the streets were wet from melted snow.

"I'm sure you're used to snow, *já*," she said, "but we haven't had any for more than a week. It's spring now. We may not get any more, *já*."

She had a strange way of speaking, always saying "yaw" like I always said "yeah" — so maybe we really were sisters. I guessed the way she spoke was Canadian style or maybe it was Iceland style. It was not the same English my teacher in Nuuk spoke. My sister sounded like Sister Katerina, the way she spoke English but you could hear some Danish under the words.

I asked her in Danish if she spoke Danish.

"Oh, my goodness, no!" She laughed, said it was her worst subject in school. She was a bad student, never paid attention. "So let's use English, all right?"

"I speak some English," I said.

"Lovely!"

She walked with me into a room full of cars. We went up to a high level, then walked along one row and back along another row. Finally, she pointed to a car. We went over to it and I saw a man sitting in it. She put my bag in the back of the car, locked away in a little room. Then she opened the door for me and I got in. It was so small — I only rode in a bus before, back in Nuuk —

so I bumped my head on the ceiling.

A little girl sat there in her own seat which was tied down to the car's seat like she was a wounded dog who got to ride on the sled instead of pull it.

The girl awoke when I sat beside her.

"Dear," she called to the man, "this is Anna. My sister. Anna, this is my, mmm, *partner*, Eric."

"Nice to meet you, Anna," said the man, turning to look back at me. "Welcome to Canada."

My sister also turned to me. "Yes, welcome to Toronto, the largest city in Canada. Your new home."

Then she introduced me to her daughter. "Thora, dear, this is Anna, my sister. That makes her your aunt. She's going to be living with us."

The girl stared at me, probably not sure if I was real.

"Anna, this is Thora. She's five." My sister patted her belly. "And I'm not sure what this one will be." She looked me over. "And you are...fifteen? I think that's what you wrote."

"Sixteen," I said. Probably I was fifteen when I first knew I had a sister. Maybe I wrote that in the first letter.

"You're so cute I thought you were younger."

"Just relax," said the man, facing forward. "We'll be home in about fifteen minutes. We live close to the airport. It's different from Toronto. It's another city called Etobicoke. On the west end of the metro area."

The man drove the car out of the room of cars and we went on a scary ride through the streets of this city, more scary than running a sled over an ice shelf and you can't see if there is open water or broken ice beyond the next pressure ridge because of fog or the snow blinding you. On the sled we go slow so we do not die. Yet in a car we had to go fast so the other cars would not catch us. When we arrived at the house, I knew we won the race.

I was sure I was about to awaken and see it was all a dream. Yet it was not a dream. Before I awoke, I was on the mountain again and Dirk was with me and the sun was shining. We lay naked beside each other. Then Mama called me to come down from the mountain and start cleaning the seal she had shot. I felt bad because I was with Dirk instead of helping Mama.

I heard a bird making noise. I opened my eyes and I was in a bed, like the bed in the Children's House, but the blanket and the sheet were so pretty. The walls were white but around the window and the door was blue paint with little snowflakes here and there in the blue stripes. I remembered my sister saying she painted it that way for me.

No more the sounds of all the children getting ready for the day or me washing and dressing them. Only silence. And a bird singing. It had to be a dream!

Sitting up, I saw I was wearing a nightgown. I pulled my feet out from under the blanket and I had on white socks.

I listened to the bird outside the window singing. I rolled onto my belly on the bed and tried to look out and see the bird. Instead of snow everywhere outside, there was yellow grass covering the yard, and some brown leaves blown into the corner where a wooden wall caught them. There was a tree standing in another corner. Beyond the wall was the top of another house.

I got out of the bed and walked around the room. My sister said it was *my* room, where I could sleep and put all my things. She said we needed to go shopping for clothes because I did not bring very much with me. And we would have a great lunch at the *mall* called Sherway Gardens. She was trying to welcome me to Canada but it was so much I could not take it all at once.

Other than the bed there was a table and a chair. There was a small machine called a *television*. We had one at the Children's House but the Sisters only turned it on for emergency news. Sometimes there was a film showing. The Sisters might let me watch if the film was in English or Danish because then it could be my lesson.

I saw two doors in my room. I could not remember which door opened to the rest of the house. I tried the door on the right but it was a small room with my clothes hanging from a wooden pole. I had three clothes hanging there.

So I tried the door on the left and it opened to a long hall.

I needed to pee so I thought there must be a toilet in this house. The Children's House had one yet the house in Tasiilaq did not and I had to go outside to another place. In Mama's hut we only had a bucket and emptied it each day. My sister gave me a tour of the house when we arrived so I knew where the toilet was. I did not have to go outside.

I walked along the hall, keeping quiet, and found steps going to the upper level. I remembered her showing me the washroom there. At the top of the steps there was a door open on the left so I looked in. The red-haired girl was asleep there, in her room.

There was noise from the next room so I stopped. I was not sure if it was a hungry bear growling or not. It was not loud but it was very rough. I leaned forward to look around the side of the open door and I saw my sister naked on the bed. She was sitting on top of the man who drove the car and he was naked, too. She was bouncing up and down on him, shaking the bed.

I stepped back but my foot made a sound. My sister looked back over her shoulder and saw me!

"Anna," she called, out of breath. "You all right?"

I backed away, into the hall. My sister stopped bouncing and waved at me to come back. She got off her partner and he pulled the sheet over himself. Yet my sister stayed naked.

"You need something?" she asked.

I tried to smile. "Toilet."

"Oh, yes. Remember? I showed you where everything is. Yours is by the kitchen. Downstairs."

Now I remembered. Yet since I was already upstairs, she got off the bed and showed me their toilet, through a door from the bedroom. She didn't worry about putting on clothes, just walked with me into the toilet room. I could see her pregnant belly now.

"You see? It has everything."

She pointed to the shower room and to the long countertop with two basins. And there was the toilet seat.

"Help yourself," she said and stepped out, closing the door.

So I lifted the nightgown and sat.

I could hear them outside in the bedroom talking. I could not hear the words clearly but there was some laughter. Maybe they thought I was strange. Maybe they did not want me to use their toilet. Maybe I should not see them playing their sex game. I did not know what the rules of this house were. I was only a guest.

After I finished the toilet, I stepped out and my sister and her partner were still on the bed with a sheet over them yet I could see they both were still naked. It's not wrong, I knew. It's the natural thing to do.

"Feeling better?" my sister asked from the bed.

The sheet was down enough that her breasts showed yet she didn't seem to worry about me seeing. I guessed they wanted to finish their game. So I nodded, hurried out.

"Strange girl," I heard the man say as I went down the hall to the stairs.

"She'll get used to being here," my sister replied. "Remember she came from an orphanage."

I stopped at the top of the steps, listening to them.

"She never saw people making love?" asked the man.

"Shhh! She's very innocent."

"Then we should start closing the door."

"No, I don't want Thora to think we are closing her out."

"Well, there is private time and public time," he said.

"I want our daughter to understand there's nothing wrong with sex between men and women."

"And your sister."

"What?"

"I mean, let your sister know, too. Tell her there's nothing wrong with sex between adults."

"I'm sure she knows that."

Maybe it was private time now. Nobody was supposed to be out of their rooms yet. So I went back to my bed and pretended to sleep until I heard new sounds.

I opened my eyes and saw the red-haired girl peeking into my room, my door open only a finger's width. When she saw I was awake, she opened the door wider.

"Good morning," said the girl. She waved at me.

I sat up, rubbed my eyes. "Good morning."

When she saw me smile, she came into the room and climbed onto the bed. I welcomed her like I used to welcome Aq and Arna. She and I talked for a while on my bed.

"Mama and Daddy shake the bed every morning," she said. "Saturday and Sunday are the loudest."

I laughed. She was so cute!

She told me everything about the neighborhood, the schools, the playground, and the shopping mall. She asked me questions about where I came from. I told her all about Greenland. She seemed interested in stories about bears.

After a while, my sister looked in on us. She had pulled on a robe but her hair was a mess.

She invited us to have breakfast. The man called Eric was making cakes in a pan, she said. Her daughter cheered. She liked that food. It seemed like Danish food. Mix the bread crumbles with the eggs and the milk and pour it all into a pan. Then you put wet, mushy fruit on top with melted butter.

The daughter watched me as though she wondered if I knew how to use a fork. I watched them eating, too, all of us grinning between bites. We sat in our sleeping clothes, eating breakfast. So different from the Children's House. Only a few days before, I had a dozen children to get up and ready for the day. Wake, wash, dress, clean, then eat. I'm good with children, the Sisters said, so I would try to be good to this child. She was my *niece*, after all. And I was her *aunt*.

So I settled in and their house was my home. It was comfortable and I learned the rules. I got the schedule fixed. In the morning my sister got up first, drank coffee as she checked the messages on the computer machine. She had a list of all the messages from her friends. She usually typed answers back to them. Sometimes there were pictures.

Then her daughter and Eric got up and he would make a breakfast. Then I got up. We ate and then my sister took Thora to the school a few streets away and her partner drove the car to his school to teach some classes. During the daytime, my sister kept the house neat and sometimes she painted a picture. She had a big room under the house for that.

In the afternoon, she went back to the school to meet Thora and they returned home or they stopped by the park to play. She got the dinner ready and her partner would come home in time to eat it. Sometimes she would buy food that was already cooked and bring it home, ready to eat. After dinner they would look at the television or read books.

At 8 on the clock, Thora had a bath and then went to bed. My sister always read a story to her. Since I arrived, however, it was me bathing her and reading to her. The same time I did that, my sister and her partner, Eric, would play sex games in their room. I had to talk louder sometimes as I read the story. Then I turned out the lights and said "Goodnight" to Thora.

At first, my sister showed me around the neighborhood, to places I might want to go. She showed me the grocery store that was close to the house, the store for female hygiene things and medicine, a place to get coffee, a snack shop, the post office, the park where Thora played. She could sit and watch Thora on the swings and roundabouts. There were so many trees, it looked like the forests I saw in books.

In the early days of my life in Canada, my sister took me shopping. She chose clothes, made me put them on. She looked me over, nodded or shook her head. She asked if I liked this clothes or that clothes. I really didn't know what I liked.

"I don't like dress," I told her. I knew that much. My legs were not long and thin like hers, not so white. My legs were hairy and thick, full of muscles for climbing mountains and pushing sleds. I didn't want people to see my legs. I also did not want sandals. My feet were short and wide with little toes, not long, narrow, and white like her feet. I had bear feet! And she always painted her toenails red.

So we looked for trousers for women that were called *slacks*, and leather shoes with low heels, good for walking. She showed me shirts and sweaters. It was spring, she reminded me, so we better get a swimming suit, too. She liked to swim. When I put on the swimsuits, I could not show them even to her. They were too tight, too small. Everybody could see a lot of skin. Standing before the mirrors in that little room, I realized I did not look pretty. Maybe Dirk was being kind to me. I was good enough to go on a journey over the ice with him but I did not look pretty here in Canada.

I didn't like any of the clothes.

"All right," said my sister. "We can look another time."

Next my sister took me to get my hair cut. Not cut all the hair off, just cutting a little so it would look better. The woman also trimmed my thick, dark eyebrows. She made a comment about the little hairs on my upper lip, too. My sister said I was from Greenland.

"Oh, an Eskimo, eh?" The woman gave me a serious look, like she was searching for clues who I really was. "That explains it. We don't get many First Nations people in this shop."

"*Já*, she's my sister—half sister. So I'm treating her to a make-over today."

The woman smiled sideways. "Might take some work...."

So I'm not a pretty girl. That is not my life, anyway. I don't even care if I'm girl or boy. I'm *me*. I'm Wolf. I do what I want and I don't say excuses. I got brown skin and dark eyes. I got a thick body and short arms and legs. I got hair on my lip and the hair on my head is all out of flow. And I got lots of hair under my arms and between my legs, too!

My sister took me to a shop where a woman would cut all the hair between my legs. That idea was not comfortable for me so I didn't let her do it.

"Don't worry," said my sister, "we can do that at home. It was strange my first time, too."

"So I gotta do it?"

"You don't *gotta*." She grinned, almost laughed. "But when it gets hot here in summer, you'll want to shave. It's much more comfortable. You never experienced the kind of heat we have here in summer."

"Nuuk got up to nineteen last summer."

"Nineteen Celsius? That's not high. Here it could be thirty-two in July. You'll want to be hairless then, *já*."

"Is that what proper Danish girls do?"

She laughed for a long time. "You're worried about being a proper Danish girl? Is that it, Anna? You're not Danish. Neither am I." She put her hand on my shoulder. "*Já*, I'm sure proper Danish girls do not have a lot of hair down there. Or under their arms, either. Let's not compare ourselves to them, *já*?"

I looked down. I was only a hairy, brown creature from the land of the dark. I wanted to go home. My eyes got tears.

"Hey, now, Anna. Don't feel bad. I didn't mean anything by that. We don't have to be like anyone else."

She sighed, then looked around the mall, almost spinning on her foot. She seemed to be looking for a certain store.

"I just don't know what to do with you, Anna. I want to help you fit in, *já*, so I thought I could take you around and change you as you like, however you want to be. So if you want to look like some Danish princess, we can do that."

I looked up. She was as confused about me as I was confused about her. Maybe we really were sisters.

"I don't fit here." Tears filled my eyes.

"Nobody fits in here." She let out a very big breath, patted my back. "I wrote you about my first years living here, didn't I? I didn't know much English and my mother did not give me any attention, so busy with her new husband. And then she had the twins! So I really didn't fit in." She wiped her eyes. "I thought...I want to make it better for you, easier for you, than the way it was for me."

"Thank you," I said. Then, "I'm sorry."

She put her arm around me. "This isn't Greenland, my dear. I don't know what life was like there, but it's a lot different than here, that's for sure."

Waving her arm around at all the shops in the mall, she told me which ones she goes to. She didn't shop very often in the mall but when she needed clothes for work, she bought them in these stores. She dressed up for school. Sometimes she taught art class when a teacher was sick at home. Sometimes she worked in an office and answered phones. Those jobs were easy, she said. She only needed to sit at a desk and let men look at her when they arrived.

She pointed to several stores ahead of us.

"How about jeans? Everyone wears jeans. Or shorts. If you don't like dresses you can wear shorts when it gets hot. And you will need more underwear — if you wear them."

She often went without underwear, she said. No brassiere or panty. I smiled. She seemed more like me, after all.

The Sisters made sure I wore everything that a proper Danish girl was supposed to wear. Yet, living on the ice, I wore only one set of clothing, a sealskin parka and anorak, trousers of bear fur, and *kamik*s — my boots. I only wore other clothes under them if I wanted to be warmer. I looked in these stores and there were so many clothes, yet none of them right for living in Greenland.

"Of course, not!" My sister laughed. "We are in Canada. And here in Toronto, it's a lot like New York City, all the fashions and frivolous shit anybody could possibly want. Whatever you want, we have it."

"I just want Kit-Kat."

Her eyes narrowed. "What?"

"All I want now is Kit-Kat."

"Oh, chocolate. You like chocolate?"

She took me down the mall a short walk to a chocolate shop with rows of chocolates in many colors and shapes, all protected under a sheet of glass.

"Here's the best chocolate in the city," she said.

Yet I knew what I wanted, so we left the mall and took a bus back to her neighborhood.

We went to the grocery store near the house. Walking up and down the aisles, I put whatever I wanted into the basket. Then my sister pulled out a purse, opened it, and took out a bunch of paper money. She handed some money to me.

"Here. You can start with this."

"Why?"

"Just want to give you some money. For...let's say helping with the laundry. Or getting Thora to bed on time all week. To say thanks."

"What do I do with it?" I asked.

"You spend it."

"I got everything."

"You have to want more. Sometime, anyway — right?"

"What should I want more?"

She stared at me. "That's a good question. What are we going to do with you, Anna?" She shook her head, then turned away. "Shit, that doesn't sound right. Sorry." She bit her lip.

I took the Kit-Kat out of the sack, opened the wrapper, and took a big bite.

"I mean, what are your plans?" she asked.

I took another bite, chewed.

"What are you thinking of for your life? Are you going to get a job? How about school? Did you finish your school there? You want to get married? What are you going to do with your life?"

I swallowed the last bite, tossed the wrapper into the sack.

"I don't know."

"Já, you sound like me."

She led me out of the store, each of us carrying a bag.

"First, you need to learn how life works in Toronto. The rules are different here." She laughed. She said Eric took her to a place called Texas long ago when they lived together in America. "*Já*, he warned me the rules were different there. I said didn't matter, I didn't know what they were, anyway."

She got me laughing. "What were the rules?"

Her eyes went blank. We stopped. "It really wasn't a good place to visit. I shouldn't mention it. We got into a fight and then I left him and returned to Iceland. I wrote you about that."

"Yet you came back to him."

She smiled, seemed like she didn't want to. "*Já*, I did. Things work out right sometimes." She sighed, put a finger to her eye and wiped away something. "And you have to keep working on it every day, or everything can fall back to the way it was, to the bad times."

I nodded and we continued walking home. She checked her watch. It was close to the time to meet Thora at the school, so we changed directions. It was like my life, I saw. Walk straight until you get a new idea, then change directions. I wondered where I would go next.

"After you learn how to get by in Toronto," said my sister, "then you will be able to make decisions about what to do."

At the school, the children were already running out. Thora saw us and ran to us. My sister set down her bag, ready to catch Thora in a hug but she jumped at me!

I caught her in my arms.

"Auntie, you came, too!" shouted Thora.

"I did. I want to see your school."

"We've been shopping the whole day," said my sister.

I set Thora down on the sidewalk.

"But all Anna wanted was chocolate."

"I love chocolate, too!" said Thora.

"Perhaps we should all get some. Or, how about ice cream?" She turned to me. "You like ice cream, don't you?"

I knew I liked ice. And snow. So it seemed like a good thing, so I agreed to get ice cream on the way back to the house.

Already the sun was warm and my skin felt hot. I felt water run down my back. My shirt had wet patches. My sister told me it was the first sign of summer coming. Perspiration. To combat it, she said, we wipe *deodorant* under our arms.

We got the ice cream. It tasted like chocolate. It was cold and creamy! I liked it. *I loved it!* I would always love ice cream from that day on! I planned to eat ice cream every day! It was worth the whole trip to Toronto!

As we sat outside the shop eating ice cream cones, we talked about what to do with me. I had all my certificates proving that I knew about numbers and words and geography and history and taking care of health. My sister wondered if I needed to attend school until I was eighteen. I was only seventeen, so we decided I should go to the neighborhood school for older students. Then I would learn everything about Canada by sitting among the real Canadian students.

My sister stopped, felt her big belly.

"It's getting closer," she said. "He must like ice cream."

My sister had her baby in July. She was very happy to have a new baby but her partner got so angry. The little boy didn't look like him. She said her son looked like Chinese. It started when they went to California. That was the month she didn't write to me. Her partner had to attend a meeting there. After the meeting there was a big party and there were many people there—many men. Many Asian men. So I got the idea of what happened. My sister still had a wild life, even though she said she stopped.

I knew they liked playing sex games. Sometimes they would introduce somebody, a young woman or sometimes a man, and call that person their *friend*. Then I would see them together in the big bedroom. I looked fast because it was not my business. I got a house to live in so I worked at my tasks and kept my area clean. I took care of Thora and the new baby. I knew how to care for children, changed a lot of diapers for her baby boy. He had black hair and his eyes were different.

Eventually Eric accepted the blame for pushing her into the party. He welcomed the baby boy into the family. He gave him a name. There was a city called Austin in that Texas place my sister hated. Eric was from Texas so he liked that name. So the house became calm again. My sister and her partner knew they better start living right and not play with other people.

I brought my sister breakfast each morning. I carried a tray of food into the bedroom and she would be sitting on the bed with the baby at her breast. I helped her by burping the baby while she ate.

After the summer, I started school. I sat quietly and listened to the teachers, and the other students didn't bother me much. Sometimes they called me 'Indian' or 'Eskimo' and said I was stupid and shouldn't be in their school. My sister came to school to defend me. She complained to the headmaster. I took a few tests and passed everything but English. So the man my sister slept with tutored me. I passed the test and got my graduation certificate!

My sister had a celebration party for me. Every time I did something good there was a party! Yet after the party there was always a hole inside me that I had to fill with whatever pictures were in my head. If I could not fill that hole, I would fall into it and not be able to climb out. Toronto was a very big hole!

"Now you can do anything you like," said my sister.

I didn't know what I wanted to do.

My sister took me to the University of Toronto. She showed me the campus. She went to school there before she ever knew about me. She studied art, became an art teacher. She still went there to model for art classes. Yet I was not good at art, so she asked me what I was good at.

"I'm good at taking care children."

"Taking care *of* children," she corrected.

I repeated after her.

"So, perhaps being a teacher would be a good job for you."

"I like helping people, too."

"That's also good. You could work with people, like helping them, if you study Sociology. Perhaps be a social worker."

"Social worker? What do they do?"

"They talk with people who have problems and try to find a solution to the problem."

That seemed like a good job for me so my sister signed me up for the classes. Because I got the certificate from the high school proving I passed equivalent classes in all subjects, they let me in. I was called *indigenous* on the registration forms, yet everybody thought I was from the north part of Canada, not Greenland. As a "First Nations" student, I got a seat.

I was so happy to be in a classroom again I wrote a letter to the Sisters about my new life.

That September I started the college life. I got myself up early and rode a bus to the campus and went into a building with my books and papers, sat in the room and wrote what the teacher said. It was what I did in Tasiilaq. Most people didn't bother me. To the students sitting around me, I was just a ghost—another *indigenous* nobody trying to fit in by acting white.

I wanted to say to everybody that my father was white but

anybody looking at me would not believe it. My sister said she looked like her red-haired mother and I looked like my Inuit mother. So our father did not count for much.

In the winter, when the snow fell, I danced around the yard behind the house. I loved being outdoors and I sat in the snow. Some people on the campus laughed at me, said it was typical for Inuit to sit in the snow instead of going inside where it was warm. I didn't care about them or what they thought of me.

I'm Wolf. I do what I want, go where I want, and I eat what I want! This Anna Tasiilaq student in the Sociology department is actually a girl from a hut on the island of Ammassalik on the east coast of Greenland and her Mama called her Wolf. I smiled because I knew the secret and everybody around me did not. At any time of the day or evening, I might burst into a furious fury of terrible terror and they would all be scared of me!

"You don't really want to scare anyone like that, do you?" asked my sister.

"If I have to, I will bite them!"

"But they don't really bother you, do they?"

"Nobody knows I'm there."

"If anyone should harass you, let me know. Or tell one of the counselors. You know where the office is?"

"They told us in orientation."

"Good. But you keep alert. It's still a big city. There's a lot of crime here."

I promised her I would be careful.

When I was back at the house, I cared for Thora and Austin. I did the cleaning. I kept my room clean. I read the books for each class and I wrote again everything I wrote in the class. I was a good student. When I was on the campus, I went any place I wanted, did whatever I wanted. I got ice cream every day at the snack shop. I watched students run around the field. I watched them move around like I was in a cloud looking down on them. Even if they looked in my direction they didn't see me.

I got to use the computer, which made it easy to write words, much better than the typing machine. I could type very fast but not very correct. My sister showed me the place on the computer she went to talk with her friends. Some of them were far away, in other countries of the world, yet they wrote messages to each other all the time. I wanted some friends, too, but I didn't know what to say to them. I wondered if anybody in Greenland had a computer. I wondered if Dirk had gone north or if he still lived in Nuuk, maybe thinking about me. I wanted to send messages to him. So I signed up for it on that *internet* place but I never visited that computer place very much until later.

I also found the library on the campus. It was the place to go every day. Besides having computers, there were a lot of books, more than I ever saw before. I liked having books around me, so many books, so many stories to tell. It was amazing! I went to a desk in the back corner, away from everybody, and read many books. Sometimes I took off my shoes, put my feet on the desk to be comfortable. A library person might come by and tell me to put my feet down, then mumble about Native people's ways. Yet in the back corner I could sink into a book and not know what time it was. The thick "classics" books were the best.

Sometimes I went over to the indoor swimming pool to hide from the world. The girls of the swimming team practiced at the same time I usually went there. I sat on the metal benches and read my books while they jumped in the water and swam as fast as they could. The echo of their voices was like the wind in my ears back in Nuuk.

One day, sitting by the swimming pool, I had to pee. I went into the room for changing clothes. When I finished, suddenly the whole swim team was naked in the room and I was the only girl wearing any clothes there. I thought nobody could see me. So many different bodies, sizes and shapes and skin colors! The girls took showers and returned, got dressed and left.

Only one girl remained.

"What're you looking at?" she asked from across the room.

I froze. All my clothes were on me, many layers for being out in the snow. There were no clothes at all on that girl. She stood and flipped her short blond hair back and forth, combed it.

I shook my head, staring at her golden skin and thin body.

"No? What does that mean?" she asked.

I stepped toward her—it was the same way to leave the changing room—yet she kept talking. She noticed me sitting on the bleachers reading a book and wondered why I always came there to study. She asked if I liked swimming. I didn't answer so she asked if I knew how to swim. I didn't.

She gradually put on clothes, taking a lot of time, like she had to remember what clothes went on next. So many layers to keep warm in the Toronto winter. All the time she was talking to me I didn't answer, just nodded or shook my head.

"I get you're an introvert," she said after she dressed. "It's okay. Lots of people are. Sometimes it's good to be quiet."

I smiled when she said that. I didn't know the word *introvert* until later, but she said it was *okay*.

She came over to me and introduced herself. She held out her hand and I reached for it. She grabbed my hand, shook it. Her name was Gigi—actually it was the letters of her name, G. G., for Gardenia Grace, with the family name Wolversen. I smiled. She was Wolf, too! She came to school here from South Africa and her home was as far away from Toronto as any place on Earth.

"You must be Native, true? What tribe are you?"

"I'm Inuit," I said. I told her my name, the same name I used at this school. I moved to Toronto from Greenland.

"So you're a long way from home, too."

Gigi was kind to me so I looked for her every day after my classes. She was studying to be a physical therapist. She was on the swim team in exchange for the tuition cost. Back in her home country there were not enough of these doctors so she thought it would be a good job. Later she practiced her massage techniques on me.

I was studying to help people with their problems, maybe go back to Greenland to help there. She thought it was a good idea, to give something back to my homeland. We talked a lot about everything. She told me about her country, all the animals there and how hot it was. She could never get used to the winters in Toronto. I told her I almost died during the heat of the summer in Toronto. We got along. Gigi was my first friend in Canada.

After the winter break, she started to ignore me. I learned some of her swimming team asked her why she was my friend. That Native girl always comes to watch you swim, they said. Is she your girlfriend? That was how they teased her. She told me not to worry yet I knew she wanted to stay away from me.

I didn't know how to swim so Gigi decided she had to teach me. I wore a panty and t-shirt at first, then I got my sister to buy a swimsuit for me, a one-piece that covered me from shoulders to thighs. Gigi always wore a very tiny two-piece suit called *bikini* that showed almost all of her thin body.

One day after my swimming lesson, we were showering and we joked about really being girlfriends, like everybody thought we already were. We got dressed. She came over to me, hugged me. I was surprised, but it felt good to have somebody hold me.

She leaned down, looked into my eyes, and kissed me.

"You are so cute, Anna, I have to kiss you!"

And I kissed her, too.

I went to Gigi's room in the residence hall and we played on her bed. Gigi liked being with me.

One time my sister sent a message on the computer saying she was on the campus, modeling for the art class, so we should meet and have lunch. We met near the library. Gigi was with me so I introduced them to each other. Gigi was taller than my sister and I felt smaller. Gigi put her arm around me.

My sister grinned. "Why don't you join us?"

So we three went off the campus and had lunch and talked.

Later, at home, my sister was happy I made a friend. She also had girlfriends in her life. She said it was good to take a break from men. I wanted to tell her it was not a break but real love. She told me about a few girls that were her lovers in the past. I also knew about the girls her partner brought home for games. My room was under their bedroom so I heard all the noise.

I stayed over with Gigi some nights. My sister got worried. She said I was allowed to do it but I had to let her know. She was getting to be like the Sisters in the Children's House.

I already had eighteen years, so I could do what I wanted, yet because my sister paid for my school, I didn't want to complain. I had a nice room in a big house and I got some snow for half the year. I got plenty of food that I hardly ever had to cook, and I never had to go hunting. I didn't even know where to find any animals to hunt. I only saw dogs and cats in the city.

And I had a girlfriend!

Until she got tired of me. Even though her friends stopped teasing her, she spent less and less time with me until I noticed the semester had ended and I didn't know where she was. I could not understand why she left me. I always did what she wanted. The way we always lay together, touching, was so good. I guessed she wanted to go back to boys.

I met some boys, too. They were in my classes. They were big, tall, and scary. They looked at the First Nations girls and got interested. We were mysterious, I guessed. A few of them said "hello" to me like they didn't expect me to understand English. I only nodded or I said "hello" back. I always kept walking, not wanting trouble.

In the summer, I took more classes even though it was hot. I understood what my sister said about wearing shorts. She never wore pants except the coldest days of winter. She looked good in dresses and skirts with sandals whenever she went to an office. I didn't get a skirt, just shorts. I could not stay outdoors for a long time, anyway. It was too hot, like sitting on a brazier. I loved the cold air in the library and in the house.

My sister always kept the house very cold by using a cooling machine. I liked to stand in front of the openings of the machine and feel the cold air blowing against my skin. It reminded me of Greenland.

Sometimes my sister went around in the house without any clothes on, just to stay cool. She didn't mind who saw her. She even went out to the yard behind the house in the evenings. Her partner joined her, also without any clothes. The daughter and the baby had no clothes, also. Yet the high fence and all the trees kept everybody from seeing them.

"I'm not really a nudist," said my sister, "but when it's this hot, I really can't stand wearing clothes. Besides, I'm quite used to being nude from modeling."

She explained what nudism really was: some people think it is healthier to live without wearing clothes, no matter the season or the weather or if other people visit them. For her, though, it was only a summer thing. Or for art.

"You can't do that in Greenland," I said. "You freeze your skin off there. You get the frostbites."

She laughed and her breasts jiggled. "Lovely!"

Through that whole summer I got used to seeing them with no clothes on. My sister said I could do it, too, if I wanted. I preferred to stay in the house by the cold air machine. I was used to wearing lots of clothes just to stay warm in Greenland. Now people were taking off their clothes to keep from being too hot. The world was upside-down!

Later in the summer we went on a trip north of the city, into the woods, and we stopped at a lake. The trees shaded part of the shore so the sun wouldn't burn us. My sister took off all her clothes, like she was going to step into the shower at home. She folded her clothes neatly and set them on the big towel spread on the ground. Her partner also stripped down, yet the children wore swimsuits. I wore short pants and a shirt I usually wear to class. I knew we were going to a lake yet I only wanted to have a look, to get out of the city for a day, not go swimming. I didn't bring my swimsuit.

"You are free to join us, Anna, if you like," said my sister.

I told her I was comfortable sitting on the towel.

As the afternoon went on, she swam in the lake and played with the children. Other people there were naked, too.

The sun got hotter and my body got wetter. The clothes were sticking to my skin. I never felt so miserable. So I pulled off my shoes and socks. I took off my shirt, let it slip off my arms. I was not wearing a brassiere like a good Danish girl. So there were my boobs for everybody to see!

My sister noticed. "You're finally ready to get comfortable?"

"My clothes sticking to all my skin!"

"Then take them off. Be comfortable."

I stood and slid down my shorts. And my panties. Suddenly I

had nothing on under the whole sky! I looked around the shore of the lake. Everybody was nude or half nude. Yet nobody was looking at me. I pulled my knees up to my chest and wrapped my arms around my knees, hiding.

"Feel better now?" She looked me over. "You really do look quite lovely, you know."

She pointed to my brown arms and legs then to the pale skin that was covered by my clothes.

"You got stripes!"

Her partner returned to the shore with the children.

"You finally joined the club," he said. "Good for you!"

I didn't know what club he meant. My sister told him not to stare at me. I stayed bunched up for some time, afraid people would look at me. I had stripes!

Then my little niece Thora asked me to go into the water with her. She held out her hand, so I took her hand and got up. We went down to the water. When I went in, the water was so cold I had to run right out!

I was standing on the shore completely naked, screaming at the cold water. Now everybody looked at me!

To escape from their eyes, I rushed back into the water. Thora cheered. I tried swimming like Gigi taught me and I could move across the water. I tried swimming on my back, too, and the sun was so warm on my skin. Very different from Greenland.

I got out of the lake after a while and lay flat on my back on the towel. I was too tired to think about covering myself. I liked the warm sun on my skin. I liked feeling free, the breeze blowing over my skin. I closed my eyes and fell asleep.

Then I felt hands on me.

"You need lotion or you'll get sunburnt," said my sister.

She rubbed lotion over my body. It was relaxing, like one of Gigi's massages. I turned over on my belly and my sister put on more lotion, from my feet up to my neck.

She awoke me when it was time to go. My body had dried by then so I got dressed and we drove back to the city.

A few times in the summer they had a party in the back yard of the house. Some of the people who visited did not wear any clothes. I got used to it. In the house, I got used to not wearing clothes, too. And I never slept in a nightgown again.

In one of my Sociology classes I met a regular Canadian boy. Stuart had white skin and brown hair. He sat next to me or sometimes behind me during most lessons. One day he dropped his pen and it rolled under my desk. I leaned forward to pick it up. He thanked me. After class, he asked if I liked ice cream. Of course! So he showed me where to get ice cream on the campus, like he was doing a favor for me. I already knew where it was but I let him get a thrill showing it to me.

We studied a lot together after that, yet I got better scores than him on tests. He was jealous. He said he needed to study harder, even though he didn't like Sociology and didn't really want to help people. His mother thought he should study it. She was some kind of doctor.

He invited me to study at his apartment near the campus. His mother was paying the rent while he was in school so he said I was welcome there any time. I could even sleep overnight there, if I wanted to.

It was a small apartment, only one bedroom, a washroom, half a kitchen, yet enough for a student. He gave me Dr Pepper to drink every time I visited. It was ice-cold and very delicious! The first time I visited, we sat on the sofa and watched a show on the television. Before it ended we were making out, kissing and touching like we had always wanted to but we were forced to wait.

I had to catch my breath!

"I'm sorry, Anna," said Stuart. "You are just so hot I couldn't help myself! How did you get to be so damn *hot*?"

While we continued making out, I wondered why he would think I was hot. It was already October, autumn arrived. Also I was from Greenland where it is always cold. Maybe I was hot because I wore too many clothes.

So I took off my shirt to cool down.

"Now I'm not so damn hot," I said, folding my shirt.

"I mean," he said, putting his hands on my breasts, "you are so absolutely sexy, I just wanna take you into the bed and fuck you all night long."

I knew a lot of English words and I was learning more every day at school and studying every night, checking a dictionary for new words, yet Stuart was so hungry I didn't care what he said. We went to his bed and I liked what we did there, even though it did not last all night long.

I went to his apartment all the time and we always went to the bed for a while before I had to go home.

Iris worried about me, so we had a sister-to-sister talk. She thought I was a virgin since I lived in the Children's House. No, I told her in a lot of serious words, I had a lot of experience with boys and men. Yet not all of it was good. Same for her, she told me, good boys and bad boys.

"It's not a bad thing to play sex games," I said. "It's what girls and boys do. If they like each other."

"If they *love* each other," my sister insisted.

"Doesn't have to be that. If you like playing together, you can do it."

"You must be careful," she said. "Be sure he uses a condom."

I got angry, the way she treated me like a little girl. I told her I had eighteen years. I reminded her of the wild life she had. Her partner was still bringing home a girl from his school sometimes and they played with her. At least I was *playing* with only one.

"That's how we, as you call it, play," she said. "It's always by our mutual consent. *Já*, it's possible to have fun that way without having to make so many rules. Nobody gets hurt."

"That's what I do, too, Sissy. Mutual consents and nobody gets hurt. It's my right to do it."

"But you don't know what you're doing. I mean, you're not being careful. You can't just sleep with anyone. You don't have the experience like I do."

"Yeah, you got *experience!* I know! That why you got a baby and he look different from your husband."

That upset her and she slapped my face. Then she was in shock as fast as me. She covered her face with her hands.

"I'm sorry," she cried. "I'm so sorry, Anna! I didn't mean to do that."

"You can hit me any time you want. It's your house and I gotta do what you want."

"No, it's not like that, Anna. You're not a—a servant here."

"Then I can do what I want."

We kept arguing all night. It seemed to me she had rules for me but not for herself or her man. They did what they wanted. And the people that came to play with them also did what they wanted. They played together and I watched the kids. That was the reason she didn't want me staying out with boys, I guessed. She needed me at home to watch the kids.

So my sister asked to meet Stuart, to check him out for me, make sure he was a good boy. Yet I didn't want a good boy.

"I'm your sister," she said. "I have to look out for you."

"I lived on my own in Greenland, you know."

165

"Perhaps, but the streets of Toronto are far more dangerous than the place you lived over there."

"We got ice bears."

"We have rapists and murderers. And there's nothing more frightening than encountering another *human* who might decide to hurt you for no reason but his own entertainment. A bear only wants food. That's predictable and you can handle that situation. Humans want…they want to hurt other humans."

I never could believe the city was more dangerous than living on the ice. We had rapists and murderers there, too.

"I want you to be careful. That's all. These boys only want to take advantage of you, get what they want. I don't want you to get hurt."

"I understand. Yet Stuart is a good boy. Yeah, he's bad, but in a good way. I make him good."

"*Já*, I hope so."

After that, my sex life really got big.

I spent more time on the computer, answering messages from boys on the campus and other places in Toronto and also places far away. I learned how to *flirt*. I wrote a sexy sentence and got hundreds of clicks. I posted pictures of me wearing a small two-piece swimsuit, or with no top on but my hand over my boob. Nudity wasn't allowed on the site, yet Stuart took photos of me with a towel or sheet covering the private places and I posted them. I got lots of friends very fast. I joked with them about sex. Like I was a sex princess who went out every night with lots of men. Of course, I didn't really do that. It was just fun playing that kind of game on the computer. After I got more than 1000 friends on that site, I decided to try to get 5000 friends because that was the most that was allowed.

Stuart was a member of a *fraternity*, which is a club for boys who don't like school. They had parties every weekend. In the middle of the week, too. Sometimes he took me with him when they had a party. He introduced me to his brothers. They were not his real brothers, just club brothers. Some of them recognized me from that website. We flirted there already.

During one of the parties, one of Stuart's brothers asked him if he could borrow me for an hour. Stuart said yes so his brother took me by the hand and led me into a bedroom and closed the door.

He tried to kiss me so I pushed him away.

"I didn't say yes," I told him. "He doesn't own me so he can't give me to anybody."

"But he gave you to me." The boy looked surprised, like I didn't know the rules of the house. "We're brothers, so we have to share. You have to do what I say."

"No, I don't. I'm Wolf. I do what I want."

"Wolf? What's that mean?"

"It's my name."

"Hah! Your name?" He shook his head. "What a stupid little Native slut!"

He pushed me down on the bed, so I kicked my foot out at him. My foot got him between his legs and he cried. He rolled on the floor, howling. Some brothers rushed in and at the same time I ran out.

Stuart asked me what happened. I cursed at him. Then I left the fraternity house and went to my home.

It took a while but eventually Stuart apologized. He said he was drinking and didn't know what he was saying that evening. He stopped going to their parties.

I started seeing other boys, anyway. And some girls. I got lots of dates and we usually had sex. I took some condoms from my sister's dresser drawer and always made boys use them. Most of the time. I started to wear short pants and tops with no sleeves.

And I never wore a bra! I was still quiet but there was always a boy who wanted to get to know me.

When Stuart made me his friend again, we made love like in the films, with music and special lights. He promised so many things to me that I had to say yes. I visited his apartment a lot more and I slept over with him.

Stuart had a friend called Jeff who seemed to visit a lot. They both liked computers. Some evenings all three of us watched the television late into the evening, then Stuart and I got the bed and Jeff got the sofa.

Stuart let me use the computer in his apartment so I could check messages without going to the library. That was important because in the library you couldn't let any bad pictures show on the screen because other people could see it. Stuart and Jeff liked to look at all the nude pictures on the computer.

Instead of looking at porn, I just went to the site where I had so many friends. When I got to 4,997 friends on that site, the silly people who owned it decided to stop me. They sent a message to me, said I was using the site *improperly*. They closed my account so I couldn't log on. I was just flirting. It wasn't real. I thought they wanted everybody to get lots of friends. Just not more than 5000. I didn't put any fully *nude* pictures there and I didn't talk about drugs or hating people that were different from me. Stuart said maybe somebody didn't like the way I flirted, or maybe I didn't give enough attention, so the guy reported me. You got to keep everybody happy or you get reported!

Stuart knew everything about computers, so I believed him. He spent a lot of time playing fighting games with other guys on the computer and he got along with them. He talked about changing his subject in school to computers, no matter what his mother said.

After a few days feeling sad, I made a new account on the

same site that wants everybody to be friends. I promised to be good. No more flirting or sexy pictures. I would be an innocent virgin. Maybe act like a proper Danish girl. On the computer you could be anybody you wanted to be, good or bad. So the new account would belong to a girl called ANNA GOOD.

I got to nineteen years in that spring semester and I had a happy life in a very big city, yet I was going crazy. I loved pizza and hamburgers so much and always ate ice cream. I ate a Kit-Kat every day, so I got fat. I always had the Inuit shape, thick body and short arms and legs, right for living on the ice, yet this shape was fat in the eyes of Canadians. And I got fatter during the winter. I still went to my classes and studied but I was learning less. My scores went down. I caused my sister more and more trouble all the time. She was getting frustrated. We argued a lot.

She kept telling me not to go to fraternity parties yet I kept going. I guess I liked getting attention. She said don't have sex with boys I don't know. Yet it was better to play with the boys I didn't know because I wouldn't have to get into a relationship and have to see them again.

My sister kept saying to always make them use condoms. Yet sometimes there wasn't time to get it out. She reminded me to stay away from alcohol and drugs, and don't take any food or drink if I hadn't kept my eyes on it. Somebody might put drugs in my drinks, she warned. I tried to follow her rules yet I was a wild girl. Everybody knew it was very easy to get me out of my clothes and on a bed. Or some other place, like the veranda of the fraternity house, or in somebody's car. I really liked boys and they sure liked me!

Except one time when I went to a party at a fraternity house, even though I knew I shouldn't. The boys wanted to play games. They got me to join a game and I lost so I had to strip naked. It was all for fun but then they wouldn't give my clothes back to me. First, I acted like it wasn't a big deal because I was already comfortable being nude, like my sister when she posed for art classes. Then I got angry, shouting at them to give my clothes back. They kept tossing my clothes over my head. Being short, I couldn't catch it. I got frustrated and just crouched down in the middle of the room, wrapped my arms around myself. The boys laughed.

I felt sick and let out a lot of gas from my backside. They all laughed. Then out came a long piece of shit on their carpet!

Everybody got quiet very fast.

"Now gimme my clothes," I growled.

The boy who had them at that moment handed them to me and apologized.

I grabbed my clothes and went out the door. I got dressed on the porch and went home.

Later Stuart called and apologized. He wasn't there because he was working on computers with Jeff and other friends. He said I shouldn't go to any parties without him to protect me. I shouldn't go at all, he said, if his buddies were going to treat me that way. I told him I didn't need any boy to protect me. I had always been on my own and took care of myself. Yet I knew he was right. I liked boys for the wrong reasons. He laughed. He said he would take care of me if I would only be with him.

He said I could live in his apartment full time, and gave me a key. Actually, he hid the key and wanted me to search him for it. I patted him all over and I put my hands into every pocket until I found the key. He said my hands tickled. I said it was because I didn't want to hurt him.

It seemed like I was a different person now than the person I was in Nuuk. I wrote a few letters to the Sisters when I was new in Toronto yet now I couldn't tell them about my life here. They would not like reading about me eating bad food, playing with boys, not paying attention in class or sleeping through the class, missing it, or staying out late to have fun. I also stopped saying words to the Lord of Denmark. I didn't write any letters.

Like the Sisters did a long time ago, my sister tried to talk to me about life — big letter L, she called it, like she had everything figured out. She was trying to protect me from all the bad things she already experienced.

Then she got pregnant again — yet she was telling me to be careful! At least this time it was with Eric, her pretend husband, so they were happy.

Even after she got over the spitting up every morning, I knew I still did not want to learn any lessons from her.

Yet my sister had to rescue me from yet another fraternity party. It was all by accident. I walked by and they invited me in. The boys knew me, wanted me to join them. They complimented me so much I had to go in. My sister got me a pocket phone at the start of the school year so I could call if I needed a pick up or to let her know if I wasn't coming home some night. I really needed the phone that night because the boys were trying to fuck me one after another yet I didn't want that. I grabbed my phone, locked myself in the washroom, and called my sister.

A short time later she burst into the house shouting my name and the boys were stunned. My sister was pregnant. Even with her belly standing out she pushed her way through the boys, checking the rooms until she found me. She ordered the boys out and tossed my clothes at me. I could tell she was angry yet she didn't say anything to me. When I was dressed she took my arm, led me out of the house. She told them if they ever touched me again she would *kill them!*

At home she talked to me again about getting involved with boys at parties, how it could be dangerous—"And you saw that tonight, *já*?"—and how much she cared for me and was trying to protect me. I still thought she was trying to make up for her own wild life by being strict with me. I had to learn on my own.

"I know, I know," I said after she told me I don't think these decisions through.

"It's not that I want you to treat everyone like the enemy. But there are bad people out there."

"I can take care myself!"

"It's not like being in a small town in Greenland."

"Here is big buildings yet people are people every place."

"Exactly. The more people in a place, the higher the chance of meeting bad ones."

I stared at her, not wanting to give in.

"All these things you do…. You know, it seems as though you are simply crying for attention." She pinched her lips. "*Já*, like I did. I did a lot of crazy things, too. So you can learn from my mistakes."

"I learn a whole lot from you, Sissy," I said in a sour voice. I wanted her to leave my room so I could relax. "So what's wrong with getting attention?"

"Depends what kind it is. That's what you want most of all? I thought you were an introvert."

"Yeah, but sometimes I want attention."

"Be careful what you want," said my sister, patting my head like I was a little girl.

Then, a few weeks later, after my classes were done for the day, I was walking near the campus and a woman came beside me, started talking to me, asking questions. She looked a little older than me, probably a graduate student, and she was very friendly. We went to get ice cream. As we left the ice cream shop, she asked where I was going and offered me a ride. I thought it would be a short drive to the other side of the campus. It was hot and I was sweating, so I agreed. She called on her phone and a minute later a white van pulled up beside us. The door opened and another woman waved for us to get in, so we did.

Inside were other women and girls. They looked happy. We talked. Then it seemed the drive was longer than it should be. I panicked so the man in the back of the van put tape over my mouth and around my wrists and told me to relax. They were taking me and the other girls to another city! That wasn't what I wanted, so I kicked and fought with them until the man hit me in the face a few times and I stayed quiet.

As soon as the van stopped and they opened the door, I jumped out and ran as fast as I could. It was night by then and the city was quiet and dark so I hid from them. I got the tape off and found a store that was open. I went inside shouting that I was being kidnapped and the clerk called the police. They got me connected with my sister, and she and Eric drove down from Toronto to get me. The people in the van took me all the way to Windsor, across the river from America. They were going to sell me to people in Detroit!

On the return trip to Toronto, my sister sat in the back with me and held my hand. She didn't blame me. She wanted me to be safe. I caused her a lot of trouble yet she always saved me and never cursed at me. Eric told me about reports of sex trafficking, girls being taken off streets, forced into prostitution. It seemed like that was what happened to me yet I got away. I worried about the other girls in that van who didn't get away. I gave the police a lot of information and hoped they could catch them.

The best thing I ever felt was stretching out on my perfect bed in my own room after a long, hot bath in the big washroom upstairs. After the bath, my sister combed my hair and rubbed my shoulders. She told me that no matter what I did she would always save me, but she hoped it would be from something easy, like missing the bus to the campus, or spilling ice cream down my shirt. I cried in her arms and she held me close for a long time. I promised to be good.

"I am so lucky to have you here," she whispered into my ear. "Life is full of tricks. They are lessons, *já*. We have to learn from them."

"Thanks," I said, wiping tears from my face. "That's what my mama always told me."

I really tried to be good. On that website I was good. I was ANNA GOOD on there so I had to be. I got some of the friends that my sister had. I learned how to be friendly without flirting. I joined some groups there and read the messages people posted about their problems and their achievements. It was like sitting in class and listening to everyone talking, or reading it in a book. I still read books, but more of them were story books instead of books full of information like for a class.

I kept dating Stuart. His friend Jeff came over a lot and we all ate the dinner I cooked then played computer games together. Sometimes it was so late when we stopped that Jeff had to stay overnight. He said the sofa wasn't very comfortable, and then after I got my period on the cushions, he refused to sleep on it. So we let him squeeze into the bed with Stuart and me.

Of course, Stuart and I still liked "making love" so we did it even with Jeff next to us. He didn't mind watching. We joked about him getting excited as he watched us, so he took care of himself as we made love. Then, sometimes I helped Jeff. Stuart liked Jeff, too, so they played with each other, too, as I watched.

One night I awoke in the dark with a warm body against me and my legs pushed open. I wrapped my arms tight around him and we got our love made. I returned to sleep. In the morning I had to wonder which of the boys was the one during the night. I guessed it was Stuart, my boyfriend, because it was only him I let go inside me. Yet the way Jeff treated me in the next few days I believed he was the one with me during the night.

Stuart got angry at Jeff when he confessed it was him.

"She's my girlfriend!" Stuart shouted like I never heard him before. "You can't be fucking her without my permission."

"But you're my boyfriend," Jeff insisted equally loud. "So I thought we shared everything."

"Not her! She's mine."

"But me and her are sharing *you*. That's allowed, isn't it?"

"Hey, guys!" I stepped between them. "Is anybody asking me? What about me?"

They both stared at me like they forgot I was in the room.

"I'm the girl in this relationship. Remember?"

"We know," said Stuart. He looked at Jeff.

"And we want you," said Jeff, turning to Stuart.

"And I want both of you," I said. "You can share me. I don't mind. We can share each other."

After a week, they got tired of fighting about who I belonged to and returned to their computer games, fighting aliens from space. They were friends again. So we decided to be a *triad*. We took turns with each other.

And that was how I got to be pregnant.

By then, we were like a family and I talked about my two *husbands* to anybody that would listen, even though we were not actually married. It was me and my boyfriend and his boyfriend living together in that little apartment.

When I told them I got all the signs of pregnancy they were

surprised. They never thought of babies, only computers. They got scared, asked me what I was going to do, like I had to make a decision.

"I'm not ready to be a dad," said Stuart.

"You don't have to be ready," I told my two husbands. "It just happens. Babies don't think about you being ready. They come out when it's time, whether you want them or not."

"Don't worry, Anna," said Jeff, patting my belly even though I had nothing to show yet. "We'll be ready."

They promised to take care of me and our baby. It would be "our" baby, with three parents. And I promised myself I would not say who the father was. I didn't know, just guessed, but my sister said there were tests to identify the real father.

I still went to classes that semester, and Stuart and Jeff had their classes, too, but they went less and less. They liked to play computer games all day and night. I warned them they would not have a good life ahead if they didn't learn things at school. It was the voice of my sister I was repeating to them. I reminded them we had a baby coming so they better prepare for a career.

One weekend, I officially moved out of my sister's house and into that little apartment. It was my new home. I had a man—two men—and I loved being there! I was almost twenty then and I could hardly remember living on the ice. I was a city girl now. I had responsibilities. Besides my classes, I cooked and I kept the apartment clean for my husbands.

My sister was happy for me but she wanted me to stay in the house so I could care for *her* new baby, a little red-haired girl she called Freyja. It was an Icelandic name, like her other daughter Thora had. Yet I was an adult now and I had to take care of myself. And the baby growing inside me. I was on my own, she told me, but not in a hard way. She would always help me.

I laughed as my belly got bigger. It was funny how I walked

and how I squeezed into the desks in the classrooms. Everybody smiled at me. Some people wanted to tap on my belly, like I was carrying a spirit drum under my coat. I was a short girl with a big belly. I almost fell over a few times, like a cartoon character.

It was my turn to have a baby yet I wasn't prepared for it any more than when I was in Greenland. I thought about it while I was playing with Dirk. What would we do? To be good parents we had to get married. And Mama told me stories of how I was born and what she did, pulling me out of her belly when it was time. My sister told me not to worry because in Canada we go to the hospital and the doctors pull the baby out. It was easy.

When the day came and water went down my legs, I called my sister. She said she would meet me at the hospital. I didn't know where Stuart and Jeff were, somewhere on the campus. I called them but no answer. I left messages on the phone and the computer. I said "Baby time!" and "Come home!" Then I left messages on their phones saying "Going to hospital!" and "You gotta hurry!" Still no answer.

I took a taxi to the hospital and my sister was there already, waiting for me. She went with me into the delivering room and everything was done so fast I didn't know what they did. They put me on a seat with a hole below, kind of like a toilet, with me wearing a gown, almost naked. My sister told me what to do: breathe and push, breathe and push, breathe and push.

"I got it already!" I snapped at her.

Then out popped my baby!

With just six hours of laboring it was done.

My sister held my hand all through the pushing and she saw my baby boy first as he came out of me — feet first, his little toes wiggling so fast.

"Have you thought of names?" my sister asked.

I could barely breathe but I told her "Atka."

"Atka? What's that?"

I took deep breaths. "It means wolf."

She laughed. I explained before about my Inuit name.

"Like you, *já*? A wolf boy for a wolf girl. Lovely!"

My baby was small yet so was I, so not much surprise. The doctors said it was too soon for him to come out but he was healthy. As a spring baby, he didn't need fat on his body, my sister said. But he needed to stay at the hospital for a few days to check him, so I stayed too. Then we could go home.

My first thought was that I was going home with my sister. I thought of the flowers outside my window and the sunshine striping the room in the afternoons. My birthday was coming, too, so this baby was like my birthday gift. I would have twenty years and a baby!

Suddenly I remembered I actually lived with two husbands in a little apartment near the campus. And they were *somewhere* —not here with me and our baby. I got angry at them, yet I stayed calm in the hospital room so nobody would know.

Now I was really a woman, like my mama. I was a mama, and my baby would love me like Mama loved me. We didn't know what love was in that cold hut a long time ago yet she took care of me until she died. And I was going to take care of this boy until I died, too. By then he would be an adult and be big and strong himself and maybe he would have babies, too, with a woman he loved. And this was how the world went around and around, I understood. I smiled and nursed my little Atka, a boy called Wolf.

So Atka and I did go home with my sister and we stayed in my room there for a few weeks as I recovered and my baby got used to me and life in the big city. My niece and nephew were very interested in seeing the new baby, especially when I fed him. My sister put her baby girl next to my baby boy and we tried to call them twins, almost a year apart in age, yet they looked different.

Atka had dark hair and dark eyes. He definitely looked like me. He had thick eyebrows and round cheeks and small nose. I could not see either Stuart or Jeff in my baby boy's face. I still loved him so much, no matter who he looked like.

Eventually I got a call from Stuart asking where I was. He got my messages. They decided to go on a trip, on the moment, and their phones didn't work. When they returned to the city they got the signal again on their phones and got my messages.

"I got the baby," I told him. "You missed it."

"So what did you name him? Stuart junior?" he asked.

I was angry so I told him I named him Atka. He said it was a stupid name, so I pushed the button to end the call. He tried calling again but I never answered. Then he came to my sister's house with flowers for me and he got to see our baby.

Later, after I returned to that little apartment just because it was my home now, Stuart always called our son "the baby" or "your baby" — never by the name I gave him. It seemed like he thought our son was all my responsibility. Stuart acted like he was my brother. Or Jeff's brother. Not Atka's father.

Jeff was better at accepting our baby. He never learned how to say his name right. I explained his name was Greenlandic. Sometimes they seemed to forget who I was, where I came from, like I had always been in this city. I told Jeff my original name and how it changed for each place I lived. He preferred Anna to Anuka or Aynur. By then, I was used to being called Anna.

I got fat being pregnant. After Atka was born I stayed fat. I didn't try to lose weight. I was too busy caring for Atka. Once in a while my husbands would tell me I was fat, like I needed to be reminded to lose weight. I didn't look sexy any more. Stuart said he didn't want to make love with me. In the early days of living together we were nude a lot, because it was hot in the summer, then because we just liked looking at each other. I continued that after Atka was born, wanting to attract him again, but Stuart told me to put on clothes because he wasn't excited seeing me naked. So I cried a lot. I knew I was not really a fat girl, I had pregnancy weight that would come off as I nursed our baby. Those boys didn't know how women's bodies worked.

My husbands didn't go to their classes. I didn't know if they even signed up for classes for the term. They stayed home and played computer games. If they went anywhere it was to the lab on the campus where they put together computers and tested them. They spent a lot of time together while I was always at the apartment with Atka.

I knew I wouldn't have time for school so I didn't even sign up for classes. I shopped, cooked, and kept the apartment clean for them. And took care of our baby. Whenever they came home, they ate fast and left again or they played computer games until late, then went to sleep. Usually I took Atka to bed with me and they would stay up all night, sometimes making too much noise playing their computer games. Yet if our baby ever cried they complained about his noise!

"I'm so tired," I said to my sister. "I take care my baby all day and night and I gotta do everything for them yet they don't do anything."

She shook her head slowly. "They are little boys, *já*. They will never grow up. If they aren't interested in finishing school, they should at least get jobs to help pay for things."

"Yeah, but his mother pays the rent and utilities bill."

"Does his mother know about Atka?"

"I don't think he told her. Not yet."

She shook her head again.

"What about food? Who pays for that?"

I confessed I didn't sign up for classes and I used the money she gave me for school to buy food. She was not happy.

"He does bring home food sometimes," I said, then laughed. It was not funny, it was pitiful. "He brings home extra food from the school cafeteria and thinks it's still good to eat."

My sister groaned. "You need to leave."

"I can't leave them, they are my husbands."

"You are not married to them."

"And you aren't married to your man."

"My man has a good job."

"I can get job, too. I checked already. I can work somewhere. Now I passed citizen test, I can."

"Then who watches your baby?"

I smiled at her. "You?"

She didn't smile back. "I'm only saying, if they do not respect you—and show you respect by helping to take care of you and Atka—then they do not deserve to have you there. They need you more than you need them. You're more like their mother than their wife—girlfriend, or whatever you call it."

I thought a moment, not liking the choices.

"So where do I sleep? You got another girl now."

When I moved out to be with Stuart and Jeff, my sister and her partner found a girl to help care for the kids. The child care girl moved into the same room I used to sleep in. It felt strange that somebody was sleeping in my bed. That meant I had no place to go. I tried to laugh about it, calling her Anna Number Two. Her real name was Sola Muangnakim and she was from a country in Asia, maybe Thailand or Indonesia.

"I don't know, Anna, but you always have a place to stay if you need a place. I promise. *Já*, we will find a way."

Before I could move out of Stuart's apartment, there was a big drama in my sister's house. I knew there would be drama when that girl started living there. She was sexy, so my sister's partner got *seduced*. He gave in and soon she was pregnant. My sister was angry. That girl, Sola, moved upstairs into the big bedroom and my sister slept in the room on the ground level where I used to sleep. I felt bad for my sister so I decided not to take her offer to move back.

I tried to stay with Stuart and Jeff. They never kicked me out but they ignored me. Except if they wanted to complain about Atka crying or about dirty diapers in the bucket, or the food I cooked wasn't good. They didn't do anything to help, so I got a job. By then I was an *official resident* of Canada and never had to leave. I could get a job. I was good with words and numbers so I got a job at the city library. They sent me to a branch library on the north side of Toronto.

I worked in the evenings mostly and some weekends. I sat behind the desk and checked books out and checked books in. I put books on the shelves again. I worked fast and they liked me. If nobody needed help I could sit at the desk and read a book. On Saturdays I read books to children, just like I did at the Children's House in Nuuk. I was very popular with children. Yet the job meant I had to let my sister watch Atka. I tried letting my husbands watch him but I came home too many times and found him dirty and crying, ignored by his papas. All they did was play their stupid computer games!

When I picked up Atka from my sister's house, sometimes it was too late to go all the way back across the city by bus, so I slept there. I slept on the living room sofa and Atka had a basket on the floor beside the sofa, like a little wolf pup. It was easy to pick him up and nurse him. In the mornings, I ate breakfast with the family. I was happy to see my two nieces and my nephew.

And I could see that girl from one of those Asian countries was very beautiful. Her chocolate skin was like a Kit-Kat. Her straight black hair was shiny, down to her butt, and her big, dark eyes were *hypnotizing*. She had big breasts and long, thin legs. I could see why men would get hooked on her. I wished my husbands would get hooked on me again like that.

My sister said they eventually tried some three-way play like I used to do with Stuart and Jeff.

It was not so strange to make love to two people at once. Now my sister had the same experience with two women and one man. They tried every position three people could do. It was good the two women were not shy with each other. My two husbands liked to play together, so every time we were together it was wonderful. Except when they played with each other more than with me. My sister confessed she liked Sola when they were in bed together. She also said Sola was good at child care. She happened to be a little better at husband care.

With another baby on the way, my sister thought about making it official, letting Sola join the family. They had that kind of arrangement with other people before I arrived in Canada, I remembered her saying. Other people lived in the house like one family. Everybody had somebody to love every night. Then one by one they slipped away until only my sister and her partner remained in the house. If they made a family like that again with Sola, then he would have two wives.

Just like I had two husbands. Except my two husbands didn't care about me or our baby. Stuart admitted he was *bisexual* and Jeff was gay, yet it was Jeff who the test company said was the father of my boy. Jeff was kinder to me and Atka than Stuart was. Still, they avoided helping with the apartment, or getting some money, or taking care of Atka.

So I followed my sister's advice and I left them. I packed up all my things, put them in the car when my sister arrived, and we drove away. Neither Stuart or Jeff even called me for a few days. Maybe then they noticed we were gone.

It was sad to know they didn't miss me or our baby. Maybe they were glad we were gone. Yet mostly I felt sad for Atka who would not get to know his father.

6

The Province

All I felt was the ice against my face. Everything hurt. My ears were full of roaring and I wondered if it was all a dream. Was I still living in a hut on Ammassalik island? Did I ever go live in a big city? Did I really have a little boy?

The wind became screaming voices, a whole chorus shouting at me. I heard the wind calling my name so I opened my eyes.

"Where am I?"

A man's voice answered, too close: "You're in Winnipeg."

"What's that?" I asked.

"It's in Manitoba."

"Manitoba?"

"Yeah, Manitoba. Canada. In case you forgot that too."

"How did I get here?"

The man laughed. "That's what the reporters wanna know!"

I opened my eyes, saw my manager, Ralph, leaning over me.

He checked my face, turned my head from side to side. He grinned.

"I've seen worse."

I took a deep breath and my ribs hurt. My shoulders hurt. My face hurt. I thought I was about to die yet Ralph said he saw worse, so I knew I would live.

"Don't worry," he said, "you won. But that bitch sure did coldcock you good. It was after the bell so it didn't count. You won on points. Now you're number two in Manitoba."

I just lay there with a big smile on my bloody, lumpy face. I tried to scratch my nose but the gloves covered my hands. I held up my left hand and saw the pink glove that I always used. My lucky gloves.

Outside the crowd was cheering: "An-na! An-na!"

Ralph leaned over me. "Think you can talk to reporters?"

I nodded. I didn't know why anybody wanted to talk to me. I did my talking in the ring. But if he thought it would be good for me, then I would do it. I got some things to prove, after all.

"Let's get her cleaned up," he said to my trainer. "This one's a winner—again!"

Sitting behind the table, bandages on my face, I tried to smile at the people sitting in front of me. I imagined what they might be thinking about how I looked. Like a wolf. A beaten, bloody wolf. A wolf that was still alive—still on her path!

"Anna 'the Wolf' Tasiilaq," one reporter called to me, "after tonight's victory over Hannah Gold, do you think you're ready to take on Jaime Little Bear again for the title?"

I swallowed some blood draining down my throat.

"Title?" I asked, still a little dizzy.

"We hear the purse is fifteen-thousand for the winner."

I looked out over the heads, not thinking of money.

"Yeah, I guess so."

"You're twenty-two and four now. How do you think that matches up against Little Bear's thirty and two?"

"No problem. Her two losses was against me. Both them by knockout."

"Will you make it three?"

"Yeah, three's good. I can do it."

I felt dizzy. I couldn't feel my hands. The room got darker.

"Anna, how did you get this far so fast?"

I pursed my swollen lips, trying to smile, remembering how it felt to get punched in the face. It made me want to punch back. Instead, I threw my hands up to shield myself but the punches kept falling on me. I called to the Lord of Denmark to make him stop but he didn't. As long as he was angry he kept hitting me, until he got tired. Then he got a chair and threw it at me but it only landed on the floor at my feet. I was crying loudly and he told me to shut up! When I opened my eyes and didn't see him, I worried he was looking for my boy, wanting to hurt him. I got to my feet and felt like I would spit up, but I rushed into my room and my boy was there. He was scared but he was not hurt.

I grabbed Atka and ran out of the apartment. I left everything behind because I wanted to get out while I could. I didn't know where he went but I thought he might come back and still be angry. I pulled my phone out and called my sister.

"He beat me up," I cried into the phone.

"What? Who?"

"Sola's brother."

"Where are you?"

"I'm outside."

"Go to a main street and get a taxi. Are you hurt?"

"Yeah, I'm hurt. Maybe my nose is broke. My eye swollen, too. I got bruises."

"Get to the hospital, let them treat you, then call me back."

My sister's family moved from Toronto to Winnipeg in July. She had returned to school and gotten a degree in counseling, thinking she could help sexual assault victims or anybody else who had trouble like that. After she got the degree, she was hired by a college in Winnipeg. When they left, I had to find another place to live so I moved in with Sola.

Now it was March and living with Sola was supposed to be good. She worked in her family's restaurant in the evenings and I worked at the library during the day. We watched each other's kids. Yet I learned they did not treat Atka very well when I was working, just left him on his own and didn't feed him or change his diaper. In the evening I cared for Sola's baby girl as good as I cared for Atka.

They cleaned me up at the hospital, fixed my nose. I called my sister again.

"What happened?" she asked.

"I don't know. I was on the computer, on the internet talking with my friends and he just stopped in. He saw me using the computer and went crazy. He pushed me out of the chair and slapped me when I got up, shouting not to use his computer."

"That doesn't sound very rational."

"He must be drunk or on drugs. Probably he didn't want me seeing all his porn. But I saw it already. He started hitting me and he didn't stop until he got tired."

"Where are you now?"

"At the hospital. Atka's here, too."

"Is he hurt?"

"No, but he's very scared, holding me so tight now."

Then my sister told me what to do. She said not to go back to the apartment, just go to a hotel. She told me which one and said she would call and pay for it over the phone. She wanted me to rest. Then she would send tickets to Winnipeg for me and my son. She was tired of the way we were treated by the people in Sola's family.

I arrived in Winnipeg with my boy and only one small bag of almost nothing. Time to start over, I thought. Always moving. Always a new place. Maybe a new name, too. I talked to Atka. He understood. Nothing matters but family. My sister saved me again.

The same as when I arrived in Toronto, Iris prepared a room for me and Atka. It was smaller than the room in the Toronto house but it was freshly painted and had a new single-size bed, the only size that would fit in the room. It was an older house with several rooms, so there was one for me and my boy.

When Atka and I arrived, we stayed in a hotel by the airport. I looked bad. In fact, they almost didn't let me on the plane because of how I looked. I told the airplane people I was going to live with my sister because my roommate's brother beat me up. They let me on the plane. My sister cringed when she saw me at the airport. She didn't want me to scare her kids the way I looked, so she put me in a hotel for a few days.

Finally, we went to the house and it was like the first days when I arrived in Toronto. I sat on the bed and held Atka. I cried sad tears and happy tears and they washed together, wetting my shirt, the new shirt my sister bought for me because the shirt I wore on the plane was too blood-stained.

I swore then I would come back and punch him in the face as hard as he hit me — no, harder! I would never let anybody hit me again, not without me punching back as hard as I could.

"So, Miss Tasiilaq, what made you get into boxing?"

"I got beat up." I squinted at the reporter. "Actually, people been picking on me all my life. Even back to Greenland. I got raped there. Yeah, my mama got raped, too, so here I am. People don't wanna talk about that kind of thing but it happens. Yeah, it shouldn't happen. Just a lotta assholes think women owe them something, ya know? Instead of trying to work together and be partners, ya know? So I said to myself it never gonna happen again, so I learned boxing to take care myself and my son."

"And now you're ranked number two."

"You never know how things gonna turn out."

It's important to get the story about Sola and her brothers straight because that's the reason I'm here at all. How did I get to Winnipeg? Sola's brother sent me. True story.

After she got pregnant, Sola moved out of my sister's house, got her own apartment. It seemed the best way. My sister's partner paid for it and he could go there to be with her instead of getting my sister upset at the house. He and my sister were not married, so he could do whatever he wanted and go where he wanted. Yet the house was his because he had the big job. Not being married, she couldn't get any divorce, so they agreed to that arrangement. He still slept in that bedroom when he was at the house, and my sister slept in the bed with him but probably they didn't have any sex.

Then there was a big storm that blew into Canada, up from the east coast of America and it was called Irene. It arrived in Toronto on the day Sola's baby girl was born so the baby was called Irene. My sister's husband was happy and wanted to be a good father. It seemed fair now because my sister had a baby with another man and now he had a baby with another woman, so they were equal. They agreed to stay calm about everything.

There were a lot of children depending on them being calm.

He slept half the week in the house with my sister and other nights with Sola at her apartment. On the nights he was at the house it was like nothing ever happened and nobody ever heard of Sola or baby Irene. The nights he was gone it was like he was working late or on a business trip, and nobody said anything about Sola or baby Irene.

Until we got the report from the same test company I used for Atka's father.

"Seems he is *not* the father," my sister sang out. She had a big grin like I never saw before. "The man is over the hill, got low sperm count." She laughed, dancing around the room.

So Eric came back to the house, bag in hand, like a dog who just got neutered. He could still perform, my sister cheered, but he could not impregnate.

"So she was cheating on him all the time he thought he was cheating on me! Fooled him! The world is back in balance."

I was happy for her. It was good to have her partner at home and the family together again. Plus me and Atka part of it. Now we just needed a dog.

All this time neither Stuart or Jeff ever called me. They never left a message on the computer. They had no questions, didn't want to know why I left or where I went. They seemed happy I took their son away so they wouldn't be bothered. They could keep playing their stupid computer games all night and eat their frozen pizzas and cups of noodles and drink beers. It was better to be away from them. They were not the *boys* I wanted my son to call his father.

I kept working at the library and did not return to college. I already had two years of classes so it was like a mini degree. I had the evening schedule so my sister was at home watching the kids then. If she had to model for an art class, Eric was the babysitter. He was actually very good entertaining the kids. He was like a big kid himself.

My sister was always telling me to learn something so I could get a career, so I did and I worked in the library. She decided she better learn something useful, too, in case her partner ran off with another girl and she needed money to pay for everything herself. She needed to start her career before she got too old to be *entry level*. As she got older, she couldn't expect to keep on modeling. So she signed up for school and started the classes to learn about counseling—since she thought she was so good at giving advice! Sometimes she would stop at my library branch to study away from the kids and we would catch up. Even though we lived in the same house again, we were on different schedules.

"You heard from Sola lately?" my sister asked one evening.

I looked around like I didn't know anything.

"Not much," I said after a moment.

I didn't want to tell about Sola. She actually was a kind girl, and really wanted Irene to be the baby of my sister's husband. She wanted to stay with him and my sister. They were having so much fun being together as a *triad*, but it couldn't continue. Too much bad feelings now.

"Atka and me visited her a few times," I told my sister in a plain voice. "The kids like playing together."

Actually I was hooked on Sola. Sometimes she came to the library, too. She usually brought her baby. First, we talked, then we made a play date for our kids. The next date was for us, the mamas, even though the kids were with us. We got hot for each other. After a few dates like that, I had to call my sister, tell her I wouldn't be coming home that night, because I was...visiting Stuart and Jeff. Just to talk. That seemed a good excuse.

My sister cautioned me not to listen to any of their attempts to woo me back. They couldn't be trusted. I had to stay strong and do whatever was best for Atka.

"I know," I told her, "and I will."

Instead of seeing Stuart and Jeff, I went to Sola's apartment, the new one. Watching Atka and Irene playing together was the best thing. They were good friends. And Sola and me sitting on the sofa making out was good, too. We fit together somehow even though she was older than me. And we matched, me from the cold north and she from the hot south. We both had brown skin and dark hair. We could almost be sisters except she was beautiful but I was just called "cute" by her four brothers — three older than her, one younger.

After everybody learned that baby Irene's father wasn't my sister's husband, Sola had to move out of the apartment he was renting for her. She moved into the apartment where two of her brothers lived. The oldest brother there got married so he moved into a new place with his wife. The lease was still active so Sola moved in. The other brother, Dōli, moved in with a different brother so she had it all for herself and Irene. Dōli still visited a lot. After all, most of the furniture and electronics was his.

"So, what do you think?" Sola asked me at the library.

"You want me to move in? Really?"

"That's what I said. Then your problem is gone."

I could feel my face full of smiling, eager to be with Sola all the time. Yet I felt bad, like I was betraying my sister. I shook my head. I would get my own place when my sister's family moved to Winnipeg. Somehow.

"Please, Anna," said Sola. "It would help me, too. I need you to share the rent."

"My sister wouldn't like me living with you."

"Your sister isn't involved with what you and me do. And she's moving away, so no more checking up on you."

"Yeah, you're right."

We gazed into each other's eyes. I saw another world there, full of steamy jungles and tropical beaches, places I could never imagine, not even in dreams.

"I guess so," I said at last, blinking my eyes back to reality. "If you really want me and my boy in your life full time."

"Full time," she said, grinning, "and all the time."

She leaned over the check-out counter and gave me a kiss on my cheek. She caught me by surprise and my co-workers saw it.

Sola's family owned a restaurant that served Asian food. The brothers cooked and served it while Sola greeted customers. Her brothers also liked delivering food to our apartment. They just wanted to get a look at me—probably because I spent a lot of time there without wearing any clothes. Sola didn't mind. In fact, she went nude in our apartment, too.

Sam was Brother Number Three, the third oldest, just above Sola, and he liked me the most of her brothers. He invited me on a date. We went to the family's restaurant for dinner. Then he took me around to meet his friends, showing me to them. It was like he wanted to prove he could get a girlfriend. I never knew what he said to them, speaking his language, yet he treated me in a special way. I liked being treated special. So I became Sam's girlfriend—or, at least, he thought I was.

"Let me get this straight," said the reporter, "so you went into boxing as a way to be able to defend yourself?"

"Yeah, that's it," I said. "But there's more to the story than that. I got a lot to prove. Like to all of you. I mean, to everybody in Winnipeg. No, everybody in Manitoba. Or Canada. And to my family, to my son. To the Sisters at my orphanage. And most of all to my mama. So I push myself."

I took a long breath. My throat was so tight from everybody staring at me. And my body ached yet I had to go on. I couldn't let anybody see me quitting.

First my sister finished her school and she thought she knew everything about counseling. She had to do something called *clinicals* where she practiced counseling on people, mostly at free clinics and shelters for people who got beat up—like me.

She liked helping people, so the next step was to find a job where she could do that. At the same time, Eric couldn't keep his teaching job in Toronto but he found one in America. It was in Oklahoma, which is near Texas where he was born, and because he wrote a big book about *linguistics* they wanted to give him a lot of money.

My sister couldn't get a job in counseling in America because her license was only for Canada. It looked like they were going to split again. Then my sister was offered the job in Winnipeg. She took the job. They planned to drive there in the summer and find her an apartment, then drive down to that Oklahoma and find a place for him and the kids.

You know how men and women can be. Enough hours being together in a car, driving from Toronto to Winnipeg, and you feel sexy when you get to a hotel at night. It happened to them. They found a good apartment in Winnipeg but she found a job for him there, too, so instead of an apartment for only her, they got a house for the whole family. Eric decided not to go on to Oklahoma, not even for a lot of money. He stayed with my sister and the kids.

But it was a big problem for me! I had to move out of that big house in Etobicoke, where I first lived when I came to Canada. They were selling it. So I took Atka and we moved in with Sola and Irene.

I worked during the days and I was at the apartment in the evenings, taking care of Atka and Irene. Yet after bath time and story time, the kids went to sleep. Sola was still at the restaurant, so I would get on Dōli's computer and visit the places where I had friends. You know everybody wants to be friends with a cute Native girl from the north who doesn't like to wear clothes at home. It was like a party on the computer and everybody was very nice to me. I stayed on the computer a long time, until Sola got home, typing messages to my friends. Being on the computer made me realize I could talk a lot, just not with my voice or in front of too many people.

I joined an *introvert* group on that site and I learned more about it. I decided that was the kind of person I was, like Gigi said before, yet I didn't think it was a bad thing being quiet. I learned to speak out on the computer, and say what I had in my mind without any worry. Then I learned I could speak out in real life if I had to, if I wanted to!

Also I joined a few groups where people liked talking about naturism and living without clothes. Of course, they all liked having another girl to flirt with. Mostly, they wanted to change laws and share information about places where they could be nude. Some just liked showing off their bodies, wanting to get some compliments, yet not me.

Actually, I did meet a photographer. That was after Atka was born yet before my sister's family moved away. We met on the campus when I was modeling for an art class. Charlie liked how I looked, a "rough, wild" nature girl, not the usual kind of tall/thin/sexy models in magazines. We went to a park north of the city early on a Sunday morning and I took off my clothes and posed among the trees. It was like I was in an art class, but he wanted me to walk around as he took photos. It was very easy and I felt free and natural. Nobody else was there. I was a little fat in those first pictures, so I stopped eating and we went again later. I looked better in the second set of pictures. I continued dieting to lose weight. I hated it but I wanted to lose that baby fat. I tried eating even less and we took more pictures after that. I started to look sexy by the third set of pictures. He suggested we sell them to a website that specialized in "natural" girls. I agreed and we split the money.

I had to grin at the reporters.

"But those pictures got shared around the whole internet, like they always do, and now you can't put them back in the box and lock it closed."

"So where *are* those pictures, Miss Tasiilaq?"

I laughed. "Yeah, everybody wants to see me!"

"You're not proud of those pictures?"

"Proud doesn't mean anything. It was only for fun. I only got about four hundred dollars, total, for all the pictures. You know I'm not one of those sexy models, not like in the magazines that get thousands of dollars for showing off."

The reporters looked disappointed.

"You can look for them, but I didn't use my real name." I was enjoying teasing them. "I don't even know what my real name is anymore. I was just born someplace far away, nobody cares where. Maybe I'm Anuka, or Aynur, or Anna, or just Taz, like my coach calls me."

"Would you consider doing another photo-shoot now?"

"I don't think so. I'm a boxer, not a pornstar."

As I got more fit, I went without clothes more often at home. The summer was hot. And I never wore anything for sleeping. I got into the habit, like people in those groups on the computer. Some never ever wore clothes. On the computer we talked about why the world doesn't let people go without clothes if they want to—especially why women have to cover their breasts in public but men don't. It was about *topless equality*. Everybody agreed the world was not fair. I wanted to change that.

"So you got into boxing because you liked nudism?"

"No, that's not it at all. They only got one thing in common, and that's I do both."

One guy raised his hand and I nodded at him.

"You ever do any nude boxing?"

"You're funny! Tried it for practice once but there's too much jiggle. It's distracting. So I wear a sports top for workouts. Good shoes, too. Gotta use good equipment if you wanna be the best."

And I want to be the best at something.

After I got beat up, my sister welcomed me to Winnipeg like she did when I arrived at Toronto. She made a room for me and Atka to have. She also helped me get a job.

"I talked to a few people at my school," my sister told me. "I think there's a job you can have. It's in the fitness center at my college. I've never been there but they need a check-in person."

"A check-in person?"

"Probably it's like checking in books but it's people there."

"I hope I don't have to put them back on the shelfs."

"No, they put themselves away after they workout."

"Everybody exercises there?"

It seemed strange to me that people went to a special place to run and jump and lift things. I remembered life in Greenland. Every day was a workout just to live on the ice. Every day there was something to do, like mending dog harnesses or fixing nets or hunting seals, and hiking or running, pushing the sled. Now people have to get checked in. And checked out when they are too tired to go on. And they stare at themselves in a mirror to see if they look good.

"I know it's not a great job" said my sister, "but at least it's something to start with. Until we decide what to do with you."

I frowned.

"Everybody always deciding what to do with me!"

"You came in the middle of the semester, so there's not many options at the moment. Be happy you have something to do that will give you some money."

"Yeah, thanks, Sissy. I know you always looking out for me."

We hugged. She didn't used to be a hugger yet after she and Eric got back together, she started hugging everybody. I guess that counseling job required her to hug a lot.

So I went to the campus about four o'clock in the afternoon and I stood at the check-in desk and put people's names into a computer and typed in the time when they left. Sunday through Thursday closing time was ten o'clock. It was eleven on Friday and Saturday. It was easy work yet boring. I tried reading at that standing desk but it was too noisy with clanking machines and loud music playing. It was too hot there, too.

To start, I dressed nice, like for the library, but my clothes quickly got too wet to be comfortable. Because it was so hot, I changed to workout clothes like everybody wore. Like t-shirts and baggy shorts, then a small "sports top" that looked like a bra and very short shorts that didn't even cover all of my butt. The better my body looked, the less I cared about people looking at me or what they might think of me. I did what I wanted to do. I made my own path.

I had the computer for the job, but I could also click over to those websites where I talked with friends from everywhere. So I typed status updates about my job and the fitness center and the strange people around me. A couple other people worked with me, a girl who was bitchy and a guy who was friendly. I wasn't taking any classes then so I got a lot of work hours.

"And how're you doin' this evening, An-na?" one guy would always say as he waited for me to check him in. He was blown up into big muscles, yet he kept working out.

"I'm good," I always said.

It was true. My name on all those internet places was Anna Good. This was a new life, after all, so I wanted to start fresh by being good.

One guy always shouted, strutting in: "Yo, Anna! I'm here, so check me da fuck in!"

At first I thought he was crazy, then I laughed every time he arrived.

I got used to people coming in, saying "hello" as they signed in. The guys always flirted with me, maybe because I wasn't the tall, blonde, sexy girls who were working out there. I was safe. They didn't have to impress me. The girls ignored me. I guessed I wasn't competition for the guys.

I stood at the desk to use the computer. After standing a long time, I had to go over to the walking machines to move around. I sweated a lot and noticed I lost weight. I tried some of the other machines. I liked feeling my muscles cry out in pain. If my body hurt, I felt tough. Soon I was moving between one machine or another and the front desk, between exercising and playing on the computer, between sweating and typing.

Sola apologized for her brother hitting me. They sent a few boxes of my things from the apartment. When I got the boxes, they reminded me of everything that happened. I was working in the fitness center that evening. I was still very angry. I walked around the machines, then found a back room where there was a big bag for hitting. I went over to it and I swung my fist as hard as I could, pretending it was Dōli's face. I kept punching the bag until I couldn't lift my arms any more and sweat was running off me like a rushing river. It was a good workout.

"You know, you're doing it totally wrong," said a tough-looking guy who came in while I was hitting the bag.

I stopped, stared at him, sweat dripping from my forehead and chin. I could not hit the bag even one more time.

"You have to keep your wrists straight or you'll get hurt."

He came over to me. I was so sweaty and smelled bad yet he got behind me and showed me what to do, how to hold my fists, how to push with my whole arm, driving into the bag with my shoulder and turn my hips with the punch. I tried it.

"You do have a wicked punch," he said. "I see your arms are wired tight. Short, too. A very compact punch. Most boxers have to throw their whole arm into a punch to get power, but you have strength even in a short punch."

His name was Ralph Doolittle. He used to be a boxer. Now he only coached. He didn't look that old yet he had muscles and a mean face. I wouldn't want to meet him on a dark street. Yet he smiled at me and I wasn't afraid.

"And you should tape up your hands before you take on the bag. Your knuckles are bleeding."

He was right. Yet I was so angry I didn't think about any of that. I wanted to hit the bag as hard as I could, wishing it was Dōli's face. I knew right then I was going to go back to Toronto someday and punch him in the face until he was bleeding.

I kept seeing Ralph working out, mostly in the back room where all the boxing equipment was. He showed me techniques and gave me advice. I started going early to workout on my own before it was time to check-in people. I pushed myself as much as I could, until I couldn't go further. People asked me if I was trying to kill myself with exercise. But it was my heart telling me to keep going. It said "Show me what you can do!"

Ralph said he would train me if I wanted to really learn the sport. He quit because of a concussion yet he was still involved in training and promoting fighters.

"Yeah, me a fighter. Nobody saw it coming, huh?"

"But you rose quickly through the ranks," one reporter said for the record.

"Yeah, I started fast. I hit hard and I did my training like a religion." I looked over at Ralph. "I gotta give this guy half the credit, never pushing me. So it was always up to me to push myself."

"That's one-hundred percent correct," said Ralph from the corner of the room. Everybody turned to him. "I never pushed her much because she was already pushing herself so far down the track. Nobody can push her more than she pushes herself."

"Yeah, pain is just your body begging you to let it be lazy and soft. And I don't want that. Pain for gain."

In the fall semester, I started back to college. I quit the fitness center job and signed up at the University of Manitoba on the other end of the city. Because I liked books, my sister thought I should get a degree in librarianship. I could be a real librarian, not just a desk clerk. That seemed like a good idea. I already had two years of classes from Toronto.

I had experience in the library in Toronto, too, so I got a job in the library on the campus. I liked being in class again. Nobody knew who I was and nobody bothered me. I kept quiet in classes and elsewhere on the campus, yet on the computer in the library or at home I was very loud. I got more friends in those groups on the computer sites. I found a group for *athletes*. I never thought of myself as athlete. I did what I had to do, running or hiking, lifting or carrying, whatever had to be done to survive on the ice. When I arrived in Canada, I lost that survival focus. I got soft. I got lazy. And fat. It was the years I had a lot of sex.

Now I was back, got focus, knew what I wanted to do. I kept

boxing and training at my sister's school. Sometimes I ran from my campus to her campus as a warm-up for my workout, about 10 kilometers. I lifted weights and pushed the machines till they broke. I punched the big bag and I worked the speed bag for hours. I jumped a rope and tossed a weight ball up on the wall. I raised myself on iron bars. I squatted until my butt and legs would not hold me up.

Ralph said I was ready to learn some moves. I had classes in the mornings and training in the afternoons. Then I went back to the U Manitoba campus for my evening job in the library. When I finally got home at night, my boy was asleep. And so was I about a minute after my head touched the pillow.

"You're like a mean little wolf," said Ralph after one killer training session. "You know?"

I looked up from my squatting position, number forty-two, heading to fifty, sweat running off my body like Niagara Falls. I couldn't lift any finger by then. I fell back on my butt, breathing hard. I could have done more but the weightlifting took some of my energy away.

"Yeah, I know." Big breaths. "That's actually my name."

"What is? You mean 'wolf'?"

"Mama called me Wolf."

"Not Anna?"

"It's long story. I'm not from here. Not First Nations person. I'm from Greenland. But I'm citizen of Canada now."

"And you happened to walk into my gym one day...."

I laughed. He always made me laugh when the workout was done. My body hurt so much I didn't want to laugh.

"Then we should think about getting you some opponents," he said. "Sparring would help you put all your moves together."

"I fight other girls?"

"That's where we're heading."

What started as just getting out my anger became a great way to lose weight and get fit. Now it was getting serious. I never thought of fighting anybody. I only wanted to beat Dōli's face into a pulp. Break his ribs with my punches. Kick him between his legs. Make him hate me and fear me!

"If it's only for fun, I guess so."

"I've got a few other girls that need a partner, so I'll set up some matches. Let's see what you can do."

We pretended there was a square circle around us but it was only the back room where I trained. Ralph said "Ding, ding." We moved around and tried to swing our arms at each other. The other girl was a little shy, I saw. I pushed her around the pretend ring as Ralph and the other girl's trainer counted our punches. We got points for each punch that landed. At the end, I won.

And I won the next sparring bout. I knocked her down three times.

The next opponent was aggressive. Until I knocked her out.

Ralph was worried about me. I had a wicked punch, he said. Yet not every boxing match is won by whoever hits the hardest. He told me how to keep my feet moving. I called it dancing. He taught me how to defend, how to keep the action going instead of going for a quick knockout. Fans want to see the fight keep going, not have a quick end to it.

I worked on defending. I worked on dancing.

I lost a couple sparring bouts on points but won more.

All along I wondered why Ralph wanted to help me. He said he saw a champion when he watched me workout. He never saw any girl push herself to the edge like I did. I told him I didn't know where the edge was. Working out about four hours every day, I dropped the last of my pregnancy weight and replaced it with muscle. I built my shoulders and arms, tightened my belly, strengthened my back and legs, and got my footwork and timing down. I had no life but the gym and the library. Even the library was boring so I would drop behind the desk to do some pushups or squats. I carried heavy stacks of books up the stairs several times before I finally put them back on the shelves like I was supposed to do.

What Ralph wanted was for me to get in a real ring and fight some real boxers. He believed in me!

"You think I can win?" I asked him every time he teased me about getting my license and setting up real fights.

"I wouldn't be doing this if I didn't think you could win," he said. "I'm counting on you putting my kids through school with my share of your prize winnings."

He didn't actually have any kids. But he was serious about winning, so I said "Yes" to real fights. He did the paperwork and I got my license. I could now fight for real.

Yet the closer it got to my first fight, the more worried my boyfriend got.

Did I mention I got a boyfriend? Not just a boy to play sex games with but a boy I could give my heart to and he would take care of it for me. That kind of boy. Joel Grainger, my fiancé.

It's funny how we met. We had a class together. It was about the principles of marketing. We talked about identity, who we were, who we wanted to be. The professor taught us about *branding*. A brand is whatever symbol, name, or idea you want tied to who you are or whatever product you're selling. The first assignment was to make a poster with our brands on it. Because all my life I never knew who I was, I could be anybody. We got the poster paper and we went to work. My brands were nudism, books, children, snow, and boxing.

"Really? Nudism?"

The tall red-haired guy in my group couldn't believe I would put nudism as one of my brands. I grinned.

"So you *practice* nudism, eh? Is that how you say it?"

"No."

I stared at him, wondering if he was going to be one of those jerks. Yet those blue eyes of his twinkled at me and the curve of his cheek twitched in a very cute way. I liked his smile.

"I don't need practice," I said. "I got it down already."

He chuckled and the others in our group smiled.

"Yeah, nudism," I answered. "Anything wrong with that?"

The three guys and one other girl shook their heads.

"Everybody is born nude, you know."

"I guess so," said my pretty redhead boy.

He kept looking at me, like he was imagining me nude.

When it was my turn to share, I stood and felt very nervous, yet I made myself push ahead. I remembered my boxing training and I got tough. I was not a little girl, not a girl who was afraid of anything. Nobody was going to make me feel small or think I didn't count for anything. I wasn't afraid of speaking in front of a class, being in front of students and a professor, telling them I was a nudist.

Maybe I wasn't, like some friends in the internet groups said, but I thought I was. It depends on how much time you're nude. I explained that I liked not wearing clothes at home or outdoors if the weather was good. It was for my comfort, not for showing off to other people.

"That's very interesting," said the professor when I finished explaining my brands. He gave me a strange look, like he didn't believe me. "And you said *boxing*, too? That's quite a collection of brands you have."

Outside it was getting to be cold so I wore a lot of clothes that day. I still had all the layers on in the classroom. Nobody could believe I didn't like clothes. Probably they didn't think I was a boxer, either. Nobody could see my muscles under the coat. That didn't bother me because I was Wolf. I made my own path.

"Now think how can you bring them all together," said the professor.

"I'm a librarian who boxes and reads nude and loves playing with children in the snow!"

The professor nodded, grinning, then waved the next student to come to the front of the room.

My sweetheart was a boy called Joel Grainger. His brands were hockey, dogs, computers, rockets, and... "boxing librarians who read nude and play with children in the snow," he said.

Joel was very tall. He could put his elbow on my shoulder if he wanted to—if I *let* him. His curly red hair made me think he could be my sister's grown up boy. He was from Brandon, a city west of Winnipeg, but he lived in a residence hall on the campus.

Following me out of the classroom, he kept asking questions about nudism.

"I said it already," I told him, feeling annoyed. Or maybe I was acting annoyed to tease him. "When I'm at home I don't like wearing clothes. Like you take a shower but don't get dressed after it. That's all."

"I bet you will wear clothes when it gets cold here."

"How cold does it get here?"

"It's like at the North Pole here. Winnipeg's the coldest city in Canada, without counting places in the arctic. All the arctic air blows straight down here and kinda stays here. Last winter it was colder here than in Greenland."

So he knows about Greenland. I smiled at him.

"Actually I'm from Greenland. I was born there. So I know about cold."

"That's sick. Really? How'd you get here?"

"It's long story. If you got a lot of time I'll tell you."

"I got another class now, but when it's cold you can tell me if you think it's as cold as Greenland."

"Yeah, when it's cold, really cold like in Greenland, then you can come over and see if I wear clothes then."

"You want me to come visit you? And you'll be naked?"

"Nude. Not naked. Big difference."

"Not to me. Not if it's you."

We kept jabbing at each other until we decided we better get lunch. He skipped his class to talk about nudism with me.

When we chose a table in the warm cafeteria, I took my coat off, then my sweatshirt, getting down to my sports top as we talked. He saw my arms.

"Holy shit, you got guns!" he said. "How'd you get muscles like those?

"I workout a lot."

"Geez, you got bigger biceps than me! And I play hockey."

His grin was so cute. I really wanted to kiss him.

"Remind me not to get you angry," he said.

"Why you wanna get me angry?"

"I don't. That's why I said it."

When we got up from the table, our arms accidently bumped. He pretended like it hurt him. I didn't feel anything. Except my heart beating fast.

"My boyfriend's a hockey player. Backup goalie for the Bisons. Why you wanna know?"

"A lot of athletes only date other athletes."

"Yeah, I guess because they know how to workout or they

like working out together. I mean exercise, not sex. Yet he is so great in bed it's really sick."

"You said he was nervous about your first fight.... How did you feel going into your first fight?"

"I didn't think anything at first. It's like sparring but now it counts. My boyfriend, he didn't want my pretty face messed up. He had to have something cute to kiss!"

One thing I noticed right away was only ethnic girls were fighters. White girls didn't fight. So I was matched with a Cree girl called Jaime Little Bear. She was 3 and O while I was O and O. Ralph got the fight by convincing Little Bear's manager that I would be an easy, warm-up fight for her next opponent. Because I was nobody, we got an early card, before all the good fights.

I did my warm ups and focused, tried to get mean, think like a wolf—just like my card name: ANNA "THE WOLF" TASIILAQ. Yet when I went out of the dressing room and got into the ring, I saw all the people, everybody staring at me, and I got nervous. That slowed me when the bell rang and Little Bear came at me, throwing punches like she wanted to end it fast with a knockout. All I could do was defend, keeping away from her. But my feet were so heavy I couldn't move.

Ralph shouted to keep moving, duck and cover! So I danced away, got light on my feet, but she kept chasing me around the ring. I got in some jabs and threw a power punch that barely missed her jaw. I heard people calling "boo" like they were not entertained. I had to be tough, even though she was hitting my right side a lot, my ribs hurting. I tried to keep my elbows in but she got around them. I lost my balance, fell on my knee. When I jumped up, she was right there and punched me hard in the face. She got me with a couple more hard hits. I got angry, remembering getting beat up by Dōli, and I rushed at her with my fists flying but the bell rang.

Ralph said during the break I better throw more punches if I wanted to get points. My face hurt so much I was really angry so when it started again I went right at her. We traded punches and locked up a few times. People started to cheer. We swung hard at each other and missed so we both fell. I hit my knee on the mat again. I was feeling good besides that, full of confidence. I could beat her, I suddenly knew. I had her against the ropes, got power punches into her belly. She escaped when the bell rang.

By the third round, I was in rhythm. Ralph told me the weak spots in her moves so I went right at her, punching hard to her face and ribs, and all she could do was defend and try to escape. People cheered! I got hard punches through her defense. She got a bloody nose! My combos landed! She fell down twice but got up. I wasn't tired at all. I was used to hard workouts. I felt good but she was getting tired. I went back to jabbing and punching until the bell rang. Ralph said I only needed to stay even with her in the final round and I would win on points.

Little Bear came out a little slow, maybe tired or afraid of me. She seemed to be waiting for me to make the first move. I kept moving, traded jabs. She tried a few punches but I was ducking and dodging! Then she swung a hook at me and I leaned back so her punch missed. At the same time, I brought up my right arm to block her punch but my arm chopped down on her punching arm, turning my body to my left. So I swung back with a left hook! I drove my whole body into that punch and it landed on her jaw. She went flying across the ring and crashed on the floor! I thought I really hurt her so I said "Sorry." The ref counted her out! She was shaking her head as she got help to stand up and go to her corner. That was about a minute into the final round.

I won! By knockout!

"Were you there? Did you see it?" I asked the reporter.

"No, sorry. I had no idea it would be such great a fight."

"My sister said it was the most exciting fight that night. The others were too evenly matched so not much action. Or all one sided. My fight was the exciting one that night. It had come from behind victory!"

"Sure wish I'd been there, Taz."

Ralph told everybody I had a hard punch. Something about my short arms being wired tighter than those taller girls, like Little Bear, who had a longer reach. If I can get inside, I can hit hard but those tall girls with long arms can't defend against me when I get inside. I proved that against Jaime Little Bear. All week it was promoted as *Bear v Wolf*. At the end of the fight, everybody was calling "Wolf! Wolf! An-na! An-na!"

I told my sister and Joel not to come watch me. If I knew they were there I wouldn't be able to focus. Because I was in an early fight, I returned to the dressing room after my win and got my face fixed. I didn't go out again until all the fights were done.

After I took a shower, I called Joel to pick me up. Some guys have to go pick up their girlfriends after the fights. It's the guy's duty, no matter how bad she looks. But he was right there outside the dressing room! He and my sister watched my fight!

They hugged me, looked me over. Joel was not happy with my face being red and swollen. I told him it would get better in a few days.

They took me out to dinner at The Keg and I got a big bloody steak! Victory dinner. But the waitress looked at me and thought I was a spouse abuse victim. She gave Joel a hard stare, but he never did anything.

"It's not what it looks like," said my sister. "She won her first boxing match tonight."

"Then the other one looks worse, eh?" said the waitress. She gave me free dessert. Chocolate cake.

At home, I had a long hot soak in the bath tub and fell asleep there. I awoke when the water got cold. My sister made an ice bag and I held it against my face, one side then the other side. The kids stared at me, asked why I got in a fight. They reminded me fighting isn't allowed at school.

"I guess I had to prove something," I told them.

"What's that?" asked Thora.

"That I was tougher than the other girl." I thought a moment. It was not about school, it was really about life. "That I could be tougher than anybody."

"Yeah, that's right," I told the reporters. "Everything you do is about proving something. Most people, it's about proving you're better than somebody, like you're stronger or smarter or more popular or sexier, whatever. Everybody gotta rank themselves somehow, so they know where they stand in life."

Some people said I got in a lucky punch on Little Bear. So my second fight would really show if I had it or not, if I got what it takes to be a winner. Ralph set up my next match against Jamie Yoshikawa. Another "Jay-mee" opponent! She was 1 and 1. And I was now 1 and O with a KO. It was going to be the opening fight again because we were both low-ranked.

I came down from my win against Little Bear. My workouts were not as hard for a while. When the date was set, I started pushing myself again. My body was feeling it but my head was slow to follow.

The day of the fight, I was sitting around all morning worried about being ready, yet I never had any thought that Yoshikawa would beat me. I felt strong and ready when I got into the ring.

Ralph said I needed to make it last all four rounds so people would feel they got their money's worth. Nobody likes a quick win. I asked him about "money's worth." When I got in the ring, I asked Ralph if he bet on me.

"Of course I did. I only bet on sure things."

I grinned. "How about tonight?"

"My money's on you. So go out there and make me rich! I got kids to put through school!"

Yoshikawa was taller than me and thin. She came out slowly like she didn't know what to do, waving her long skinny arms like a monkey! I danced around as she jabbed at me. Neither of us threw many punches, just defending and dancing, deciding where to attack in the next round. I started working inside and throwing combos—jab, hook, cross, jab, then a belly buster. I knocked her down with an uppercut. She got right up but the bell rang.

Her manager probably told her that she better start throwing more punches. Ralph told me that, too. Working on points! We came out fast in the second round, throwing lots of punches, very wild. I got her across her jaw a few times and she went down but got up before being counted out. I went after her hard again but she danced around, staying away from me. She was smiling like she thought she would win! I hated that. I had a lot of punches that didn't land because she was always ducking and dodging. She got a few punches on me before the bell rang.

I needed to keep throwing punches, make sure they landed, said Ralph, or I wouldn't get enough points to win. In the third round I came out fast and Yoshikawa went back to dancing out of my way. I got angry at her for not giving people their money's worth and punched her hard a couple times, knocking her down both times. But she got up both times. I was getting frustrated— but not tired. Fight day is a light workout for me.

In the final round, Ralph said I was ahead on points so I only had to keep even with her. He said not to worry about getting a knockout, just keep landing punches. We were dancing again, not fighting hard. Finally, I got her against the ropes and after a series of combos she dropped to her knees. I went to a neutral corner but she got up. I almost knocked her out but she got up at the final count. So we danced again, jabbing, until the bell rang.

I won on points. Even though I knocked her down five times she always got up. No knockout! I never went down and I threw more punches. Not too tired after this fight. My face was clean. Ribs a little sore. I wasn't nervous before this fight, either. I knew what to expect and I was ready. My sister told me "Trust your training" and I did. I had confidence all the way. The people got their money's worth.

"Is it true, the rumor you had a thing for Yoshikawa?"

"Yeah, she was very hot, " I said to the reporters. "But I had to hit her instead of kiss her. That's how life goes sometimes."

"And then you had the rematch with Little Bear."

"Yeah, after I KO'd her the first time she wanted a rematch. I thought I could KO her again, so I said 'why not?' Ralph set it up, but it wasn't until after I had five more fights. I was six and one by then. Four knockouts. Little Bear. Then Carly Gambino at a minute in the first round. Taylor Calderon in the second round. Janette Malone also in the second. My only loss was the split decision against Sharla Jackson. We fought through six rounds. But she was impressed with me. She grabbed my hand, held up my arm with hers, like we both won. We went out to dinner after the fight. Then I met Little Bear again, second time. And you know what happened, don't you?"

"That was a great fight, for sure."

"Yeah, I KO'd her again. She was out cold. Third round. She was eleven and two after that, yet her only losses were against the Wolf."

When I wasn't working out, I hung around with Joel. Both of us being introverts, we were happy just being together, not doing anything. We could just sit together and study without saying a word. We could feel each other's thoughts. Actually, Joel was more shy than me and the fact he was a year younger made me feel in charge, even though he was tall.

Joel was a perfect boyfriend. He let me do whatever I wanted and he never complained. He never acted like it was his job to protect me or help me, yet he was always ready to. He knew I could take care of myself. Except if there was something too high for me to reach. Then he would act like a giant and raise his hand to get what I needed. Although we were different sizes, we matched in bed. I would climb on top of him and make him feel like God. I knew that because he always shouted "Oh God!"

We got the idea of going to a party for Halloween, so we had to choose costumes. I thought of Eve and Adam, the first couple, because we could go to the party nude. Or mostly nude if we wore a leaf or two. Joel wasn't comfortable with that idea. His friends would be there and he didn't want to be nude in front of them. Maybe he didn't want his friends to see me nude, either. I remembered the parties back in Toronto, so I gave in. We only stopped for a short time, wearing a white sheet called *toga*. Then we returned to my house had our own party in my room. Atka and his cousins were out getting candy from the neighbors so we had the room to ourselves.

When my sister and her partner decided a Winnipeg winter was not for them, they went all the way south to the coast of Texas with the kids. They were gone for two weeks during the Christmas holidays. So Joel and I had the house for ourselves—

with Atka.

Joel was very good with my boy and Atka liked him, too. Joel was tall so Atka liked riding up on his shoulders whenever we went out, like for shopping. It was like we were a family already. Then, on the Valentine holiday, Joel asked me to marry him and I said yes—but only after I finished school.

I went to classes in the mornings, worked out all afternoon, then took a shower and went to work in the library until closing. I hardly ever saw Atka except when I was going between places, but he knew who his mama was. One time I took him to watch me workout but he got scared seeing me hit that bag so hard, looking so angry. He saw me get beat up in Toronto so he was afraid of violence. I had to hug him a lot.

Violence became a part of my life. I wanted to be so strong nobody would hurt me or even think of trying. When I was on campus one night, a boy from one of my classes followed me to the library. I was going to my job there but he kept teasing me, asking me to flash my boobs. He said if I was really a nudist I would show him. Just as we entered the library, I couldn't take it any more.

"If you don't leave me alone, I'm gonna punch you," I told him, taking off my coat. "I'm a boxer."

"Hah! You?"

He didn't believe me, laughed at me.

As I started away, he grabbed my shoulder to hold me back. I spun around and swung my fist into his belly. He lost his breath, fell to his knees on the carpet, and emptied his stomach.

The boss of the library suspended me from the job. He said we can't have librarians punching students. My sister, being a counselor at her school, called Dr. Denton and explained how I had sexual assault experience in my past so I reacted that way to defend myself. I got triggered by that guy when he grabbed me.

Because I had boxing training, I was supposed to hold back from using my skills. I warned him before I hit him. Witnesses agreed with me. So I got the job back.

While I was suspended from the library, though, I watched a lot of television. Once I saw an advertisement about Indigenous soldiers. The video showed them in the snow up north. It got my attention. They guarded the arctic border, called it Northern Patrol. Not many people wanted to go up there, yet people who lived up there already were happy to do the job. I got interested. I just wanted to be a *badass*.

"And that's when I decided to join," I said to the reporter's question. "I got my citizen already so I wanted to do something to serve my country. I got a boy, too, and I want him to be safe. So I went off for summer training in Quebec. It was nothing like my boxing training, too light for me. Yet I learned how to use many weapons and work in a squad."

"So how was it? Did you out-workout the other recruits?"

"I never show up anybody. That's not me. Everybody got their own speed and their own strength. I knew mine, so when I didn't get enough PT—that means 'physical training'—I just ran around the base or did more running on the treadmill. If I don't sweat enough, I don't feel I did anything."

"But what about the military aspects of the training?"

"You mean did I follow the orders? March around properly? Yeah, of course. I was so badass I got to be squad leader first. Then again later when we rotated it through the platoon. I was introvert, like I said, yet if you're gonna be the leader you gotta learn to shout at people, so I shouted."

Canadian Forces training was hard enough yet we trained indoors on computers simulations before going out for live fire exercises. Every day we got up and did PT, then got our areas cleaned and went to breakfast. When I was squad leader I had to be sure my squad members did everything properly. It was like being in the Children's House again, looking after the kids, but with guns.

Eventually, we went into the woods for field training. It was a big reminder of living alone on the ice. Except no ice, just trees. A lot of trees to fight in. I got confused under the trees. I needed to see the sky, feel the wind. Even so, I was good at shooting. I fired a rifle when I was young. In the Forces training, I got top scores hitting the targets. I remembered how I had to be patient when waiting for a seal to pop up.

If the training was for Northern Patrol, they didn't actually train us how to live and fight in the snow and ice. No training for how to drive dogs or run a sled over the rocks and ice or through deep snow. This training was for all soldiers, no matter which group they went to after initial training. For me, I was in reserves. After my initial training, I would go train every month at the base in Winnipeg.

What I really wanted to do was go north and patrol the arctic border. I dreamed of a dog team pulling my sled over the snow and ice through the wind. I would stop for the night and build an igloo. I wanted to shoot a couple seals, dinner for me and the dogs. Yet nobody talked about dogs or sleds or arctic living.

After I got home, I went to my first training in Winnipeg. I wore my green camo uniform, of course. They welcomed me. I saw Captain Smythe. When I first went to sign up, the recruiters told him I did some boxing. The captain said he did some boxing, too, a while ago. Suddenly, he took a stance like we were going to fight. I didn't want to hit him because he was going to be my boss. So I faked some jabs and tapped his cheek with my fingers. He was surprised I got through his defense so easy.

When I returned after training he saw me, recognized me.

"Here's our girl back from training! How did it go?"

"It was fun, sir." I saluted and stood straight. "Not as hard as my boxing workouts, sir. But I learned what I was supposed to learn. I'm ready to fight."

So they had me show them what I learned, like how to take a C7A2 assault rifle apart and put it back together again, find my way on a map, and radio procedures. They were impressed, but maybe it was because I was a girl or because I was Indigenous, a First Nations soldier. They were impressed that someone like me could learn all that.

They knew I worked in the university library. So they knew I was good at keeping my area clean and putting things in order by numbers and letters. One of the sergeants showed me to an office.

Inside, there was a desk covered with a lot of folders in stacks. My task for the weekend was to put all of them in order by file number, then put them into the cabinet, each drawer by number, making labels for the folders. And if I found certain folders, I should set them aside. If there was any time leftover in the weekend, there were some documents to be typed.

I sighed and rolled up the sleeves on my uniform to begin the secretary work I learned how to do back in the Children's House in Nuuk.

"Yeah, I coulda had more fights," I told the reporters. "Yeah, I coulda been right up there with Little Bear by now. But I took time out to join Canadian Forces and get trained. You know, it's my duty as citizen, gotta be ready for anything. I even had to sign papers for my sister to be guardian of my boy, in case I got killed in a war."

I glared at the reporters. They were silent.

"So now you know I can type and file."

"And box," said one of them.

"Yeah, that too."

"I'm sure you'll get to the arctic someday."

"Maybe. I still got a lot to prove. You know? But right now, I just—any more questions? Right now, I just wanna get some ice cream."

7

The Nation

I push the button to end the call, holding my breath, wondering how I'm going to get to Yellowknife. My bag is almost packed, has been for weeks. I can leave any time. They will assign me a weapon when I get to the headquarters.

Rushing down the stairs to the living room of my sister's house, I see that Atka and his cousin, Austin, are racing toy cars across the floor. My sister, Iris, sits at the dining table working with her laptop. Her husband stretches out on the sofa, reading a book. Little Marky, the husky pup I persuaded my sister to get to teach the children responsibility, a year old now, lazes on the lounge chair. The red-haired girls, Thora and Freyja, are in their room upstairs drawing pictures of Vikings and princesses.

"Sissy, I gotta get to Yellowknife by tomorrow afternoon!"

She looks up from the laptop. "You what?"

"Captain says if I get to Yellowknife I can go with them. If not, I gotta wait another year to go on Northern Patrol."

"Yellowknife? Why there?"

"It's the headquarters. In Northwest Territory. Then they fly us north for sovereignty patrol."

Her husband gets interested, sits up on the sofa.

"Sovereignty patrol?"

"Yeah, we gotta check the border, make sure nobody coming here illegally."

He laughs. As an American by birth, he has to tell me about all the people that cross the border into the U.S. from Mexico. He stands up as he gets excited talking about it.

"This is about protecting resources," I say. "Another country could be taking our stuff and we don't know it because nobody lives up there to report. So we gotta patrol the border."

"All right, calm down," he says.

"Can you check flights for me?" I ask my sister.

She logs off Facebook, goes to Google. She types in a lot of words, then waits.

"There's a flight tomorrow morning, leaving at six-thirty. But it goes through Calgary."

"Does it get there before noon?"

She checks. "Yes. Ten-forty."

Then it hits me. I gotta get myself there. No free flights. So I return to the living room where my sister's husband is about to drop on the sofa again. I come up behind him, wrap my arms around him.

I use a sexy voice: "Can you buy my ticket to Yellowknife?"

"How much is it?" he asks, turning to me.

My son looks up from the floor. "Why is the knife yellow?"

"It's six hundred forty-two dollars," my sister calls from the dining table.

"Whoa! That's a lot for a trip to a backwater mining town.

Are you sure about this thing?"

"Because they got lots of copper there," I say to Atka.

"Oh. I want a yellow knife."

"I'll bring you one."

"That's a lot of money, you know," says my sister's husband. "They can't expect you to foot the bill every time."

"I know."

We sit on the sofa side by side.

"Captain thought I lived up north. Most patrol members live there already. He forgot I'm in school here. So they're gonna go without me. I told him I signed up specially for Northern Patrol. I have to go. I wanna go."

I feel like I'm about to enter the ring for a match. So much trouble! Yet I'm burning inside and must go.

"Joel is gonna be so angry at me. And I need to tell the library I'll be gone, too." I call to my sister: "Can you tell the library for me on Monday? I got vacation time coming, anyway."

"All right," she replies.

"Can't wait until next year?" asks her husband. "Didn't you just return from training not too long ago?"

"Eight months ago. That's long time for sitting around."

"They don't expect you to get right into it so soon, do they?"

"But it's eight months already! I wanna get right into it. It's why I signed up."

"That's a lot for a ticket. Are they paying you back?"

I lean over and hug him again. "I can pay you back. When I win the title fight, I'm gonna get fifteen-thousand dollars. I can pay you back from that. If you can wait a couple months."

He laughed like he didn't think I would win. "You're going to spend your prize money on a ticket to Yellowknife so you can ride snowmobiles for a couple of weeks?"

I smile. He gets it. "Yeah, that's right!"

It took a lot of words to get Joel to understand why I signed up but my sister's husband gets it right away. Maybe because he used to be a soldier down in America for a few years when he was young, long before he met my sister.

"Or you can say it's my birthday gift."

I stare at him, smiling. He stares back.

"If you wanna," I say.

He grins as my sister joins us. "We ordered a cake for you. It was supposed to be a surprise, *já*," she says. "Now you won't be here to eat it."

"Please give my share to Joel."

She shakes her head, looks sad, then gives me a hug.

"I hope they appreciate how dedicated you are."

"Newbies usually are dedicated," says her husband.

"I won't be a newbie after this patrol." Then I smile at my sister. "And you take care my boy when I'm gone?"

"*Já*, of course." She hugs me again, like she is afraid to let me go. "Same as we did when you were away for your training."

We all turn to watch the boys playing: Atka, almost five, and Austin, seven. They have been best friends since they first met.

"Don't worry," she says, and turns to her husband. "You're getting up early to take Anna to the airport, *já*?"

He yawns, tries to make it as big as he can. "If I have to."

"It's Saturday," she tells him, "so you can go back to sleep after you drop her off."

"Yeah, and you don't even have to go in or wait for me," I say. "And you can stay here with the kids, Sissy."

"Lovely," she says with a sigh.

"Great! Everything fits."

I kiss each of them, then grab my boy and we go up to our room. It's our room yet he prefers sleeping with his cousin. Even though I graduated from the university last year, I still work in the school library. It's my full-time job. I live with my sister's family to save some money so Joel and I can get our own place together after he graduates. Then we can finally get married. My sister is already showing me wedding dresses she likes yet there is no way I would look good in dresses like those.

I sit Atka on the bed and we have a talk about Mama going on patrol in the arctic.

"Only two weeks," I tell him. "Depends on how many bad guys we find." I laugh but his face is so serious. I kiss his chubby cheeks. "Oh, you be a brave boy, okay? Mama gotta do her duty. Maybe I see an ice bear."

"Please don't go, Mama."

"Mama's gotta go. It's my duty. But Aunt Iris is gonna take care you. And you got your cousins. Same as when I'm working late in the library and I get home after you're asleep."

A tear pops out of his eye. "Don't go...."

"Remember how I come in and give you a kiss? You're asleep so you think it's angels in your dreams, sent all the way from the Lord of Denmark. Yet it's really me kissing your head."

He frowns so hard his lips pucker. More fat tears roll down his cheeks.

"Atka, my beautiful boy, remember you're a wolf. Like me. You make your own path. You gotta be strong. You gotta be tough, like Mama. Nobody gonna give you anything you don't fight for. Only family gives you anything without you fighting for it. Remember that."

Still pouting, sad eyes.

"Atka, you gotta do something for me."

He stops pouting. "What, Mama?"

"You gotta take care of Joel. He's a big boy on the outside but he's a little boy inside. You gotta be sure he isn't sad. Can you do that for me? Take care of Joel for me?"

He frowns his prize-winning frown, lower lip sticking out, and makes tears line up in my eyes, ready to fall. I hug him tight, then kiss all over his face until he swipes his hands to keep my lips away. I laugh and he laughs. I know he will be all right with his cousins.

I give him his bath, then lie on the bed with him.

When Atka is asleep I call Joel, get him to come over to the house. While waiting for him, I see the printout on the kitchen table, my flight reservation, paid by credit card.

Everything is dark as I welcome Joel into my arms. We sit on the sofa, making out in the dark. He seems fine with me going. Besides, he knows he can't stop me if I set my mind on it. So he smiles and says he loves me.

"You know, we were going to have a surprise party for you. Cake and ice cream," he says. "Not a surprise now, eh?"

"Why?"

"For your birthday, silly girl."

"Oh. Yeah, I guess it is. It's just the day the Sisters chose."

"Hey, I certainly want to celebrate you being born."

"Thanks, lover! You gotta say that."

He whispers into my ear: "I miss you already."

We kiss. "Miss you, too."

And he keeps repeating he will miss me.

And I say I'll miss him, too.

He promises a big date night when I return. Depends on the hockey playoff schedule. If the Bisons get in, he might have a game when I return. Either way, he promises a big steak dinner followed by some hot lovemaking. He knows I like lovemaking. And steak.

It is after two when Joel leaves. I get my bag and set it by the front door.

At four, I hear the alarm clock upstairs.

After a few minutes, my sister's husband comes down to the living room, dressed in jeans and a Winnipeg Jets sweater.

"Ready?" he asks with a yawn.

"I been ready all night."

He pulls the keys from his pocket. "Then let's go."

I'm too excited to sleep on the flight from Winnipeg to Calgary, yet I fall asleep on the plane soon after leaving Calgary. I awake as we approach Yellowknife in the Northwest Territories. I can't remember the dream I was having, just Captain Rogers' words over the phone. He wasn't angry with me. He was surprised. Maybe he didn't expect me to fly up to Yellowknife so he said it as a way to stop me from coming, save me the trouble. Yet here I am, and the plane is landing.

I pass a vending machine on the way to the exit and stop to stare at the Kit-Kat. Knowing I'm still in training, I don't want it. I fight Jaime Little Bear in a month. Yet I'm going off to the arctic for a couple weeks first, so I go ahead and get it, stuff it into my bag for later.

My bag is in my hand as I step out of the airport. My sister gave me some cash for a taxi. As I look around I don't see the town, only the forest.

There seems to be only a long road into the town. I think of Nuuk, a town without trees. Here there is no harbor, no iceberg-filled strait, no bare mountains rising behind the town. They have a big lake here. I saw it from the plane, but I can't see it now that we've landed. Forest spreads out everywhere. Dirty snow dulls the scenery. Piles of old snow rise everywhere.

Standing in my green camo uniform and boots, I don't see any taxi so I start jogging along the winding road away from the

airport. I only have an hour to get to the armory. After about a kilometer, an old black pickup truck stops and the man driving asks if I need a ride into the town. I say I'm going to the armory so the man, covered in a big red beard from his nose to his waist, drives me there.

"I can't believe my eyes," says Captain Rogers, getting up behind his desk when I enter the office. He steps around the desk, his hand extended. "You're Private Tasiilaq?"

I nod, set my bag down and salute. "Yes, sir."

The captain is tall, the whitest Canadian I have ever seen, with short cropped blond hair, so short it doesn't cover his head. He's about my sister's age. He probably thought I would be a big man with a mean face and muscles. I have muscles, yet they are under my parka so nobody can see them. But I'm short. And a female.

"Private Tasiilaq reporting for duty. For Northern Patrol."

He sits back on the top of the desk, looks me over.

"How old are you?" he asks.

"Twenty-four, sir. I'm short, I know. But I'm strong."

"For your size, perhaps." He rubs his chin. "We have a lot of gear to stow. Then a lot of heavy things to carry with us on the machines. I thought you were...larger."

"I carry my weight. I do my part."

"Yes, I'm sure you will."

"Sir, you said if I get here by today, by twelve noon, I can go on the sovereignty exercise. It's only eleven-thirty."

"I did say that." He grins, holds back a laugh and shakes his head, but not in a happy way. "I sure never thought you'd make it here. You bought your own ticket?"

"My sister's husband bought it."

"He's a real trooper, doing that."

"I didn't want to miss another chance." I stand at parade rest.

He waves at me to relax. "I just got back from training last time, sir, so I missed it. This is what I signed up for, so here I am."

He nods a few times, thinking, deciding about me. Then he calls to another soldier to take me to get outfitted. Weapons and arctic clothing.

"I won't go back on my word, Taz." He starts to walk away, then turns and calls back. "I don't know if you can handle it, but…. You're likely to be a pain in the neck, but I said you could go with us and I won't break my word."

"Thank you, Captain." I salute again.

I take a breath. At least I wasn't shown to a desk with a lot of folders to organize. I didn't come all the way from Winnipeg to be a secretary. I'm not some stupid girl. Captain Rogers knows I'm Indigenous. Almost everybody here is, except the captain and a couple others. They all live in the north.

After being issued my C7A2 assault rifle and arctic gear, I stumble carrying it all in my arms as I go from the supply room to the barracks. A few men in the barracks laugh, wondering who is hiding under all the things I'm carrying.

"Private Tasiilaq," I grumble before dumping the load on an empty bunk at the end of the room. I unsling the rifle from my shoulder and lay it carefully on the bunk.

With my arms free, I stand at attention in front of everybody. All eyes are on me. They look surprised.

"Listen up, men," says Sergeant Haines, who helped me get all my gear together. He looks half-Native, older than Captain, broad shouldered with a serious face. "This is our new soldier."

"You're our new member?" asks one guy—Corporal Black, his uniform tag says. He is clearly First Nations, a skinny boy, his uniform not very neat.

"We heard some reservist from Winnipeg was due in," says Sergeant Tagaq, a handsome Inuit man, proud to be in uniform.

A few of the men step forward or jump down from their bunks. They shake my hand. A few say "Welcome" or "Good to meet you."

"Your first patrol?" asks a younger man. He has on Master Corporal insignia. His name tag says Qaaviauq. He is definitely Inuit.

"Yeah, I came all the way from Winnipeg for this."

"Winnipeg? What're you doing there?"

"It's long story. I was in college. I work in the library now."

Some of the men laugh. To them, library and arctic patrol don't mix. College student and soldier don't mix, either. I am the odd one. I look around and do not see any other females. So I'm a charity case, they must be thinking. Just a poor girl from the Children's House. Now they have to look after me.

"Hey, stop it, men," says Sergeant Haines. "You know who this is, don't you?"

They do not know me.

"This is Anna Tasiilaq," he says.

Yeah? Who's that? they all wonder.

"This is Anna *the Wolf* Tasiilaq. She's a boxer." He turns to me. "Ain't that right?"

"Yeah, I do some boxing."

"Some?" He laughs, then explains to them that I really am a boxer. After twenty fights, I'm number two in Manitoba. That seems to impress a few of them. "And how many knockouts?"

"Eight. But two were technical."

Sergeant Haines heard of me. His sister's boyfriend is the brother of Lisel Métis, one of my opponents. I knocked her out in the second round of my eighth fight. I apologize to him.

"It's no problem to me," he says with a chuckle. He turns to the others. "So you men better not fuck with her." He stares hard at a few of them. "I'm serious."

"But that's girl boxing," says Corporal Black with a sneer.

I know I could knock him down easy, skinny as he is.

"You wanna match up with her? You sure?" asks Sergeant Tagaq with a laugh.

"I had some boxing lessons," says Black, jutting his chin out.

"We got a patrol to prepare," Sergeant Haines barks. "You can fight it out after we get back."

"I'm not gonna hurt anybody," I say. "No fighting. I'm on patrol duty now."

They chuckle like I have been fooled. Maybe they don't take the patrol seriously, only a snowmobile ride for fun. Yet for me, this first patrol, I want to learn all I can and do my part. This is what I signed up for.

The rest of the afternoon we stow our arctic gear in crates, both personal stuff and the patrol's things.

I keep hold of my C7A2 rifle, tape it up in white camo. I like it, the same kind of rifle I used in training. I got expert ranking in my final testing, shooting targets at different distances and from different positions, both stationary and moving. I had the fifth highest score of everybody in the training regiment. They asked me how I could be so good at shooting, so I told them how I lay quietly on the ice for an hour waiting for a seal to pop up at an air hole, then fire one shot to get dinner for me and my dogs. I didn't have many bullets so I didn't dare waste any of them. Of course, nobody believed me.

Dinner is whatever we happen to get in the ration packets Sergeant Haines tosses to us. Some of the soldiers trade. Mine is noodles and sausage. Raisin cookie for dessert. One of the other privates gives me a small tin of brown beans.

Before dawn we board the choppers and head into the arctic.

"No, I missed it last time," I tell my seatmate, Master Corporal Oakes, through the headset. The noise of the chopper almost drowns out our words. "I just returned from training yet they already left on patrol."

"So what did you do?" asks Oakes. He joined us only that morning, ten minutes before the choppers arrived, so he didn't hear my introduction. His bus from Fort Simpson broke down.

"I went back to school. University of Manitoba. Studying for a degree in Librarianship."

"You learn how to put books on the shelves?"

"There's lots more than that."

"Then you decide you want to go off riding snowmobiles in the spring?"

"Whatever my duty is. Besides, I prefer dog sled."

"Dogs? That's old school. Nobody uses dogs in the Canadian arctic any more."

The chopper rattles, hitting some rough spots in the arctic wind. My belly tightens.

Below, I see the tundra is still white with snow, a few spots glimmering with patches of ice under the gray sky. A few trees, shorter than me, squat around some of the small lakes. A ragged herd of caribou startle, try to run away.

"And I had some fights," I say, turning back to my seatmate.

"What? You were fighting? Why? What happened?"

"No, I mean I was boxing. It's like a side job."

"Hah! You beat up people for a living?"

"It's a sport. I get prize money. It's how I paid for school."

"Oh, I get it. Cool."

The choppers enter a broad turn, drop low over the frozen strait, the ice as smooth as glass, almost clear, dusted in long streaks by powdery snow. We leave the mainland, crossing to one of many islands in the Canadian arctic, all stitched together by ice and snow.

Being only a private, nobody tells me anything. No mission details, no locations. One guy said we were going to a village to get snowmobiles. Then we would go on patrol. Patrolling the coast was all I knew. Maintaining sovereignty. A border patrol mission. The wind in my face is all I wanted.

Looking out the window of the chopper, I see we are really out in the wasteland, not even small settlements of subsistence hunters below. White everywhere. Still winter up here.

The high arctic. I think of Dirk out on the ice, maybe at the ice edge far past Qaanaaq, hunting walrus. He could sled across the frozen strait between Greenland and Canada. He could live his life free as a falcon. I stare at the vast white world for a while, thinking about what I want, what I've fought for.

Energy surges through me, like I'm coming home at long last, waiting eagerly for the first sight of Mama waving to me outside the hut. I know it is actually far away, in another country, yet everything is so white below, it could be there. Mama watches me, I know, and I want her to feel proud of me.

Soon we are landing near a pair of gray metal buildings half-hidden in snow drifts, our view blocked by the quick blowing, horizontal snow. Captain gives us instructions. We tumble out of the choppers, unloading our gear, taking it into one building. Inside are rows of snowmobiles and other gear on shelves along the walls. Soon they close the doors and we get in formation.

The noise of the choppers fades away as Captain tells us our mission, where we will patrol, what we are looking for. Some of them grumble yet I smile as bright as July sun. I'm ready.

"Any questions?" Captain asks us.

I raise my hand. "Where are we, sir?"

Several men laugh. Captain grins. "Classified. We'll tell you when we're leaving."

The men start to get up, ready to start their tasks.

Captain raises his voice. "And let's keep all the chatter down. Radios, too."

Yet I have to know, so I follow Captain. He senses me behind him and turns. I ask again.

"Can't tell you, Taz." He shakes his head. "You should know security protocols. Didn't they teach you in your training?" He exhales hard, puts his hands on his hips. "Listen to me. You're here in the arctic. Like you wanted. Now let's follow orders and not ask questions. All right? Two weeks is a long time to be putting up with each other if we can't come to some workable arrangement."

"Yes, sir. I understand." I salute. "I wanna do all I can. I don't wanna be secretary. I thought if I knew more I could be more helpful."

"You don't salute in the field," says Captain. "Your standing order on this mission is to help where you can and stay out of the way when necessary. Got it? Watch and learn. That is all."

"Yes, sir."

I follow the others over to where they are doing their tasks. Maintenance of the snowmobiles. Checking weapons. Mending arctic gear. Whatever is needed. I look around for a sled. I listen for dogs. Outside, the wind blows harder, whistles through the seams of this steel building. I look over shoulders and squat to watch what others do. I hand a tool to somebody. I don't know anything about snowmobiles or engines. Yet I can help with the weapons. I know weapons. Nobody talks to me except telling me to move out of the way.

Probably it's classified to say, but we have twenty members on patrol. Besides Captain Rogers, there is Lieutenant Illivat joining us from Iqalit over on Baffin Island, and Sergeant Haines from Fort McMurray in Alberta. There are a few Indigenous sergeants, some corporals like Qaaviauq, and a little private who doesn't know anything — Anna Tasiilaq.

"If you must know," Master Corporal Qaaviauq whispers to me in Inuktitut. That's the Canadian Inuit's language yet I can understand him enough. "We're either outside of Repulse Bay or Cambridge Bay. Those are the two choices. We're not allowed to go into the village, anyway."

I tell him I don't know where those villages are but I thank him. Either way, we are in the far north. I continue my task: putting bullets into magazines.

Most of the patrol call me Taz now, like soldiers in my unit in Winnipeg do. One corporal named Jaybird calls me Anna. He is on his second patrol and he started growing a mustache for this one. There are two other men about my age who looked Inuit, both privates. I guess they are from the arctic, know the territory. They do not talk much except to each other and they sure do not want to talk with me, a woman.

And I am the only woman here.

Captain Rogers comes over as I watch the men working on the snowmobile engine. I look up. He flips through a few papers, my papers.

"Looks like a happy birthday is in order, Taz." He smiles at me. Then he calls out to everybody, his voice echoing through the large steel hut. "We have a birthday today. Private Taz is twenty-five. And on her first patrol. Instead of having cake and ice cream, she's serving her country. Let's give her a cheer."

There are half-hearted shouts of "Happy Birthday" around the room. A few clap their hands.

"Shall we sing 'Happy Birthday' to you?" asks Captain.

I shake my head. Then I realize he is being tricky. He didn't really want to celebrate my birthday. It is only a way to tease me.

Yet I mutter under my breath "I'm Wolf. I make my own path, so nobody is gonna hurt me." I want to throw a hard left hook at his face yet he is the captain and I want to stay on the patrol. Instead, I pull out the Kit-Kat I bought at the airport and eat it slowly. I pretend it's my birthday cake. Yet I miss the ice cream.

We work into the night on the machines, testing them, repairing where needed. We have enough of the machines working for the patrol. Captain Rogers complains the previous patrol members didn't take care of the equipment. Yet we are ready.

The next morning we load up and head out.

"You ever ride a snowmobile?" asks Sergeant Haines.

"I always used dogs and a sled."

"You don't say. Where was that?"

"Greenland. I'm from Tasiilaq. I mean originally. I was born there. I had some dogs and I—"

"She can ride with Jaybird," Captain snarls like a dog that got his trace tangled and lost his footing as the sled dashed on over rough ice.

I was about to tell him how I lived alone when I was thirteen, how I went hunting, driving the sled all over Ammassalik. But I stop myself, climb on the machine behind this young corporal. I hold the strap on the seat behind him instead of putting my arms around him like I always see girls do while riding motorcycles with their boyfriends. I just met Jaybird and I got my fiancé Joel back home waiting for me.

At that moment I really wish we made love the night before I left on this trip. I don't know if I can make it two weeks. I don't know why I didn't push him into bed. Or right on the floor! We spend so much time in bed together as it is.

I almost feel I am home again, surrounded by so much white, all the shades of white. The sky is overcast, gray, snow-bloated clouds ready to let loose. The ground is mottled, snow and ice sewing the bare brown rock together, patch by patch. The world I see is flat, only a low hill sometimes, or a distant crag or cliff. No trail or road or sign of human settlement anywhere. Who would want to invade here?

Captain said it's part of the Barren Grounds. There is not much soil covering the rocks so nothing grows here. Only a poor flower or a few tufts of grass fighting for life in the cracks and crevasses between the rocks — if you look hard enough. The snowmobiles can't go over the rocky patches, which limits our route. Without snow cover, it would be impossible to use the snowmobiles, so we patrol before the snow melts. April is our last chance. Once the snow and ice melts, the landscape becomes a sloppy mess, too difficult to cross by any kind of vehicle.

We run north along the coast a few days, stopping at caches, taking measurements, marking our position, making notes of what we find. Each night we set up a temporary camp. I set up my own small tent, intended for only two people. I'm the female. Regulations. Nobody helps me but nobody bothers me. I wish I had an ice knife so I could make an igloo instead of using their arctic tents, which are bulky and unstable. The wind blew my tent over on two of the nights.

Finally, I agree to sleep in the big tent with the others. They say all their jokes about me sleeping with the men, then they get tired of it. I'm not going to sleep nude anyway. There is no *illeq*, so nobody is sharing warmth under the furs. We all got bags to sleep in and they tell me to close my eyes whenever they change clothes. I keep the same clothes on.

After a few days, we get to a strait where the ice has broken open. The lead is too wide for us to cross so we have to double back. I still don't know where we are among the islands of the arctic. Qaaviauq has not updated me yet. The landscape has a million lakes, big and little, all iced over. North by northwest from those metal buildings is all I know.

I remember what Mama told me about the ice. Everything Mama told me comes into my head. I try to give advice yet they ignore me because it is my first patrol and I am from Winnipeg in the south. I wish I had a team of dogs and a sled. Then I could go my own way.

"All right now," says Sergeant Haines roughly. "Thanks for the ideas, Taz."

I say too much. They are operating following army rules, not the rules I learned growing up on the ice.

You're never going to sneak up on anybody with noisy machines, I want to tell them. A trained team of dogs will be quiet when you stop to hunt a seal sunning itself on the ice beside its air hole. The dogs know to be quiet, yet as soon as they hear a shot they get excited and bark, want to run to the seal, to get their dinner.

After skirting the lead, Captain directs us on up the coast, then he falls back and lets Lieutenant Illivat take the lead.

Riding his machine, Captain comes alongside me and Jaybird on our machine, shouting at us to keep up with the others. We have fallen to last place. Again.

"You need to stay in the middle," he shouts. "Catch up and don't fall behind again."

"Yes, sir!" I respond.

"He forgets I'm carrying a passenger," says Jaybird.

"Somebody gotta be last, keep watch behind us," I shout into Jaybird's ear.

We find another place to cross the strait, the ice clear and hard. We stop while Captain checks the map. Jaybird and I catch up to everybody. They look at us with scowls. *Slackers* is what they are thinking. We shut off the engine and join them.

Nobody is saying anything. From my position, I can look over Captain's shoulder at the map. Army map, lots of symbols. I get an idea where we are. I can also hear radio noise leaking out of his headset. It seems that he is getting instructions from somebody far away.

He tells us to take a break, eat our rations, then we will cross the strait to another island. As we eat, I watch Captain talking over the radio to the person that's giving him orders. He looks concerned. Maybe we are going the wrong direction. Or a storm is coming and we will need to "hunker down" and wait it out.

When Captain looks up from the radio, our eyes meet.

"Everything okay — sir?"

"Yep, all's well." His face is a mask of broken ice yet his voice is full of spring wildflowers.

He waves us into a semicircle. I kneel on the front row, all the taller people behind me. He stares at the map, holds a compass in his hand. Then he looks around the group, trying to meet each member's eyes. He skips me.

"All right, here's the deal. New mission."

Some of the soldiers grumble. I guess a new mission means it's something harder. Captain waves them silent.

"We'll be changing directions," he says. "We'll be looking for wreckage."

"Wreckage? What kind?" asks Sergeant Haines.

"Yes, wreckage." He frowns. "An airplane has gone down."

Everybody gets silent. A few of them automatically look up to the sky or behind them, as though an airplane might be about to crash. None of us want to find airplane wreckage here in the arctic. Nobody wants to find people killed in a crash.

"It could be partly submerged," says Captain. "There could

be a debris field. We will know it when we come to it. We're on recon mode now. Keep in contact by radio—"

Right then the sky erupts in a great angry roar!

We spin around as a pair of Canadian fighter jets streak over us, very low to the ground, charging north as fast as they can.

"Whoa!" shout the men, watching the jets disappear.

"Probably checking the wreckage, too," someone says.

"Or *making* the wreckage."

"They're flying low to avoid detection."

"You mean they're attacking? Like at other fighter jets?"

"Shooting down something."

"But why shoot down—"

"We have our mission," Captain says sternly.

He huddles with the sergeants and Lieutenant Illivat, giving them orders and showing them where to go on the map.

Jaybird tugs on my parka sleeve like my little boy Atka does when he wants my attention, but I want to know what they are planning. I know there is a reason I came on this patrol. It is like Sila called me to be here to save people. My head fills up with sunshine even though I see all the dark clouds collecting on the horizon.

"Taz, you and Jaybird are with me," says Captain. Probably he wants us newbies to be safe.

We mount our snowmobile and follow the line of machines already heading up the coast in the direction of the dark cloud now curling into the sky on the far horizon. That has to be the wreckage. If an airplane crashed, there will be a lot of fire and smoke. We have to hurry!

Between the spot where we started and the place where the

black smoke rises, the ground is very broken. Rocks not covered with snow. Pressure ice that will not allow us to cross an inlet. Jaybird and I fall farther behind.

"Keep up," Captain snaps over the communications link in my earpiece.

"We gotta go faster," I shout into Jaybird's ear.

He hits the accelerator when we reach a flat snowfield and I almost fall off. I reach for his waist, wrap my arms around him. That surprises him. He takes a hand off the handles and presses it against my arm, maybe to check if it is really me.

"I'm not in love with you," I shout at him as we roar along. "I just don't wanna fall off!"

Because of the rough trail, we jump over rocks and berms and drop into depressions and leap up from them. My stomach goes up and down, too. It is hard to hold on. I never rode on a snowmobile before but Jaybird seems to be an expert.

I can see the others far ahead now, like little birds waddling over the snow. They are spread out in a wide formation, like a team of dogs. And Jaybird and I are on the sled behind them, calling them to push on! We hurry ahead since we are on the flat snowfield now.

Suddenly the sounds of gunfire blast over the comm set in my ear.

I tap Jaybird's shoulder. "Stop!"

More gunfire ahead of us as we slow to a halt. It continues for a few minutes in my ear. Then an explosion shocks my ear. My head is numb and I rip out the earpiece, shaking my head.

Looking far forward, I see the blast, orange flash against the white landscape, wind blowing black smoke away.

"Is that the wreckage of the plane?" I ask Jaybird, my mouth against his ear. It's the only way to hear each other in this wind.

I squint, trying to see what is far ahead. I see some people standing and other people flat in the snow, just dots to my eyes.

"Couldn't be," he says. "Who's shooting?"

"They found something if they had to shoot."

"Should we go on?"

We pause, wondering what to do. Maybe Captain will call us and tell us what to do. He keeps telling us to hurry up, keep up.

I put the earpiece into my ear again but now it is quiet. The icy wind continues to whistle through it.

"What do you think?" asks Jaybird.

We dismount, kneel beside the machine. I don't have any optics, so I can't see that far over the snowfield.

I can identify a ridge, completely white with snow, spreading from left to right. Farther to my left is the coast, the ice shelf spreading from the land out to the dark blue strait. And brown rocks. To my right, after the ridge drops, the whiteness of the arctic tundra extends as far as I can see. Rising beyond the ridge is a haze of black smoke bobbing in the wind. The wind tosses it around, then sends it away to my right, inland.

Between the ridge and where we wait, I can see the other snowmobiles stopped in a line, some bunched together.

"Better call in, see what's going on," I tell Jaybird.

"Yeah, okay."

He stares ahead, squinting.

"Are you gonna call in?" I ask.

"Maybe you should."

We don't have time to argue about who calls Captain. I check my comm set and make the call. Nothing. Static noise.

Then the line crackles in my ear.

"Taz, stay back." It is Captain speaking into my comm set. "It's a trick. Someone hit us." He groans like he is in pain.

I look at Jaybird as I pinch the talk button on the mouthpiece.

"What happened, Captain?"

"Ambush," he says, then groans again. "Listen to me. Switch to emergency freq and give our position. Call for support."

"You never told us the position."

He curses then grunts out some numbers, says it is GPS and they can find us with those numbers. They got us on satellite.

"Can you believe this?" Jaybird says, freaking out. "Another fuckin' war game scenario."

We lay bellies down in the snow, watching the distant ridge. I see tiny figures coming down from the top of the ridge. Then I hear the pop-pop of more shots being fired.

"We got trouble," I say to Jaybird.

I roll onto my back, dig the whole radio set out of the pack that was strapped on the snowmobile.

"Hello," I say when the radio comes alive and I switch to the new frequency Captain told me. "Calling headquarters. Come in, please." Suddenly I don't know what to say. My brain is all scrambled and I can't remember my training. "This is Sierra-Papa thirty-zero-eight. Captain Rogers' unit." I shake my head. Is that even right? I don't know anything.

I hear more pop-pop of gunshots far ahead.

"Follow comm sec protocol. Over," says a man's voice.

"I don't know all the numbers. I'm just on patrol, first time. We got attacked here."

"State your position. Over."

I tell him the numbers. "It's GPS. Captain Rogers said it's our position. We're north of Repulse Bay or maybe Cambridge Bay, one of them. Maybe fifty kilometers."

"Where's your captain? Over."

"He's forward of my position, about a kilometer. I think he's hurt. Can you send help?"

"Say again. Over."

"Requesting medevac."

"Roger. Medevac is for you? Over."

"Not me, but my captain needs it. Maybe others, too. We got attacked. Request medevac."

"Will confirm. Wait, over."

The radio goes silent and I look at Jaybird. His eyes ask if we are being serious enough. Is this a test? Then we both get our rifles and check them, load them. I pull off my outer parka, too bulky for fighting, and make sure my knife is still strapped to my boot. The white parka liner will be enough for an hour in this cold weather.

"You shittin' me?" asks Jaybird.

"Stay here," I tell him even though he is a corporal and I'm only a private. "Keep on the radio. They gonna send help."

I keep low, crawling through the snow on my belly, my eyes fixed on the ridge as I see more puffs of gunfire captured in the dry frigid air. I hear cries of pain as I get closer. My uniform is covered in snow, concealing my movements as I work my way to a depression and slip into it.

Over the top edge I see a dozen people not wearing Canadian Forces arctic uniforms. There are other bodies lying in the snow, too, the white-gray arctic uniforms of my patrol. The people not in uniform are going to each of them and firing a shot into each body. The attackers are wearing blue jeans or canvas pants and black or blue vinyl coats, a few with hoods. Like they are going on a ski trip, not an extended stay in the arctic. It's about minus twenty Celsius here with a strong northwest wind. They are not dressed for the arctic—yet they have guns, shooting at the soldiers of my patrol!

I am not close enough to see where Captain is, or identify any of the patrol members individually. None of them seem to move, all on the ground, lying in the snow. The attackers walk around slowly, taking their time. Now I'm afraid to call Captain. I don't want the comm noise to alert the attackers to his position.

Is this real? Or is it some kind of war game, like Jaybird said? Like we played during training camp. Maybe I shouldn't shoot anybody, in case it is only a game. I remember Captain saying one of the purposes of the patrol is training us how to fight in the arctic. Maybe this is a test. I don't know what to do.

I still have my comm set in my ear and the mic by my mouth. Yet I can only hear radio static. I take a deep breath, exhale.

Suddenly my comm set comes to life and I grab the volume control, quickly turn it down.

"Taz, you there?" It's Jaybird.

"Yeah, me."

"They confirmed our position. They're sending gunships and evac chopper."

"Great!"

"What do you want me to do?" he asks.

"You're the corporal, not me."

"Tell me!"

"Hold your position. Keep in contact with headquarters."

"Gotcha."

"I'll tell you what I see and you tell them."

"Will do. Uh…what *do* you see?"

"There's other people here. They attacked the patrol."

He lets go a string of curses. "What should we do?"

"Wait for the gunships, I guess."

"How long'll that be?"

"We're five days run from where we got the machines. How fast can they fly?"

Jaybird is silent.

"Maybe we should do something," I say.

"Like what?"

"Like fight back."

245

"You shittin' me?"

"Are you a soldier, Jaybird?"

He doesn't respond.

"Are you?" After a second I say, "I'm going forward."

"Okay…. Uh, be careful."

"Yeah. Out."

I crawl farther through the snow, seeking the next depression to roll into. This is like training camp, only then it was wet, sloppy mud I crawled through, and under a hot summer sun. Snow is much better. In a white uniform, covered in snow, white-wrapped rifle locked and loaded, I'm ready. Maybe it is not a game. Yet who would be all the way up here in the arctic waiting to attack a sovereignty patrol?

The snow field gives way to a crevasse I could not see before, a shallow ditch full of rocks, free of snow. The ditch runs out to the coast, about a hundred meters to my left. If we hit it with the snowmobile, we would flip over.

With my knees on the rocks, I lay my rifle on the edge and watch the snowfield ahead of me.

The attackers have moved into a circle, huddling together, ignoring the bodies in the snow. They start up the slope, back in the direction they seem to have come from. A few of them look back down the slope as if they are checking the bodies. The attackers seem in good spirits as they cross over the crest of the ridge and disappear from my view.

I count sixteen gray lumps in the snow.

Everything begins and ends in the dark, Mama always told me. So it does today. She also told me everything we learn in the light helps us in the dark.

Realizing this is not a game, I mutter one of Jaybird's curses.

I climb out of the ditch, crawl forward on my belly toward the bodies. It's about fifty meters.

The first one I reach has several gunshot wounds in his face and chest. Private Ilaitsuk. I never got to talk with him. I crawl forward to the next body. Also dead. I crawl through the snow to the next body.

It is Corporal Black, who thought he could fight me. Now he is dead. Ahead of him is Sergeant Haines. And Lieutenant Illivat. Here is the sergeant who grabbed me one night in the tent. And Master Corporal Oakes. And the other Inuit private. Sergeant Tagaq. And another corporal. And others. My patrol.

All dead.

Ahead toward the slope I see a few bodies that are not in uniform. A few of the attackers were killed in the shootout.

I begin to understand. Not expecting there to be people with guns waiting here on this arctic coastline, the patrol rode into an ambush. A firefight. Nowhere to hide, nothing to get behind for cover. Only the open snowfield and two lines of shooters, like a cowboy movie. And the attackers had the high ground on the slope. The patrol didn't have a chance.

Except Jaybird and me. We were always falling behind.

I can't understand who the attackers are. Not Canadian men, I think. They aren't dressed for the arctic. They could only have dropped out of the sky —

Now I am in the middle of the killing field, just another white lump in the snow. I worry the attackers might return, coming over the top of that ridge to see if the patrol is still dead.

I raise my head and softly call "Anybody still alive?"

A hand waves. I scramble up on my hands and knees and go to him. Sergeant Mikele. One hand clasps his throat as blood leaks out, soaking his glove. He cannot speak. There is nothing I can do. The evac is on the way but I don't think he will last until it arrives.

I call again and another movement catches my eye.

Corporal Meqesuq is in tears, staring hard into my eyes. He mouths Inuit words. Something about him being ready to go home. I put my ear to his mouth, keeping my eyes on the ridge. He whispers a message he wants me to give to his mama. I tell him I will. Then he closes his eyes and exhales.

I glance around, no more movement among the bodies. Yet I see the rocks along the shoreline. Beyond them is the strait. On my side of the rocks, I see stains of blood on the snow.

I sling my rifle over my shoulder and dare to get up and try to run through the snow. My legs sink almost to my knees in the snow drifts. I lumber through as fast as I can, not wanting to be seen by any of the attackers if they might be watching.

As I run, snow shakes off me and my white uniform looks more gray, easier to see now.

"Taz, you there?" It is Captain, calling through my comm set. Yet I am running as hard as I can to the rocky shoreline.

"Yeah—running."

"Good. Keep away. Most of the patrol is killed. Call in help."

"Did it!" I am breathing hard. "Jaybird's in contact with HQ."

I turn, look back, don't see anybody chasing me, so I drop down in the snow, roll around to cover myself so they can't see me. And catch my breath.

"Captain, they're sending gunships and medevac."

"God bless you."

I keep crawling through the snow and I reach the bare rock, the last of the land before the ice shelf extends out over the inlet. Crossing over the rocks will expose me. But I see movement on the other side of the rocks, shadows against the white snow. I also see blood on the top of the rocks.

"Captain, are you behind the rocks?"

"Yeah…."

I check for any attacker coming behind me. I don't see any — I can't see much of the snowfield from where I am near the rocks. They can't see me, either, but maybe they can follow my trail in the snow.

Jumping up, I throw my body over the top of the rocks and crash against hard ice on the other side.

Captain Rogers is covered in blood, gritting his teeth.

"Jesus, my leg's messed up," he moans.

I look at the blood-soaked snow, where he dragged himself behind the rocks. Beside him is Sergeant Aklassik, unconscious but alive, his arm completely missing. A belt is wrapped above where his elbow used to be. He is breathing but shallow. His white uniform is covered in blood.

Captain says they were lucky to make it to safety. He didn't intend to leave the others. There was a firefight, but he and Aklassik were at the rear of the patrol, Aklassik driving the snowcat with our big supplies. It was the grenade that got them. Even wounded, Captain managed to drag himself and Aklassik behind the rocks, then apply the tourniquet before the sergeant passed out.

Captain is worse, I see. There is not much leg left between his thigh and his foot, only bare bone. He has taken his own belt off and tied it around his leg at the middle of his thigh. Blood keeps dripping out.

"Need to tighten this more," he tells me. "You know what to do. First-aid training. Make a tourniquet."

"Yes, sir."

"I plan to make it out of here!"

I tighten the belt around his leg as much as I can, pulling it with all my strength. He clenches his teeth, then lets out a cry.

He says I need a stick, something, to get more leverage, so I dig in my waist pouch and pull out the flashlight Joel gave me so I could find my way across the campus at night after the library closed. It's about twenty centimeters long and two centimeters thick. It will do.

I slide the slim flashlight stick between his leg and the belt and twist it to make it tighter.

As I turn the flashlight around on his thigh, he screams. It's too loud and we both worry the attackers might hear him. I push the toe of my boot to his face and he bites down on it, digging his teeth into the dirty sole until I tie off the flashlight so it will stay in that position.

"I don't feel anything," he says, "so must be working."

He breathes hard for a minute, watching me. It is so cold, I climb on top of him. I lie over him with my liner open, pressing my warm body against him.

"Bet you never thought we be laying together."

He chuckles, then pain sweeps through him.

"Listen, Taz. It's up to you now. It's more than calling for an evac now. The mission...."

"Yeah, you never tell us anything."

"The airplane wreckage we were supposed to recon...?"

"I saw the smoke."

"No, it's not a plane wreck. I mean, it is—but not a crash. Our boys shot it down. The jets...remember?"

"They shot it down?"

"They *forced* it to land. Didn't dare destroy it. Because there is a bomb on that plane. A nuclear device—"

"A bomb?"

"The men out there were on that plane. Survivors. Terrorists. The plane was probably bound for Toronto or even New York or Washington. There's a nuclear device onboard. It's still there, inside the plane." He makes an ugly, twisted face, fighting pain. "Maybe I won't make it, Taz. But you have to do something for me." He is breathing hard. "You're the only one now."

"Tell me what to do."

"This is what they told me. There's a key. A key that has to be inserted in order to detonate the device. They can still set it off. They insert the key and *boom*." He sucks air a moment. "Do you have any idea what would happen if a nuclear bomb went off in the arctic? First, all the ice and snow around here would instantly vaporize. Then all the other ice and snow farther away would melt very fast and the oceans would rise, flooding coastal cities around the world."

"They're sending gunships—"

"No, Taz! They could set it off right now. One of them has the key, probably hanging from a chain around his neck, or in a pocket. I need you to make sure none of them get back to the plane." He grabs my hand. "You have to get that key away from them and keep them from detonating that device!"

"How am I gonna do that?"

He sucks more air. "You have to…kill them. Search the body. If no key, kill another, search the body. Kill anyone heading back to the plane. It's only partly submerged. They can still get inside it and…."

"And blow it up?"

"Yes."

"That's what you want me to do?"

"Yes! Kill'em, Taz." He closes his eyes tight. "Kill them all. You can do it. You have to! Not just for the patrol but…for the world."

I stare down at Captain, yet I feel a serious disruption of the landscape from the corner of my eye.

Turning my head, I see the huge tail section of the airplane rising from the water, standing tall in the gray sky as snowflakes stream by. The front half of the plane's body is submerged, the nose under the ice shelf. It looks like a commercial airliner, like what I flew in going up to Yellowknife. Yet the plane has been painted over. Now it has some squiggly writing along the side that I can't read. Not alphabet.

"Taz, I really want to order you to get as far away from here as you can, where you can be safe," he says with his jaw tight, "but now you're the only one who can stop them." His grip tightens on my hand. "You are the only one left."

Even now, I realize, one of them could be climbing back into the plane to detonate that nuclear device. There could be a big flash of light and earth-shattered explosion any moment. There is not enough time for us to get far enough away if it were to happen. Yet if they think they have killed everybody in the patrol, then they will relax and be in no hurry to set it off. They probably know they would die, too, if they set it off. What are they waiting for? Maybe they don't care about that now.

But I got a beautiful boy and a gorgeous fiancé and a lovely sister and her wonderful family, and there are a lot of other people who don't know me, and they all want to live. So I leave my waist pouch with Captain and continue with only what I need to carry out the mission.

The radio crackles and through a lot of static I hear faint voices. It's clear they don't think I can hear them. Maybe it is supposed to be confidential or top secret. Yet I hear them in my earpiece. Whoever it is, they can see me. Probably they are looking down from the satellite.

I get up from the snow, run and drop, repeat.

"Who do we have down there? I see one of ours moving."

"Comm signal is go."

"Checking signature. That would be Private Tasiilaq, sir."

I feel like waving up at the satellite yet that might catch the eyes of the terrorists. Instead, I work my way through the snow on my belly again, getting closer to the camp they made on the other side of the ridge from the snowfield where my patrol were killed. I move along the jagged shoreline to the end of the ridge.

From there, resting on my belly in the snow beside where the ice shelf begins, I see their little camp. The terrorists have made a fire to keep themselves warm. They hug themselves, pat their shoulders, pacing around the fire. They never expected to find themselves on the ice. They thought they would be safe inside a warm, comfortable airplane all the way to wherever they were heading just to kill a lot of people.

"I count twelve," says the voice in my ear.

That's the number of terrorists I see down there, too. Are they waiting for rescue? What is their plan now? They could be dead by morning from the cold. And there is the plane with that rear side door open and the yellow rubber slide extending down to the dark, icy water. I see a yellow rubber raft resting on the shore, front half on the ice shelf.

Pop that raft and they couldn't get back to the airplane. Yet the shot would alert them to my location.

Is anybody left on the plane? Or are they all on the shore, standing around the fire?

I watch them, thinking what to do.

"Who is it? A private?"

The radio voices return in my ear.

"Soldier completed initial training last summer, Colonel."

"That's it? That's who we have down there?"

"First patrol for this one, the orders indicate."

I want to shut off the comm. Or change the frequency. But I need to know if there are any new orders. All I have is Captain Rogers telling me to guard the airplane, keep the terrorists from getting back into it. At least keep them from using the key to activate the device.

"Private Tasiilaq is a girl."

Not girl. Woman!

"I'm Wolf," I whisper into the snow at my chin.

"A female private? We really are f[*radio static*]g doomed. How soon till the gunships arrive?"

"Patrol member is Anna Tasiilaq. Inuit name, I guess."

"Name sounds familiar."

"She's a reservist out of Winnipeg."

I unhook the grenade Captain Rogers gave me. I measure the distance, decide I'm close enough here at the end of the ridge, on a narrow strip of land between the ice shelf and the slope. I need to throw it as hard as I can. So I pull my feet up under me, into a low crouch. I shift my weight so I can jump up and fall back down in one fast motion.

Then I launch the grenade towards the middle of the camp. It hits only halfway but then it rolls on down the slope and stops between the feet of one of the terrorists standing by the fire. He looks down, notices it—

"Shit! You see that flash?" my ear piece roars.

"Our gal just sent them a gift!"

I switch to another freq. Too distracting.

The group of terrorists scatter. Half of them do not move, silent in the snow, bodies splayed outward from the campfire like spokes on a wheel. The others run away, run toward where the nose of the airplane goes under the ice shelf. They do not hesitate but run straight out onto the ice. They slip and fall, can't get up.

I run up the slope, my boots fighting the deep snow. I drop into a firing position at the top. I align the sights on the man closest to the airplane, even though he is still far away from it, and squeeze the trigger.

He spins around like he is hit, slipping and falling on the ice. Shoulder wound. He tries to get up onto a knee but slips and falls again. I fire two more times and he drops on his chest there on the ice yet his body slides a few meters more. He collapses hard enough to crack the ice — which cuts toward the shore.

Two of the men on the ice stop and fire back at me with pistols. They calculate my position and shoot. Their bullets do not reach me, though.

I crouch below the crest of the ridge, expecting them to come for me. Now the terrorists are on guard. They know they didn't kill everybody on the patrol. One lone wolf lives.

Two of them are marching up the slope, stepping through the deep snow with their fancy pants and expensive shoes, hoping to look down on the snowfield where the bodies are. They expect to find me there and shoot at me.

When they appear above the crest, I'm already below them in the snow, covered with snow, looking up at them, aiming up at them. Before they can notice me, my C7 rifle sings. They fall to their knees and I wait to see if they need more bullets. Then they fall over like cut trees, face-first into the snow.

I scramble to my knees, rifle ready. Searching them, patting their pockets, tearing open their collars, I do not find anything that looks like a key to a bomb.

Then I slide down the slope to the snowfield. I switch on my comm set.

"Jaybird," I call into the mouthpiece as I get up and run.

"Taz! You okay?"

"Captain's wounded. Everybody else is killed. Where's the

medevac? We still got gunships coming?"

"Where are you?"

"North side of the ridge. The plane wreck's here."

"I heard explosion."

"That was me. Grenade."

"You okay?"

"Stay on the radio. Direct them in. Gotta go!"

"Wait. Taz!"

"Quiet. I'm hunting."

The light has changed, the day dropping, the clouds melding with the snow and ice, new snow streaking on the wind, making a curtain that confuses the eyes. I back away from the bottom of the ridge. I wait, rifle at my shoulder, waiting for somebody to come over the crest of the ridge.

I wait.

Nobody.

I take a couple steps up the slope, pause. I still expect them to come after me over the crest of the ridge. I climb the slope until I can look down at their campfire again.

I don't see anybody moving there. Silent bodies. Body parts. I take a glance to my left at the tail section of the airplane rising from the black water. It looks the same. Already ice is forming around the metal body, refreezing, locking it in.

Stop them from getting to the airplane, Captain told me.

Nobody heading that way.

My eyes scan from their campsite on the shore out over the ice shelf. The crack has spread, broken open. Narrow enough to still leap over it.

Movement catches my eye. I turn to my right, looking inland.

From the crest of the ridge I see one of the men running away over the tundra. There are bare brown rocks among the patches of snow and he dashes back and forth to make his way. He can't know what is out there, probably running out of fear. Maybe he thinks he can run all the way home.

I drop into the snow along the crest, aim my rifle at the man. He is running as fast as he can, given all the rocks he must maneuver through. Ducking and dodging.

Rifle to my shoulder, I mark the sights on the moving figure. I slow my breathing and squeeze the trigger. He seems to trip, losing his balance and falls among the rocks, out of view.

I wait, watch.

He gets up after a moment and I know my shot only nicked him. Maybe the bullet hit a rock, skipped into his butt or hit his hamstring. He limps.

I know then that he is approximately 150 meters away.

He tires to run, hobbled, grabbing the rocks. He jogs left and right, trying to make it difficult to aim on him. I adjust the sight. Then I slow my breath and squeeze the trigger again.

A puff of red blooms like a bouquet of roses where his head used to be. The body drops from under that pinkish cloud, out of view among the rocks.

I wait. He does not rise.

One of them has the key that activates the device.

From my position at the top of the ridge, I don't see any of the terrorists in any direction. So I get up and step down the slope to their campsite, keeping my rifle up, ready to fire. I move through the area and get on the path of the one I just shot. I go through the rocks and over the patches of snow and come upon the body.

It was an ugly shot and tore his head off at the neck. Nothing on a chain. Nothing to hang a chain around. Nothing like a key in any of his pockets, either.

I start to get up, trying to keep my head low so nobody can see me among the rocks. A slight slope between the rocks leads down to a wider open area with deeper snow, a drift sweeping up one side.

A man is hiding there.

We see each other and in that moment he grabs my ankle and pulls me down from where I stand. I land hard on my back and he is on top of me, grabbing at my jacket. My rifle is somewhere behind me. I get my knee up between us and kick him away.

He laughs like he enjoys playing games.

I scramble up, ready to defend myself.

He stands with his back against the rock, most of his weight on his right leg, like a boxer who does not know how to dance.

I kick at him before he can think what to do next. My boot strikes the side of his knee hard. It crunches and he screams, collapsing, cursing me. He drops his rifle in the snow.

Somebody is running at me, coming from where I shot the man a few minutes before.

While this man is holding his knee, I pick up his rifle, a different kind of assault weapon that I don't know. I get my finger on the trigger. Nothing happens. There must be a safety so I find it and flick it off, then pull the trigger as the other man rushes me.

The rifle lets out a burst of shots and I'm thrown back, away from the rock wall, the shots landing in his chest, collar, throat, jaw, and eye. He drops at my feet with his hand on my leg. I kick my leg free. My training sergeants always complained about my shot placement.

The man with the broken knee is growling like a wounded bear, down in the snow on his side, holding his knee. I turn the rifle on him and try for a good shot placement, center of mass.

I check for keys on neck chains. None.

I check the pockets of both men for the key. Nothing. Only a few unopened condom packets.

Crouching between the rocks, I hook the comm set on my head again, knocked off during the fight. I replace my helmet and touch the mic.

"Jaybird, you there?"

"Oh my fuckin' god, Anna, are you alive?"

"Yeah—very alive."

"I don't know what to do—"

"Listen. Call HQ, tell them we don't need the gunships any more. But keep the medevac coming. And better send somebody to take care of the bomb in the airplane."

"What? You shittin' me? A bomb?"

"Yeah, but don't worry about it now."

"Why? What'd you do?"

"I killed them."

"All of them?"

"I think so."

There were twelve terrorists. I counted my targets. Only twelve around the camp fire. Six died there from the grenade. I shot two men coming after me on the ridge. Another one on the ice. Another one running among the rocks. And these two men at my feet. Twelve.

Maybe there are others hiding, afraid to show themselves.

I listen for voices. I listen for radio traffic in my ear. I listen for choppers. All I hear is the wind screaming across the tundra, slipping across the ice. I look north and see the entire world.

I get up, rifle in my hands.

The standard size magazine is almost empty. Captain handed me the magazine from his rifle, keeping the Glock for his own defense. I pushed the magazine into my leg pocket.

Now I see the magazine he gave me is almost empty, too. I pull off my gloves, transfer those three bullets to my magazine, reload. I got six shots left. Better to save them for long distance kills, like if I need to stop one of the terrorists from returning to the airplane.

Now to get back to Captain Rogers and Sergeant Aklassik, wait for the choppers to arrive, and think of home. I'll be able to cover the airplane door from Captain's position.

I listen again, hoping to hear choppers but I hear only the wind. It sounds like home. I take a long deep breath, finally able to relax —

I see the man below me among the rocks, his brown leather jacket helping him blend in. Having a short beard and wearing sunglasses, he is dressed for driving a sports car top-down through a tropical city like a playboy, not lost here in the arctic. He does not seem to notice me. I am so quiet — always Introvert, people say. I work in a library. I make sure everybody is quiet. Or I punch them.

Resting as still as a stone, there is no noise to surprise him. He is hiding, maybe waiting for all the others to be killed first. Then who will save him from a cold arctic night? From an ice bear? From a *wolf*?

I set my rifle down, pull the knife from my boot and hold it steady.

Aiming for the point between his collarbone and throat, like I was taught, I leap down upon him. He sees me at the last instant, a big shadow sweeping over him, and raises his two bare hands just in time to push me away. I fall into the snow, lose the knife.

Jumping up, I hold my arms ready, get into fighting stance. I make my bare fists into guns.

"You know boxing?" he asks me in English, pointing at me with his chin.

When I leaped, I knocked off his baseball cap. His black hair is short. He's almost bald, stubble like his dark beard. His eyes are dark, like he holds inside him all the dark of the world.

"You better run away, boy," he says, taking a similar position with his fists raised. "I was boxing champion. I was in Olympic."

I stare at him, never giving away my plan.

"I got Bronze medal," he says. He laughs like he thinks I have no chance. Marla Bounty was over at weight-in but I fought her anyway, and beat her with a knockout forty-eight seconds into the first round.

"Bronze is like third place," I say.

"It's fucking Olympic medal! You can't beat that."

I get ready to rumble. "I'm number two in Manitoba."

"So not the best, huh. You're just—"

Before he can say another word my left fist snaps out and smashes his nose. He grabs his face. Blood spurts between his fingers. He gets angry and his long right arm swings hard at me, clubs the side of my head before I can block him.

I fall backwards, my head going down and my feet flying up like in a somersault. I crash in the snow, a rock poking into my shoulder. He comes at me, shaking blood from his fingers. He bends over me, blood running from his flattened nose.

As he leans down, I kick out my foot and the heel of my boot strikes his chest. He falls backwards, hits hard against the rocks and tumbles into the snow on his side. I scramble to my feet, stand over him, fists ready for more. His hand grabs my ankle, threatening to pull me down. There is evil in his eyes, so I do not hesitate. I drop all my weight onto him, putting my knee on his throat, crushing his larynx.

He grasps his throat as I step away. He can't breathe. He tries to get up. Instead, he can only get to his knees, one hand on the ground, the other hand at his throat. He wavers like a bear shot in the head and not feeling it. He desperately tries to suck in air.

I wait.

"There's no peace when you're facing down an angry bear. All you can do is kill it," Mama told me. "It's the only way."

To be sure he is dead, I pick up my knife from the snow and push it through his ribs, then wipe it clean on his fancy leather jacket. The evil spirits can stay in him. He and his partners were trying to kill thousands of people who would never see the airplane coming. And that's not what I want.

I check around his neck and in his pockets. No key.

"You little piece of shit!" the bearded man shouts.

Catching me from behind as I made my way back to where Captain Rogers waits, I struggle to get free from his big arm, tight around my neck. He lifts me off the snow by that neck hold and flings me forward against the rocks. I lose my breath.

He grabs my shoulder, spins me around. His fist hits my face.

"You and me are going to heaven!"

He leaps onto me, covering me, and his hands grab quickly at my parka liner, tears it open. My dark gray t-shirt, the bright red FIGHT FEST III printed across the front, doesn't hide my boobs. He squeezes the left one like he is checking it is real.

"So you *are* a girl. I thought so. Even if a boy, no matter. Yes, a short soldier—toy soldier, like you're playing a game. But I don't play games!"

He slaps my face hard, like it's my punishment for killing his friends—and in that moment I see it dangling from his neck on a chain. Something that looks like a key. It's the shape of the letter H, about two and a half centimeters long, one centimeter wide, all silver but with a bright orange stripe along one end and some black words and numbers. The key to the nuclear device on the airplane!

I grab the chain, jerk it hard. It breaks away from his neck. He feels it and lowers his chin, turning his head to see what I did.

"Is that what you want, little princess? Some jewelry?"

He slaps my face again, then shifts his sitting position over me, pressing all his weight upon my hips.

"It's not jewelry, but it is a most beautiful thing. It is the key to glory!" He stares into my eyes. "You know glory? It's the best thing anyone can know."

I gather the chain with the key into my hand, ball it up, then fling it as hard as I can away from us. I don't see where it lands yet I guess only a couple meters.

He begins speaking in his language, like he is talking to the Lord of Denmark or lord of his own country, asking permission to kill me. He stretches over me, pressing against me with his hips, and I can feel that he is excited. His hand grabs at my belt, releases it. Opening his eyes, he shows a grin with a few teeth missing. His hand pushes my uniform trousers down, the other hand grasping my throat. I wrestle with him but he is big and holds me under the weight of his body. I can't get out from under him.

His hand digs between my legs, pushes inside my trousers, inside my underlayer, and his fingers enter me.

"Yes! A real girl!"

I curse at him, squirming under his weight.

He opens his pants, prepares himself with his hand—and I pat my leg, feeling for my knife. It's not there. It must have fallen when this man grabbed me. There is nothing in my pockets I can use as a knife.

So I swing my fist at his head as hard as I can, bare knuckles striking his temple. I bash his head again and again yet from flat on my back in the snow I don't get leverage so my punches are not hard enough.

He leans back, sitting on my hips, out of reach of my fists, and laughs. Then, angry again, he slaps my face hard.

I continue swinging my fist at his head but I only strike his shoulder. He tries to capture my arm and hold it down. He rolls off me in his attempt to grab my punching arm and I bring my knee up hard behind him, striking his butt. He raises a bit and I can bend my knee up between our bodies. I get leverage and kick him off me.

I jump up, try to run with my camo trousers slipping down my legs. I reach down and grab the key on the chain from the patch of snow where it landed when I tossed it.

He lunges at me, catches my ankle. I fall on my face and he pulls me by my foot, dragging my body back towards him, on his knees in the snow. The chain slinks out of the hole in the key and drops into the snow.

As he pulls me to him, I twist onto my back. I kick at him with my free foot but he keeps hold of my other foot. His hands grasp my trousers and jerks them down to the tops of my boots. Under my camo trousers, I wear silver and blue leggings, what I wear for daily runs on the campus. I thought they also would be good for arctic missions.

Suddenly, he has a knife in his hand. He cuts the fabric over my thigh, cutting across my thigh. Blood forms a line along the cut. He tears the fabric open with his two hands. My bare skin feels the icy wind.

He climbs up my body, hovers over me, face to face.

"Don't be afraid, little one." He kisses my cheek. His beard scratches my face. "You will be blessed in paradise." He tries to kiss my mouth but I turn away. So he slaps my face. "Give me the pretty jewelry. It belongs to me."

I have the key hidden in my fist. He reaches for it, tries to peel back my fingers. I bat him away and shove the key into my mouth.

"Little piece of shit!" He grabs my throat, trying to squeeze the key out of my mouth. "Mangy dog! Give me that!"

I swing my knees up hard, kicking him in the back. He slaps me and tries hooking his foot over my leg to hold my knees down. We wrestle a minute yet remain in the same position.

He breathes hard from our struggle.

"Give me the key and I won't rape you. It's a deal?"

I shake my head. No deal. Then I swallow.

"Shit! You're joking at me?" He shakes his head in disbelief, then hauls off and punches my face with all he has.

My nose is broken, bleeding. My face is numb. The key slides down my throat with more swallows.

As he sits over me, I see his pants are open. My trousers are at my ankles yet the leggings are torn open from one knee up to my belly and the wind blowing over my skin is very cold.

"You make it very hard for me to get to heaven," he sneers in a voice spilling over with darkness.

He shows me the knife. He holds it over my face and it glints like a shard of ice.

"It could be so easy, you know. But not now."

And the knife goes into my belly.

He pushes himself down to my knees, gets a better angle, and works the knife around, trying to open my stomach like a surgeon. Yet I can't scream. I have no breath. The blade cuts into everything. The opening in my belly widens, my guts feel the frigid air. He shoves his fingers inside my stomach.

"There it is, little dog." His fist works the knife, pulling it back toward himself. "I've got it now! And you will be dead at last, no way to stop it."

I bite my lip, then my tongue. Blood runs up into my throat, blocking my air as the rising noise of choppers echoes across the snowfield.

"Finally I kill you!" grunts this madman who doesn't know me at all, doesn't know what I've been through or who I am.

He laughs—

I have worked my fingers inside his open pants as he dug the knife through me. My fingers wrap around his testicles, squeeze them hard. He shrieks and drops the knife, reaches for my hand. At that moment, my other hand grabs the knife out of my belly and thrusts it under his lowest rib—and I push push push the blade into his heart until my hand is all the way inside his chest.

"My life counts for something," I say as I twist the knife back and forth. "Yours won't."

He gasps, eyes rolling up. He curses, spits.

Then collapses on me.

I let his body roll off of me, and gaze up at the blue sky, the clouds parted now, the sundog shining bright like Mama's smile. As the shadows of the helicopters cross the snowfield, moving into position above me, I wave my hand.

8

The World

All I feel is a wonderfully raw coldness, so pure and clean, like the world is newly born.

"Tasiilaq? Private Tasiilaq, do you hear me?"

I feel a hand on my shoulder, my ears full of whirring metal. My body vibrates against a hard surface, like Mama did against the floor of our hut when she went into the darkness.

"Are you with us? Hold on! We're evacing you. You're going to make it!"

I do not know the voice, only a man. Maybe he is part of the recovery team securing the bomb. When I open my eyes I see him, another soldier, helmet and goggles, headset, medic badge on his green uniform. I guess I am in a helicopter, just like when I left my home long ago....

Leaving the village of Tasiilaq for the airport at Kulusuk....

Lifting from the snowfield, rising into the sky and turning

toward the sun, then away, and the feeling of weightlessness, flying over the pale arctic landscape —

"Hey! Wake up! Hold on, I said. We're going to make it." He turns and speaks over the comm system, "Can you push it any faster? She's lost a lot of blood."

"Nearest hospital's an hour away," comes the answer out of his headset. "You want a level one trauma center, we'll have to go all the way back to Yellowknife. That's the closest one."

"But I can't stop the bleeding."

"We're rocking as hard as we can."

He stares down at me. Gives me a big smile like everything's all right. I know it isn't. My gut feels empty, like I got nothing there, like my whole stomach is gone.

Like I am nothing but a cloud...out there over the sea....

"You hear me? Private Tasiilaq? Answer!"

I try to smile at him. He is a handsome guy. His hands are in my gut, holding me together. But I cannot finish the mission.

I am flying, flying to where Mama is. We are going to meet each other there in the dark beyond this world.

"Stay with me! You're a hero! You have to make it!"

The dark covers everything, fills everything....

"Come on! Stay strong! Hold on!"

The dark is colder than anything....

"Stay with me, Tasiilaq! Fight! Don't give up!"

I see it first in the corners of the chopper cabin, spreading like big mountain shadows at dusk....

Everything begins and ends with the dark. Between, it fills everything, big and small. Sometimes it covers even the brightest light—

I see Mama. My dogs are there. The black sky is bright with stars and green curtains, and the land is so white.

I'm not dead. Not really.

I'm spirit. And because it is summer now, there is no north wind to take me home. So I stay a little longer to make sure my family will be all right.

I want to hug them yet all I can do is float nearby, never touching them. Still, I hear them and see them. They cry and they talk about me like I am gone, like I will never visit them again.

I know my boy Atka will grow big and strong yet kind and smart. He has his cousins to help him. I taught him everything I know except how to drive dogs or hunt on the ice. Maybe he will visit my homeland someday. Maybe he will want to see that point where a hut once stood, across a fjord from the ice cap. He might wonder how anyone could live there, how any *girl* could survive. And knowing one girl did survive, he will feel confident and powerful the rest of his life.

And my beautiful fiancé Joel pretends he is strong, yet he is a little boy inside. It's all right to be sensitive, I want to tell him. He is such a good man. He was going to be a great husband. Yet he does not need to hold on. He should find another girl to love, because he has so much to give. It's only right that he not be tied to memories of me. If he stops one night and recalls a moment we shared, that is enough.

My sister cries a lot yet she tries to hide her tears. She folds up my clothes, gathers my things, and puts them in boxes. She sits on my bed and shakes her head, like there was something she forgot to do or something she could have said that would make everything not happen. She calls me the good daughter, the one who brought honor to the family, the one who makes up for our father's bad deeds. Yet, so many times it was her who saved me.

Her husband tries to comfort her yet he fails. I brought them back together, it seems, after all of their playing around. From where I float I can see tomorrow. I know they will have another baby, a son this time. My sister always wanted a boy who looks like her, red hair and all, to replace the son she lost long ago. Next year she will meet him. And then she and her partner will finally get married! Instead of Íris Magnusdóttir, she will be Iris Schaeffer.

I heard that Captain Rogers survived, got a fancy mechanical leg to stand on. His wife calls him a robot. He resigned from the Forces, became a teacher in Edmonton, his hometown. His wife forgave him for going off to play soldier. She will get over seeing him with the robot leg. And they will have a baby, too. You see how life goes around? Some people die, yet other people are born.

Captain Rogers wrote a long story of what I did up there in the arctic. He heard everything through the comm link. That got me cited for valor. They say I am a hero. That I saved the whole world. No, I was doing my job. A hero isn't somebody who just survives something terrible. A hero has to act, has to complete the mission, whatever it is. And to save herself. I failed at that.

In the end they had to call it an accident. They couldn't have the entire world thinking everything almost ended. Couldn't let people be afraid of some terrorist attack coming down from the arctic. Who would think a nuclear device put on an airplane that was hijacked months before all the way on the other side of the world would be used that way?

No, officially it was simply a tragic accident. All units will get more training so it doesn't happen again. The official report says the patrol broke through the ice crossing a strait. Everybody drowned except me and Captain Rogers. We were the trailing element so we stopped in time. My valor citation was changed to bravery, for helping pull the men from the icy water at risk to myself. In the end the result is the same.

And Jaybird. That crazy kid.... He quit when his time was up. I see him out hunting caribou with his grandfather now. And he is a lot happier.

Before all those reports were written and read, I wandered through the streets of Winnipeg, like I was still running from my campus to the fitness center at my sister's campus. It felt strange to see Ralph working out alone, seeing him stop to wipe tears then punching the bag so hard, not doing it right, like he didn't care if he broke his wrists.

I found where they were having the big funeral service. At a Catholic church! Somebody thought I'm Catholic. Was it because I talk about the Lord of Denmark? Or because I once lived in the Children's House in Nuuk, run by Sister Margret and Sister Katerina, trying to learn how to be a proper Danish girl? Even as I kept taking my friend Dirk up the mountain to teach him about love? Yet what is love?

Of course, all I know about love I learned from Happy. All I know about life, though, I learned from Mama. And from the ice itself. From the cold and the dark and the light and the animals there in that frozen land where I was made one night long ago. I know where I am going. I could be a wisp of smoke, or the howl from a wolf's throat, or a flicker of light in the night sky, or just a snowflake falling, one among many....

My sister's husband said he counted three-hundred-fifteen people sitting in that church. Even Jeff came, all the way from Toronto. He got to meet his son Atka after the program. He told my sister he and Stuart were as close as ever, both with good jobs in an internet security company.

I recognized Jaime Little Bear sitting in the third row, head bowed, along with three other girls I fought, all dressed in black. Some people came from the university. From my library, too. And there were soldiers in dress uniforms. Several men in dark suits came all the way from Ottawa just to put a big display of flowers and Canadian flags on the stage. One of the men gave my sister a folded flag.

All those people! That was more people than I ever met in my whole life. I stayed by myself mostly, and I always kept my area clean. I can't understand how so many people could know me. Maybe they saw a boxing match I fought. Or I checked a book out for them. Or sat in a class with them. Maybe they were lovers that I forgot. Or just people I passed on the street. Maybe we shared a quick glance, or bumped elbows, or rode a bus.

You never know who they are, all those people who pass through your life. The people there in the background. It's like a photograph somebody takes of a friend yet you are behind them, caught by the camera. Then years later, when those two friends look at that photograph, they notice you in the background and they wonder who that person is. They wonder what she must be thinking as she watches that picture being taken. Who is she? What is she doing there? What's her life been like? Is she loved by anybody?

Then she is gone.

"None of us really knew her," said my sister when it was her turn. "Já, none of us ever understood who she was...this girl from a village in Greenland. I got a letter one day saying she existed. And my life changed forever. I thought I was an only-child. Suddenly I have a sister.... Even though she lived in my house off and on for a few years, even though I saw her almost every day, I still had no idea who she was...who she *is*.... She's with us now, I believe. She always will be. And yet it's clear when I look out at all of you sitting here...it's obvious how many lives she touched in one way or another. In her too short life.... Sorry...I shouldn't cry. She never did.... She touched us. But not as someone who fought for justice or fought for fame. Not as a girl who always wanted to be loved, who wanted to be *accepted* wherever she went.... Not as simply a girl who walks through other people's lives, but as...as.... I don't know. I can't explain.... I remember one time she told me her mother gave her the name Wolf, whatever the word is in Greenland. She was named that, she told me, because she was meant to make her own path. And I know now...I know *for certain* now, that *that* is exactly what she did. This girl called Wolf made her path through all of us."

Acknowledgements

A special thanks must go to Anna Good, social networking maven extraordinaire, who graciously allowed me to borrow episodes from her life in full detail, both the pleasant and not so pleasant events.

Over the course of composing this novel, there were constant discussions and negotiations, always settling the fine line between presenting the cold, hard facts and telling a compelling story. Anna approved the fictional conclusion as a profound statement of human dignity, women's empowerment, and the universality of goodness triumphing over evil.

Thanks also go to Íris Schaeffer who, as more than a character in this novel, created the cover artwork, as suggested by Anna Good.

About the Author

Stephen Swartz grew up in Kansas City where he was an avid reader of science-fiction and quickly began emulating his favorite authors. Since then, Stephen studied music in college and, like many writers, worked at a wide range of jobs before heading over to Japan for several years of teaching English.

Along the way, Swartz obtained a Master of Fine Arts in Creative Writing, which required him to study not only the Classics and the English literary canon, but also Old Norse literature. His novel, *A Beautiful Chill*, originally his MFA thesis, features the character Íris who reappears in the present work.

Swartz is a Professor of English and teaches writing at a university in Oklahoma. He can always be found writing his newest novel, usually late at night.

www.ingramcontent.com/pod-product-compliance
Lightning Source LLC
Chambersburg PA
CBHW071309200626
46813CB00015B/770